Love in an elevator

He raised his gaze from her mesmerizing breasts, covered in the same tight, black fabric as her slacks, to her beautiful face. She gave him a come-hither smile and his gut rolled. All he could think about was getting close enough to touch her, to feel her skin under his fingertips and taste those lush, ripe lips.

"I don't mean to be presumptuous, but I was hoping you might ask me to your room," she said as the elevator climbed.

Bombarded by a dozen reasons why he shouldn't take the invitation, Lucas swayed on his feet. She didn't say another word, just set her mouth into a curving line and waited.

When she followed him into the hall and stopped beside him, he prepared to brush off her request. Then he remembered the last words of advice he'd been given by the president. *You're all work and no play, Lucas. That's not good for a man, even one in the middle of a crisis. Find the time to do something for yourself once in a while.*

Pondering the sage words, he said, "Sure, why not?"

JUDI McCOY

WANTED:
One Sexy Night

AVON BOOKS
An Imprint of HarperCollinsPublishers

This is a work of fiction. Names, characters, places, and incidents are products of the author's imagination or are used fictitiously and are not to be construed as real. Any resemblance to actual events, locales, organizations, or persons, living or dead, is entirely coincidental.

AVON BOOKS
An Imprint of HarperCollins*Publishers*
10 East 53rd Street
New York, New York 10022-5299

Copright © 2005 by Judi McCoy
ISBN-13: 978-0-06-077420-2
ISBN-10: 0-06-077420-7
www.avonromance.com

First Avon Books paperback printing: September 2005

Avon Trademark Reg. U.S. Pat. Off. and in Other Countries, Marca Registrada, Hecho en U.S.A.
HarperCollins® is a registered trademark of HarperCollins Publishers Inc.

Printed in the U.S.A.

10 9 8 7 6 5 4 3 2 1

*To friends who have supported me
throughout my career:
Mary Atkinson, Katrina Murray,
Carolyn Harrell, Melissa Buehrer,
Jackie Dietzler, Renee Manwarren.*

Prologue

"So, child, the time has come."

Mira gazed at her father, the highest-ranking elder on her planet. Tall, with regal bearing and a full head of silver hair, Thane cut an imposing figure. He'd adopted her as an infant, after her parents were killed in an accident, and she owed him her allegiance for rescuing her from a lonely future as a ward of the state. Although he wasn't sentimental, he had brought her into his home and seen to it she had every advantage available as the daughter of a leader.

She inspected the pristine cubicle of the transporter room, its gray walls and tubular furniture, its impersonal ambience—a true reflection of her orderly, but stagnant, world. "What will you do while awaiting our return?"

His brows rose. "My duty, of course. I will continue to lead the council's discussion on future interaction with the people of Earth, and our scientists will search for a way to bring our male citizens back to full potency."

"But this mission—? I thought Project Rejuvenation was the answer to our problem."

Thane frowned. "There is always a possibility Project Rejuvenation will fail."

His words hit Mira like a slap. Generations of cloning and gene manipulation had left their men either impotent or sterile. Nine women had been chosen for a journey of hope, a mission the scientists had declared was their best chance to rectify past errors in judgment. She and the other eight travelers were committed to succeed, and now it sounded as if her own father had doubts.

"I thought everyone had agreed this was the only logical way to save our world."

"In theory, we believe it to be so, but your success or failure will be the truest test. And there are still some who disapprove of the idea of infusing our people with the blood of an inferior race." He squared his shoulders. "Are you prepared? Do you have questions before you leave that weren't covered in training?"

She recalled the information she planned to review on her journey, even though the details of life on Earth, the customs of its people, their speech patterns and mannerisms, had been one of her favorite areas of study. As an expert in life on other planets, she'd felt a kinship with those known as humans the moment she read about their struggles and advancements.

"I plan to go over each lesson with care. I'm determined not to fail."

Thane pulled at his beard. "Of the nine, you placed highest in testing, Mira. We are confident you will honor your oath and do as ordered. The others are near to perfect, but you . . ."

She let him itemize her supposedly stellar qualities without listening. He loved her in his own way, was proud of her accomplishments, but Thane had adopted her for one simple reason: She'd been evaluated and found exceptional. At the time of her parents' deaths, he and the other elders had been well along in their work on Project Rejuvenation. Childless and with no hope of producing offspring, he'd used his political influence to make her his heir. When she returned, he would share in her success and bask in her glory.

"I have a gift," he said, intruding on her musings. He placed a heavy hand on her shoulder. "You have the bracelet and ear chips like the others, but this is . . . special." He set a metal box no bigger than her little finger on the table.

"What is it?"

"A transmitter. It's been synchronized to link you directly to my personal communicator in the council chambers and at home."

"Why am I being given such a thing?"

"We fear there may be difficulty with your human, though not through your doing. The others are being sent to remote areas where the chance for detection is slim, but your target resides in the most powerful city on the planet. Therefore, you will be in the greatest danger. If you use it, I'll know your mission has become compromised. Be certain it remains activated, and I will make sure you are rescued."

The nine women had been told they were being sent to the man with whom each would have the highest likelihood of success. The compatibility factor with her target was 99.9 percent, as it was with all the couples. It was the individual traveler's duty to elude capture by use of her wits, mental gift, or gemstones. If they were discovered, they'd been given the wherewithal to contact the mother ship for emergency retrieval.

"I agreed to go, knowing the perils, but it doesn't seem right that I have an edge over the others. It isn't ethical to treat me differently because I'm your daughter."

"You were given this honor on your merit, not because you're my child." Thane's almost gentle expression turned guarded. "Besides, we have only one. The council members decreed you have need of it most."

Picking up the object, Mira tucked it in her bag. Though she had several character flaws, being stubborn when faced with logic wasn't one of them. She didn't regret that she'd been known as Thane's daughter most of her life, but was pleased she'd managed to carve a career for herself as an expert in the field of understanding the inhabitants of other worlds. Fortunately, this mission would give her the opportunity to further her studies and honor her biological parents, as well. Her mother and father were a traditional couple who refused to order their lone child from a list or clone her from an already perfect being. If she'd been born with low intelligence or a deformity, they still would have loved her.

A bell sounded, and she stood. Thane embraced her, his arms tightening for a moment. "Go, daughter, and fulfill your destiny."

She walked to the entry chute that would take her directly to her traveling pod. But she was already thinking of her child and the life they would share when she returned.

A child she would love with all her heart.

One

"*A*re we still tracking?" Lucas Diamond focused on the interstellar map mounted on his office wall. His body tensed in anticipation as he rose from his chair. "Stay on them, Jensen, we can't lose them now."

"Still tracking, sir," the dispatcher responded, his voice growing in strength. "We've pinpointed three touchdowns, with six to go. Make that four," he corrected rapid fire. "North Dakota, Arizona, southern Virginia, north Texas . . ."

"Hell, they're hitting ground like hailstones." Lucas speared rigid fingers through his hair. "I want the list and exact coordinates in here immediately, and bring in the others as you get them."

"Yes, sir, will do—" Jensen paused. "Uh, make that five, sir. Add Montana to the list."

Lucas set the receiver in the cradle and pressed the

heels of his palms into his eyes. He'd caught a few hours of sleep a day ago, and that was only because the president had ordered him to do so. It had been a smart move, even though he hadn't wanted to miss a moment of what he knew was the biggest event the United States—the world—had ever experienced. He'd always believed they were out there, but he'd never actually thought—

His intercom buzzed. "Yes, Peggy?"

"It's Martin. I thought you'd want to speak to him."

"Thanks. And make sure you copy the touchdown list when it comes in, then notify each team of the specific coordinates. Tell them to head for the site and begin their investigation."

He took a deep breath before he picked up the phone. When Martin Maddox had retired as director of the Division of Interstellar Activity three years ago, he'd been Lucas's superior, mentor, and friend. In all the excitement of the past week, Lucas had neglected to call him; but as far as he was concerned, Maddox had as much right to be informed as the president. The ex-director had more details on extraterrestrial theory stored in his brain than the entire department could ever hope to remember.

"Martin."

"I've been waiting for your call. Never thought you'd leave me out of the loop, son."

"I know, and I apologize." Lucas ran his free hand through his hair. "But you can imagine what it's been like down here."

"I have a pretty good idea," Martin said. "I'm anxious, not angry."

"Then you're aware of what's happening?"

"Aware? I've been tracking those stars for the last seventy-two hours. At first, I thought they were an undetected celestial phenomenon, then a meteor shower. When I saw they had a path and a purpose, I about dirtied my drawers. I have buddies as far away as California phoning and e-mailing me as if it was the Second Coming. Hundreds of amateur astronomers have locked on to those stars, Lucas. I hope you realize this won't stay quiet for long."

"I know. We're lucky they're all heading for fairly remote areas of the country. We plan to deny everything until there's something concrete to report, which will probably take a while. It's our only hope for containment."

"Containment?" Martin snorted. "How in the hell are you going to manage that? As soon as word leaks out, the tabloids will be on the story like ants on a cracker crumb."

His mentor was right, but Lucas still believed they had a handle on security. "Other than denials, there will be no press conferences or news releases until I say so. I decided to send in small teams, two or three operatives per site, which should cut down on speculation, and they've been ordered to keep things low key. Peggy's giving each team the go-ahead as we speak. The rest of the agency is in lockdown, and we've reminded everyone of the consequences of a security breach. More importantly, the military has been ordered to stand clear. I've convinced the big man it should be DIA all the way, and he agrees."

"I'm impressed with your powers of persuasion," said Martin. "And I don't blame you. The only thing those military men ever want to do is blow things up. Remember the piss poor job the army did at Kecksberg and Roswell."

"The president knows that. Thank God, he sees it our way."

"At least you have the luxury of top-notch equipment. Even with my state-of-the-art Meade, I had a hard time homing in on the closest star when they split up. Since there are two on the East Coast, I decided to keep tabs on the baby headed your way."

"I didn't think you'd bother tracking the craft aimed for Canada, when we have one veering toward southern Virginia. It even managed to evade the NASA contingent on Wallops until a few hours ago."

"Canada?" Martin barked out a laugh. "How long has it been since you touched base with the control room?"

"About ten minutes." Perspiration broke out on Lucas's forehead. "I've only been informed of five touchdowns. I'm still waiting for the coordinates on the others. What do you know that I—"

There was a knock, then Peggy poked her head around the corner. "Lucas." She trotted to his desk. "The control room super just brought this in. You'll want to see it." She handed him the memo, then stood as if waiting for his reaction.

He scanned the page, and his stomach turned cartwheels. "They're sure?"

"Looks like it's going to get even more hectic around here in the next sixty minutes," his second-in-command said in her usual manner of not answering him directly.

"Wipe that grin off your face and call the big boss. Tell him I'll be there in a few minutes, then I'm going out to take a firsthand look at things." He remembered Martin was on the line, and realized the man was still a jump ahead of him and NASA, even though he was a hundred miles away. "You might have told me the Canadian star did a 180," he groused into the receiver. "Instead of letting me find out from Peggy."

"Don't beat yourself or your men up about it. The damn thing turned on a dime. But I would go over each team member's profile and their last interview again, just to make sure there aren't any rats in the woodpile. Harden and Griggs were self-serving sons of bitches when they worked for me. They can't have mellowed any since you were promoted over them."

"They're the same, but they know their stuff. And they weren't happy that I ordered them to stay here. The only reason I made them team commanders was so I could stay on their backs." Lucas opened his briefcase and stuffed in every page of pertinent data he'd collected as he continued to talk. "Now that I've let you in on my secret, you'll be the one I turn to if they find out."

"Gee, thanks," Martin muttered. "I think."

"You're at the cabin?"

"Where else?"

"We counted nine. Is that what you have?"

"Exactly. You have enough qualified field operatives to hit that many sites?"

"Are you wrangling to come out of retirement?"

"I would for this one. All you have to do is ask."

Lucas blew out a breath. "Then stay on alert because I may need you. We're covered for now, but not every scout is first-string."

"Too bad. How's your weather?"

"Raining cats and dogs. I had no idea we'd be lucky enough to get a backyard landing, so I'll have to put together a makeshift team and recall the pair I sent to upstate New York. The men I have left are green, but they'll be so thrilled to go on this assignment they won't care that they're mucking their way through a deluge."

"I assume you'll join them?" The older man made it a statement, not a question.

"Just as soon as I'm done briefing the president."

"Then I won't hold you up," said Martin. "Oh, and tell him I said hello."

Mira braced for the jolt as her pod skimmed the tree line on its trajectory to Earth. The transporter was only a bit larger than her body and composed of little more than a rubbery gel of electronically charged particles, proteins, and amino acids. Designed to be steered by her mind, it would shield her from injury upon impact, then dissolve in the first heavy rain. If she landed in a river or lake, the pod would begin the process immediately, disintegrating as she extricated herself and swam to shore.

Each of the landings had been programmed for darkness to avoid detection. The current heavy rainfall swamping the East Coast was both a boon and a deterrent. Precipitation would hasten the destruction of the pod, but it had thrown her vehicle off track, causing the need for a manual realignment before she veered too far from her target. The sooner the pod dissolved, the better.

Branches whipped at the craft as Mira peered through the trees, dodging huge specimens that loomed in her path. Because it was May on Earth, most of the trees were approaching full leaf. Finally, the pod skipped over a body of water and skidded to a halt. Climbing out, she stepped into what looked to be a shallow stream. Clambering ashore, she wiped the water dripping from her hair and eyes and gave the pod a final glance, pleased to see it melting into the current.

Shaking her limbs, she stretched out the kinks, shook the water from her face and hair, and headed deeper into the forest. Threading her way over fallen logs and piles of organic matter, she made a mental approximation of her landing site: Rock Creek Park in the District of Columbia, capital of the United States.

The immense size of the park would assist in her cover. If need be, she could climb a tree and hide in the V of its branches, but a comfortable bed under an outcropping of rock or in a cave would be safer. Better still, she'd find a softhearted human willing to direct her to a place of peace. She'd been told the larger cities here had shelters for homeless citizens who needed—

A dog howled, and she stilled at the familiar sound. The canine was a common Earth animal similar to a type found on her planet. Turning in a circle, she squinted into the night. To her left, lights flared in the distance, bobbing as if being carried. More lights spaced equally apart and moving steadily as if affixed to a vehicle, followed them. She heard a chorus of howls, the baying almost frantic, and guessed the creatures had caught a scent.

Since hunting wasn't allowed in these woods, there could be only one reason for the lights and vehicles— and the dogs.

Her.

She cut through the forest at a lope, keeping on an angle until she found the stream again. Dogs often lost scent of their prey in water, another positive to aid in her escape. She splashed through the rivulet at a run, ignoring her wet boots and soaked uniform. The rain was warm, as she supposed the atmosphere would be once the storm cleared. She never got sick, and doubted the damp would affect her, but she'd be uncomfortable while waiting for her clothes to dry.

Circling shrubs, she ran backward over her tracks. Executing evasive measures, she improvised a looping pattern then crisscrossed her footsteps to walk an X between the trees. Though tedious, the backtracking was necessary to confuse the dogs and buy a few more precious minutes.

The howling seemed louder. Holding her breath, she heard voices on the breeze and plunged ahead, moving faster. *Think*, Mira, she ordered herself as she ran. *Stay focused and think.* Another series of lights glowed ahead, but their bluish cast was more like the glare of streetlamps in a city. The thought urged her on. If she lost herself in a crowd of humans, their scents would mingle, further confusing the dogs.

She had exceptional sight and hearing, honed through her mental ability to suggest and manipulate. Hers was an unusual psychic skill, and one that cooperated only if she were in complete control and her subject compliant. She'd had little practice using it because so many of her people were capable of blocking outside suggestions with their own mental shields.

Before she'd entered training, she and the rare others like her had engaged in testing to see how far they could take their talents, but she had no idea how they would work on the people of Earth. Very few humans had psychic powers, and those who did only tapped into the tip of what they could accomplish. Still, she had to be careful of how she used her skill. They'd been told by their scouts that humans did not take kindly to being mentally manipulated and would be even less understanding of someone prying into their private space.

Engrossed in thought, she tripped over a fallen log and began to roll in a tangle of wet vegetation and branches. She relaxed her body and went with the motion, knowing it would be less destructive if she hit a boulder loose-limbed. Her forward momentum finally slowed. Dizzy, she lay still and caught her breath. Her mind eased when the sound of the dogs seemed farther away.

Standing, she checked for injuries. Nothing was broken, but she'd be bruised and sore the next day. Stumbling toward the rumble of motorized vehicles, she focused ahead and saw flat ground. She was at the edge of a road—a place where humans drove their automobiles and other modes of transportation.

Mira finger combed her hair and tucked it behind her ears, then brushed at the leaves and debris clinging to her clothes. Stepping onto the rim of the highway, she waited until she saw a car in the distance. Gathering her courage, she positioned herself in its path and concentrated on the mind of the driver.

If the human didn't stop, Mira hoped he or she would have the decency to go around her. If not, her mission would be over before it began.

Lucas ran a hand through his sopping-wet hair. He'd needed it cut a week ago, just about the time they'd first spotted the lights. With all the excitement, he'd never had a moment free. At this rate, it would be down to his shoulders before he could get it taken care of.

He stood on the crest of a hill, balancing carefully on a huge boulder. Rock Creek Park was over seventeen hundred acres of recreational territory accessible to the general public, and a very clever place to stage an alien landing. Encircled by a series of highways, it housed bike trails, hiking paths, a zoo, even a planetarium, which—luckily for him—had been closed this past month for repairs. The area was large, with sections rarely patrolled by the Park Police. Some places were so remote that several years ago a congressional intern's corpse had gone missing for eleven months before the cops found it at the bottom of one of the park's many drop-offs.

When the dogs had gone crazy about a quarter mile back, he'd stuck close and kept his voice low, even though stealth was impossible with the baying hounds. He'd also had his men collect water and soil samples in the area where they believed the actual landing had occurred, but it was going to be tough getting a decent lab report with the downpour washing away everything in its path.

Martin had tutored him to expect a well-thought-out plan. They also agreed that if the aliens decided to show themselves they would probably not have destructive intentions. Trouble was, not too many others shared their theory. If certain factions knew of their beliefs, Lucas was certain he'd be laughed out of his position.

Still, he'd managed to convince the president that aliens with the advanced technology needed to travel the galaxies would have the weapons and wherewithal to blow up the Earth in a heartbeat. The cave drawings were proof they'd come to the planet for centuries, but men had been too primitive to interest them in those first visits. When humans finally became smart enough and civilized enough to make it worth their while, Earth embroiled itself in a series of wars.

Once things turned peaceful, aliens sent a scouting mission to Roswell, but the ship crashed, and its survivors were taken prisoner. Unfortunately, the travelers had died, though no one in charge would say exactly how it happened. Their spacecraft, hidden a couple of miles underground in Area 51, was still being studied. Lucas knew, because he'd seen it for himself.

In the next forty-plus years, extraterrestrials had tried again and again to reach us. They'd used crop circles, shown themselves to our astronauts, even buzzed the White House. And in return, they'd received nothing but belligerence.

Things had quieted down over the past decade, but the appearance of a flotilla of spaceships over Mexico a year ago proved they were testing the waters. That night's bold touchdown told him they were again trying to communicate.

Thus his assumption that whatever had landed would be wary, probably terrified and, more importantly, well trained. The fact that they were brave enough to land smack in the middle of the District of Columbia meant they would be forced to venture out in public, which told Lucas another important fact. Their visitors didn't resemble "grays," the slang name for the slightly built, big-eyed creatures that had touched down at Roswell and were depicted in cave drawings, but looked human enough to blend in with any man on the street.

Phelps, one of his brightest but greenest recruits, charged toward him from left of the ravine. "The hounds are all over the map, sir. Rigosi is with their handler, but he's not too happy right now."

"What seems to be the problem?" asked Lucas, but he had his suspicions.

"It's wet, and damned dark—pardon my language, sir. And whatever it was ran a darned good evasive track. They—or it—were either in complete panic mode or extremely clever."

Extremely clever, thought Lucas, but the sound of heavy footsteps accompanied by the scent of noxious fumes kept him from voicing his comment.

"So you haven't found what you're looking for?"

Lucas ignored the figure towering over Phelps. "It's too late to do any more tonight. Tell Rigosi to stand down. The men should get a decent night's sleep, and we'll meet at the start point at six."

Phelps nodded and took off. Lucas peered into the darkness, willing the man climbing up next to him to disappear. "I believe the army was given orders to stay clear of all areas my teams were known to be working, Major."

"We were." Major Everett Randall shifted on the boulder, his bulk almost pushing Lucas's six-foot frame to the ground. "I'm here on my own."

Lucas gave a sidelong glance, inspecting the pompous man's yellow rain slicker, khaki slacks, and steel-tipped hiking boots. He'd always suspected the major had spies everywhere, and his ability to infiltrate a cordoned area only proved it.

"I have work to do, so if you'll excuse me—"

"Fine," the major said, after Lucas jumped to the ground. "Just know that I'm watching. And waiting." He puffed on a cigar the size of a carrot, blowing thick smoke into the damp air. "You'll need me sooner or later."

"I doubt that," Lucas threw over his shoulder as he stomped away. Hell would freeze over before he'd allow the army to ruin the closest shot human beings had of meeting an alien face-to-face.

"I'm your shadow, Diamond. You might not always see your shadow, but you should remember it's there."

Lucas turned. "Stay away, Randall. From my men and from me. If I get wind of you sniffing around my investigation again, I'll have you thrown into a cell so dark there won't be enough light to cast a shadow."

The laugh Randall barked out reminded Lucas of the devil on a bad day. Well, fine. If it was war the blowhard wanted, he was messing with the wrong man. Refusing to pay him further mind, he spun on his heel and headed in Phelps's direction.

"You going to be okay, miss?"

Mira smiled at the pleasant-faced human wearing a slightly confused expression. He'd swiveled in his seat to speak with her after he'd parked in front of what he said was an all-night mission.

"I will be as soon as I go inside. Thank you. You've been very kind."

"Not a problem." The driver furrowed his brow. "You know, I make it a point to never pick up hitchhikers. It took balls for you to stand in front of me on the parkway like that. Good thing I decided to slow down, I guess."

Balls? She tugged on her ear, but only two definitions appeared: one of a child's toy, and the other an article of sports equipment. Surely he wasn't intimating that she had *bounce?*

"I was lucky." *And you were easily swayed.* She opened her door. "It's late. I should go. I'm sure you have a home and a family worrying about you."

The man nodded. "I do, but I work a lot of overtime. It's eat or be eaten in this town."

Humans were not cannibals, she reminded herself, noting the phrase. It didn't compute, but it obviously was a common analogy with a simple meaning, or he wouldn't have used it.

"I have to go. Thanks again," Mira said with a lilt. She stepped onto the sidewalk, and implanted a subtle message in his mind. "Drive safely."

He tossed her a wave and pulled into traffic. Glancing around, she checked the deserted street. The rain had stopped, but water dripped from the awnings and flooded the gutters, pushing debris to the protective grates. Something told her this wasn't a safe part of town for a woman alone, but she didn't have the luxury of going anywhere else at the moment.

She headed toward the doors of the building behind her, noting the WELCOME FRIENDS sign covering one grimy window. Tomorrow was the beginning of the first day of her quest. She had to locate food, rest, and recharge her body.

In the morning, she'd begin her search for Lucas Diamond.

Two

*M*ira stood on the sidewalk, absorbing her surroundings. Last night, when she'd entered the crowded shelter, a woman had offered her a hot meal. She'd eaten a few bites of the vegetables while she observed the humans who made use of the facility. On her planet, everyone had a place to live and a purpose; her government allowed no one to be homeless or hungry. Aware of her disheveled appearance, she realized she was still better dressed than most of the people seeking assistance here, and refused their gift of a change of clothing.

Now, fully rested, she focused on her goal and prepared to begin her search for Lucas Diamond in the same logical manner that she approached every challenge in her life. She took in the sights and sounds of vehicles and pedestrians clogging the streets. In this teeming metropolis, it could take several days to locate her target and several more to set up a meeting.

Since this was a city of politicians and lawmakers, there was a high probability he held a position with the government. Of course, it wouldn't matter if he were a farm laborer, artist, or street sweeper. Nor would it deter her if he had a life partner. She had already accepted the possibility her match might be committed to another, but for the success of her mission she'd taken an oath that overrode her ethical nature.

Each traveler knew of the risks involved when she'd volunteered for this quest. The chosen nine had been instructed to do whatever necessary, short of physically harming a human, to get pregnant, elude capture, and reach the rendezvous site. Though the council hadn't voiced the words, Mira knew anything less than returning with a male child in her womb would be considered failure.

Her immediate concern was to obtain the essentials needed to survive: sustenance to keep her healthy; clothing to help her blend with others; a base from which to operate; and funds to continue the endeavor.

Focusing on that thought, she stopped near one of Earth's many financial institutions and observed two men interact with a machine that dispensed currency. When a large automobile pulled into a space in front of the building, she appraised the well-dressed female driver and decided she had found the means to achieve part of her goal.

It only took a moment for the woman to collect her

money and obey a mental suggestion to leave her card. After the vehicle drove away, Mira went to the machine and followed the directions that appeared on the screen. When asked for her PIN, she placed her palms flat on the glass and called up the last set of numbers used. A few seconds passed, then the message changed to an inquiry: How much currency did she wish to obtain?

She pressed several amounts before the machine expelled the card and offered bills from a slot. After pocketing the money, she continued walking until she found an establishment that served food. Choosing several items she thought were close to those available on her planet, she enjoyed a breakfast of toast, fruit, and orange juice. While paying for the meal, she began a conversation with her server and was given directions to a group of stores a short distance away.

Though interesting and informative, the experience was very different from what she was used to. On her planet, citizens utilized their equivalent of the Internet to purchase goods or visited huge, domed buildings that offered all manner of items. To choose a product, one stood on a moving walkway and passed by a transparent wall while making a selection from a display on the opposite side. There was no need for a physical exchange of funds, as everyone was connected to a currency bank that automatically debited the purchases.

Enthralled with the store's vast choices, Mira wandered the aisles, reveling in the varied styles, colors, and textures of Earth clothing, so unlike the uniform gray suits her people wore. Shoppers were even allowed to try on the articles for fit and comfort, get opinions from the sales staff or friends, and wear the items home.

After consulting a trio of clerks, she chose pants, shirts, shoes, sleepwear, several sheer undergarments, and a black, formfitting ensemble one saleswoman assured her would turn men's heads. She paid for her clothing and a large tote bag by carefully copying the name of the woman who owned the card onto each sales slip, and made a mental note to return the card to Margaret Weston with a generous thank-you as soon as time allowed.

Mira had been told the people of Earth placed a high value on emeralds, diamonds, and rubies, the stones in her ears and bracelet. Perhaps she could send Margaret a jewel, since they would no longer be needed when she left for the pickup site.

Inside the store's restroom, she discarded her old clothing and tugged on pants, a shirt, and the most comfortable pair of shoes. Back on the street, she found a shop that sold personal care items and bought the last of her essentials. Inserting everything into her carryall, she hoisted the bag over her shoulder and set out to explore.

The coordinates of her touchdown placed her within a few miles radius of her target. That meant Lucas Diamond lived close by, and probably held a job in the area. After entering several of the multistoried buildings and reading the roster of company names, she acknowledged that finding him would be daunting. She had three locator stones at her disposal; she could safely utilize two in her quest, and save one in case she had need of an emergency rescue. Since it was best to use the emeralds in a dark atmosphere, the smart thing would be to find a map of the area or study a phone directory or other name-listing source.

Gazing at the street sign that read CONSTITUTION AVENUE, she realized she was at the site of this nation's government buildings. Scanning the area, she observed groups of humans who seemed polite and friendly. She also noted an information booth on a far corner and knew it would be of use in her search.

If she were clever with her questions, she might be able to find a clue to Lucas Diamond's whereabouts without wasting one of her gems. If she learned nothing, she would wait until nightfall to use the first stone.

Lucas stood on the corner outside the Library of Congress, disengaged his cell phone, and checked off the sector that had just reported in. When he'd discovered the UFO's landing site, he'd divided the city into grids, assigned each grid a number, and given every team member a series of grids to investigate. After careful consideration, he decided it was the only way to find their target.

The stars had been an infinitesimal cluster of blips on the screen until one sharp-eyed member of the tracking team had called them to his attention. He'd watched the phenomenon grow for close to a week before he agreed they were in the throes of a visitation. When the stars breached the Earth's atmosphere and separated, volunteers in his department had lined up three deep to sign on for the chance to capture an alien. He'd handpicked the teams, but had to wait until he knew each set of projected touchdown coordinates before he could send them to the nearest major city.

Tossing and turning before catching a few minutes' sleep last night on the couch in his office, he'd mulled over what seemed to be the most logical theory. The craft were small, but their size hadn't given him a clue to the appearance of the visitors until the landing in Rock Creek Park.

It stood to reason that no being who resembled the creatures portrayed on television and in the movies would dare drop into the middle of Washington, DC, and expect to remain undetected. When coupled with the size of the UFO, he had to assume each had carried a single passenger who looked very much like a human. He also suspected the ship was equipped with a cloaking device or could be easily camouflaged, and therefore was still hidden somewhere in the park. When the search team reported in, he'd learn if they'd found anything to confirm his suspicions.

Because of the location of the landing site, it made sense that this particular being was here to speak with the president, perhaps as an envoy for the others. Then again, the aliens had arrived under cover of darkness, with no advance warning. If they were friendly, why hadn't they made contact first, stated their mission, and arranged a meeting?

Lucas blew out a breath. It seemed that each time he thought he had a handle on the whys, whens, and hows of the situation, more questions popped into his mind. He wanted to believe they'd come in peace, but the idea of a lone alien descending in secret on the District sent a chill up his spine. DC was an easy town to get lost in, a city where one heard a wide variety of languages and accents. Tourists from other countries dressed in their native garb and gathered in groups on the Mall or on street corners, and no one gave them a second glance. They stopped at embassies, walked galleries and museums, even participated in guided tours through the Capitol and White House and, in most circumstances, were ignored.

He'd already had a meeting with Homeland Security and local agencies, and impressed upon them the need for extra precautions while admitting visitors to government buildings. They had assured him the guards would do their duty, which took a load off Lucas's mind. If they were vigilant, his men could scour each sector without worrying about the president or his advisors.

He was considering their next move when his phone rang. "Diamond," he said sharply into the unit.

"Phelps, sir. Grid three is secure. I'm moving to four."

"Nothing unusual to report, I take it?"

"No, but it's early. Perhaps our target is still in hiding or has left the city."

"I doubt it," Lucas said, rejecting both ideas without a second thought.

Phelps hesitated before continuing. "It would help if we knew what we were looking for, sir. You know, a characteristic or feature that would set our quarry apart."

Lucas gazed at the men and women swarming the library steps. "I wish I could offer an idea, but their physical attributes are anyone's guess. Just keep your eyes peeled for signs of unusual activity or a subject who appears out of place, no matter how slight. I want a call the minute something warrants your attention. And Phelps, remember to remain discreet."

"Yes, sir."

Less than ten seconds later, his phone rang again. "Lucas, the president wants you to phone him as soon as possible," said Peggy. "He sounded anxious but patient when I told him you were on the street."

"Glad to hear it."

"And the men from upstate New York just arrived, but they drove through the night to get here. They're beat," warned Peggy. "What should I do with them?"

"Tell them to get four hours' sleep and check in at two, ready to roll." He propped himself against a wrought-iron railing surrounding a stone-and-brick building. "I've been on the phone most of the morning. Have there been any reports from Rigosi's team at Rock Creek Park?"

"I would have called if I'd heard," she countered.

"How about the results from those water and soil samples?"

"Not yet."

"The search teams in other parts of the country?"

"Arizona, Montana, and Texas called to say they're nearing their target areas. I'm sure we'll hear from the others by the end of the day." Peggy's tone turned caring. "Be patient. It's going to take them a while to set up a cover and scope out their surroundings without arousing suspicion."

"Thanks for reminding me," he said with a sigh.

"You sound tired. If you don't take care of yourself, this mission will fall to pieces, and I'm not about to take control. Have you eaten today?"

"Not yet, *Mother.* I'm on my way in for a bite, and a read-through on what you've amassed so far. Call the lab and tell them I want the sample findings on my desk in thirty minutes, then hail Rigosi and see what's taking him so long. And ask Janice to pull up reports from all the major newspapers and put whatever pertains on my desk."

"She's already working on it."

"Do me another favor? Get back to the president and ask him if he can wait an hour."

"Are you telling me to stall our commander in chief?" she asked in a voice ripe with amusement.

"Very funny. Just buy me a little more time, okay?"

Lucas disconnected the call and scanned the area. Intent on remaining unobtrusive, he forced himself to stroll to his office while he observed the activity on the sidewalk around the Capitol. You could always distinguish the natives from the tourists, then separate the Americans from the foreigners. Those who lived and worked in the District handled everything in stride, dodging traffic and heading purposefully to the various job sites. The people from other countries had a more reverent attitude about the capital of the free world, as if they knew the city was special. Americans, on the other hand, made a point of having fun. Brandishing video recorders or digital cameras, they ate from corner pushcarts as if they were in a government-funded Disney World.

Three distinct groups, each there for a specific purpose, going about the day-to-day grind.

Little did they know an alien walked among them.

His heart crested to his throat at the thought. As a boy, he'd been fascinated by the vastness of the heavens, but more than the beauty of the universe, he'd been enthralled with the promise of what it might hold. He'd inhaled each new series of *Star Trek*, had taped every episode of the *X-Files,* toured the International UFO Museum in Roswell twice, and had a slave computer at home hooked into the Search for Extraterrestrial Intelligence, better known as SETI.

He'd majored in political science in college because the inner workings of the government intrigued him, but the unlimited boundaries of space continued to eat at him in a way his country never could. After the tragedy of his son's death and his subsequent divorce, the possibility of contacting a being from another planet became his life's focus.

Meeting Martin Maddox had given him purpose, at the same time putting things in perspective. Martin had convinced him that the chance of either man's encountering an extraterrestrial in their lifetime was about the same as winning the lottery times ten, but it *would* happen.

And men such as themselves would pave the way.

Lucas pushed through the doors of the Treasury Building. Though he held the highest-level security clearance, he showed his ID to the guards before he passed through the scanner and took the elevator to the basement. The Division of Interstellar Activity was such a top secret agency few knew it existed, let alone its proper name or the location of its headquarters. The guards thought the men and women Lucas supervised worked on security sensitive documents, which they transcribed onto disk at a highly classified data center in the bowels of the building.

He stepped into the corridor leading to his office and was immediately comforted by the almost silent hum of activity. There were usually several dozen people working there at any given time, assessing data, compiling information, or monitoring scanners that scoured the farthest reaches of space. Today, the area contained less than a third that number. Lucas had dispatched twenty investigators to nine different states, and handpicked a dozen more to comb the Rock Creek landing site. While Rigosi's detail remained at the park to search in the daylight, he'd regained the two men he'd sent to New York.

He rounded the corner to Peggy's office, and found her talking on the phone while studying her computer screen. Her mental dexterity reinforced Lucas's belief that the most capable multitaskers were women, and Peggy one of the best. She had started out as Martin Maddox's personal assistant and worked her way to a position so integral to his team, Martin had insisted she be given a title and more responsibility.

When he'd retired, Martin had asked her opinion on choosing his successor, and gladly would have given her the job if she'd wanted it. But Peggy, a wife, mother, and grandmother, had no interest. They'd chosen Lucas and informed him jointly of their decision, and Lucas and Peggy had segued smoothly into the new regime.

She waggled the fingers of her free hand, and he stopped at her desk. Smiling, she rolled her eyes as she spoke into the receiver. "Our official statement is still 'no comment,' and that's with the approval of the president. If the television stations and newspaper reporters won't take the hint, tell them to take a hike." She set the phone in its cradle. "I'm going to have to do something about the young man working the press desk—like take him over my knee and spank him."

Keeping a straight face, Lucas shook his head. "So the rumors are true, you are into kinky sex."

Peggy's rosy cheeks heightened the blue of her eyes. "That's me, all right, the Grandmom de Sade."

She held up a sheaf of papers. "If you're up for a joke, this might brighten your morning."

Lucas accepted the computer printouts and scanned the first sheet, which contained an article from the *Arizona Republic* on a suspected meteor landing in the Painted Desert. He shook his head as he flipped through the pages, stopping to read whatever caught his eye.

"How in the hell can Florida and Pennsylvania report UFO landings, when none of those craft touched down in either state?"

Peggy leaned back in her chair. "That's easy. It's pure speculation, and I say the more lies we have floating around out there, the better. As long as we know the truth, who cares?" She read from a list on her blotter. "Rigosi's team has nothing to report. He said to tell you they won't stop searching, but it doesn't look good."

"That's impossible." Lucas frowned. "There has to be something they're missing."

"My words exactly. Oh, and those soil and water reports are on your desk. Promise me you won't have a heart attack when you read them."

Raising a brow, he walked into his office. *Now what?*

Mira had yet to establish a home base, a fact that didn't overly concern her. The morning had dawned sunny and continued to warm, drying the sidewalks and making the atmosphere quite pleasant. She'd wandered most of the day and passed several impressive hotels in her travels, any of which would be acceptable for a few nights' stay.

She'd also explored the edifices and monuments surrounding the Mall, walked the Capitol Building, where the United States Congress was in session, eaten lunch, and rested on some of the benches dotting the immediate area. In an effort to meld with the many pedestrians crowding the streets, she'd held several conversations with a rotating group of women in charge of the information booth. The women had been happy to expound on any aspect of the city, and had imparted much useful information.

Mira recalled Thane's judgmental comment about the people of this world. Her planet's scientists had searched the galaxies in hopes of finding a biologically compatible life-form that might infuse their people with fresh genetic material, and the citizens of Earth had been the only ones deemed acceptable. Though the planet was considered substandard by many species, she felt its inhabitants had potential. Once the two worlds began a dialogue on the dangers of gene manipulation and cloning, perhaps humans could be nurtured to a higher plane and taught the positive side of peace and unity. When that happened, they would learn more of her people's advancements and mental skills, which in turn would lead them to greater achievements of their own.

So far, everyone she'd met had been polite and helpful. The few minds she'd inspected were of average intelligence and nonthreatening. Unfortunately, none of them had any knowledge of Lucas Diamond. But that didn't deter her. She and Lucas had been matched for a variety of reasons, their likelihood to produce a male offspring being the most important. She would find him when the microscopic chip that had been implanted behind his left ear years ago, when he'd sold his sperm, reacted to the locator.

During her search, the chip's pulsing would intensify, while he would feel a dull throbbing, as if he were suffering a headache. In training, she'd been taught how to disable the device without his knowledge. Then they would be free to mate.

Now, with the Earth's single sun low in the clear blue sky, she felt certain that throngs of bodies would soon flow from the surrounding buildings to go to their homes. She found a public restroom and changed into a one-piece black suit, then returned to the street. No one paid any notice when she slipped an emerald into the underside of her bracelet and snapped it in place. Pleased with the stone's steady blink—confirmation the instrument was operational—she set out on her quest.

Alternately focusing on the bracelet and her path, she followed Fifteenth Street until she arrived at the Treasury Building, one of the busiest workplaces in the city. An information booth worker had told her it was inaccessible to all but those with the highest level of security clearance. As she passed, the emerald brightened while its pulsing quickened, telling her she was headed in the right direction. She widened her scope in one-block increments, and when the instrument's glow faded she went right and crossed New York Avenue.

Mira took several turns until she returned to the Treasury. Walking west on Pennsylvania Avenue toward Lafayette Park, she noted the stone had again ceased its frantic pulsing. Retracing her steps, she stopped at the corner and stared at the severe facade of the official building. Paying her no mind, men and women pushed through its doors, swarmed past her, and exited onto the sidewalk.

Heartened by the locator's reaction, she edged into the foyer and peered through the glass to inspect the lobby, where she viewed armed guards chatting to each other or people who passed. Growing bold, she slipped around the door and stood to the side. The pulsing had become more rapid, the green more intense, so she took several steps farther inside.

"Can I help you?"

Mira spun to face a young man wearing an official-looking uniform and an inquisitive expression. Smiling, she nodded. "This is an impressive building. I heard I might be able to sign up for a tour either today or tomorrow."

He raised a brow, his stare dour. "We're closed for the day. Besides, the Treasury isn't open for tours."

She raised the guidebook she'd purchased at the information booth. "I must have read this incorrectly."

He folded his arms. "This your first time in DC?"

"Yes." She settled the tote bag firmly over her

shoulder and craned her neck to peer around him. "So . . . what kind of things go on in here?"

"That information is classified. If you don't have government clearance—"

"I'll have to leave." She sighed. "I figured as much."

"That would be best. Sorry."

She held a hand to her throat and schooled her features to remain innocent. "I don't suppose there's a water fountain I could use? I've been walking for hours, and I'm thirsty."

The guard scanned her face, then her chest, then quickly moved to her mouth. By the time he remembered to look her in the eye, he was red-faced. "Um . . . sure. But I'll have to stay with you." He headed toward a far wall as he talked over his shoulder. "It's right here."

Mira bent to take a drink, knowing full well the man was assessing her backside. While drinking, she gave a sidelong glance at her bracelet and noted that the blink had quickened while the stone's hue had deepened. "You've been very kind," she said when she finished.

"No problem." He escorted her to the door and gazed at the people milling about on the sidewalk. "You alone in town?"

"Why, yes, I am. Why?"

The guard sucked in his stomach and stood taller. "My shift ends in five minutes. Maybe you'd like to join me for a cup of coffee . . . or something."

Mira glanced at her bracelet again. "Thank you for the offer, but I can't."

He frowned his disappointment. "That's okay. It was nice meeting you."

"Thanks for your help," she answered, hoping to soften their parting.

With her heart pounding in triple time, she made her way to the sidewalk and plopped onto a bench. She heaved a calming breath, but it didn't help ease her excitement. She had trained for this moment for a ninent, and it still felt unreal, as if she were enmeshed in a dream.

She had found the building where Lucas Diamond worked. Soon, she would meet him in person.

Three

Lucas rubbed the nape of his neck. Too much excitement and too little sleep, coupled with the past week's stress had given him a doozy of a headache. He opened his desk drawer, found a bottle of pain reliever, and tossed back three tablets. He had so much work on his desk, he didn't have time to walk to the watercooler.

Glancing again at the top priority report on the sample taken from Rock Creek, he heaved a sigh. If not for the diligence of an experienced lab technician, the findings would read like a freshman chemistry experiment. Not only had the technician done a rush job, suspicion, instinct, or just plain curiosity had prodded the guy to run a complete DNA scan, along with the usual tests on the contents of the creek. What the scientist had found perplexed him so much he'd handwritten a question mark on a Post-it note next to the pertinent information along with the word *impossible*.

Lucas was under no obligation to respond to the query, of course, but he understood the cryptic remark. Along with a smattering of life-sustaining electrons and a small amount of an inexplicable plasmalike substance, traces of humanoid DNA in the waters of Rock Creek would be enough to set off alarm bells in any competent scientist's mind.

Humanoid was the key word, because he knew a strand of human DNA wouldn't have shown at all. That this sample had survived was enough to arouse suspicion. It was very close to human, but far enough off the mark to indicate a species unlike any found on Earth. The man had even run a cross-check on the known animal kingdom before releasing his findings to be sure he was interpreting the findings correctly. The lab worker also noted he was willing to check a few databases that held DNA samples from archeological digs, as if he thought he'd discovered the missing link or some kind of genetic mutation.

He made a quick call, told the technician he had enough information, and reminded him that the findings were classified top secret. Under no circumstances should the data be given to anyone else. Then he leaned back in his chair to ponder his next step.

Thanks to the report, another piece of the puzzle had slipped neatly into place. With such a close DNA match, the alien would definitely resemble a human, which greatly increased its capability for covert and possibly dangerous activity. Worse, if word of the visitation leaked, and the similarity factor came to light, panic would ensue.

Knowing he had to focus on the capture, he asked himself another question: Would it be easier to find the creature there, in a city overflowing with people? Or did his men at one of the other landing sites, where there was less population but also less manpower, have a better chance of detecting the alien?

Before he came up with an answer, his phone buzzed. "Yes, Peggy."

"It's after seven. Janice left and I have to get some sleep, or I won't be worth a wooden nickel tomorrow."

The ache in his head beat out a silent tattoo of agreement, and he realized the same was true of him. "That's fine. There's nothing more you can do tonight anyway."

"I don't mean to nag, but the president called again. Said he'd be in his office, working until midnight on his proposal for the peace summit he's scheduled to attend tomorrow. He's not exactly thrilled you blew him off this afternoon."

"I did not *blow off* the leader of the free world. I had to contend with the water and soil samples. Besides, there wasn't much I could tell him."

"That's exactly what I said when I relayed your message. I know you're concerned with the test results, but you have to see him tonight, before he becomes unreachable. We both know his cooperation is the only thing that stands between us and a full-scale military intervention, not to mention a media circus. If that happens—"

"All hell will break loose." Lucas drummed his fingers on the desk. "Do me a favor before you leave. Call and tell him I'll be there by nine."

"Will do. By the way, we've heard from each team. They're either on their way to the coordinates or already in place."

"What do you mean *on their way?*"

"Hey, those landing sites are remote. The one in northern Montana is about two hundred miles from the nearest airport, and our guys have to drive in order to retain mobility," she explained. "Everyone assured me they'd be up to speed by morning."

Peggy was correct, as usual, but it didn't make him feel any better. "Okay, sorry. It's just so damned frustrating."

She paused, and he knew she had something important on her mind.

"Lucas, I think you should phone Martin."

"Has Maddox talked to you today?" he asked, fairly certain he already knew the answer.

"Once, early this morning. He wants in," she responded hesitantly. "I think you should reinstate him immediately."

Great. The last thing he needed was for Peggy to doubt his ability to lead the mission. She'd started her government career in this division, so her loyalty to Martin made sense, but Lucas thought he'd earned her trust and respect over the last three years.

"I'm the one in charge now, Peggy. I call the shots."

"I'm not trying to insult you, Lucas, but I didn't think I was here to stroke your ego or gain points by telling you how well suited you are to this job. Martin and I agreed you were the only man capable of the position when he was forced out. I'm just thinking of the years he spent building this organization from the ground up, the hours we—he worked setting the wheels in motion for a break like this. It nearly killed him to retire, but he had no choice. It almost seems unfair to leave him out now, when his life's dream has become a reality."

Her explanation made perfect sense, as well as soothed his ruffled feathers. Besides, it wouldn't hurt to have another expert brain to pick. "I'll speak with the president. If he gives his approval, I'll call Martin tomorrow and invite him back on board. How does that sound?"

"It sounds like the decision of a wise and compassionate man. Thank you."

"You're welcome. Now go home."

Lucas smiled as he hung up the phone. Maddox's astute observations and wry comments would keep him on the straight and narrow, as well as ease some of the tension in the division. And Peggy was correct about this moment being the man's lifelong dream. He and Martin had talked at length about this day and what it would mean for mankind, as well as them personally.

The throbbing in his head intensified, and he slumped forward. Damn, but those tablets had done nothing to lessen the pain. Pushing from his desk, he slipped into his suit jacket and smoothed his hair. After opening his briefcase and stowing the test results, he strode to the elevator and rode it to the street level.

Outside, he took a careful look around as he walked, noting a woman sitting on a bus stop bench, a couple on the corner waiting for the light to change and, as he passed the rear of the building, a shabbily dressed man sitting in a doorway. The local authorities had done a commendable job in the past few years of keeping the area safe and derelict-free for the tourists. It wouldn't be long before the Metro Police shuttled the guy on his way.

That gave him an idea. First thing tomorrow, he'd ask if Rigosi had thought to interact with the nearest precinct and Park Police headquarters. Could be one of their officers had rousted someone suspicious and taken them into custody, or maybe grilled them and sent them packing.

Another stabbing jolt jabbed the back of his head, and he made an effort to brush away the pain. Concentrating on what to tell the president, he arrived at the side entrance of the White House, where he showed his badge to a guard.

"Lucas. He's waiting for you."

"Thanks, Mike. It might be a while."

"No problem. I'll be here all night. Heard through the grapevine something big is in the air."

"Could be," Lucas answered evasively. "Tell me, have you had reports of anyone trying to get inside without the proper credentials?"

"Not on my shift. I can ask around if you want."

"I'd appreciate that. Thanks."

Mira waited patiently in the darkness. She'd followed Lucas Diamond to the White House, and she assumed he would exit soon. She had recognized him when he'd left the Treasury Building by the locator's reaction when he'd passed her on the bench, and the way he'd held a hand to the nape of his neck as he walked to his destination. She was saddened by the fact that she was causing him pain, but it was the only way to pinpoint him as her target.

She'd managed to catch a glimpse of his face in a streetlamp before he turned onto West Executive Avenue, and was still intrigued by what she'd seen. Tall and well built, he'd worn a gray suit, red tie, and an expression of determination. The harsh lines bracketing his sensual mouth had caused a shiver to race up her spine. His furrowed brow had done nothing to soften his features, but she'd been drawn to him just the same.

From the look of it, he'd been in quite a bit of discomfort, but because of the reaction of the microchip, that made sense. Short of sending him into unconsciousness, even the heaviest dose of medication would bring little relief.

Standing in the shadows, she considered the building, with its many lighted windows. She'd read the guidebook and knew this was the side of the edifice that held the office of the leader of this country. What kind of business would have Lucas Diamond in conference with the most important man in the United States? And why were they meeting at such a late hour?

She spotted a police car and stepped back farther, willing herself to blend with the darkness. Thanks to the outfit she'd changed into before setting out on her quest, and her nearly black hair, she'd been able to remain inconspicuous, but how much longer could she stay that way? The travelers had been warned that terrorist attacks from other countries had put the United States on alert and made it difficult for ordinary people to board planes or cross borders freely. In this city of leaders, the security was doubly high. If she were stopped, would she be clever enough to convince them she was a simple tourist taking a late-evening stroll?

The sound of a door opening and mumbled voices alerted her to activity at the side entrance. A cluster of men came through the door and stood chatting. When one person separated from the rest and walked in her direction she retreated into the shadows. Realizing it was Lucas, she followed him, matching the tempo of her steps to his so as not to arouse suspicion.

Staying at a discreet distance, she noted he was still cradling the back of his head, though he continued to walk with purpose. A block later, he entered the Hay-Adams Hotel.

Mira waited a moment, then nodded to a man who held open the door. Entering the deserted lobby, she slipped behind a tall, bushy plant and spotted her quarry heading for the elevators. At this great a distance, she wasn't certain she could affect the machine's inner workings, but she had to try. It had taken her an entire day to reach this point in her mission. She was still unsure of Lucas Diamond's profession, but it had to be important if he worked in a secure building and held late-night meetings with the president. Now that she was here, it was imperative she be clever as well as cautious. Who knew when she would have another chance to get near him in a place of privacy.

Holding her breath, she armed for battle. Steeling herself with what she hoped was an intriguing expression, Mira hoisted her tote bag over her shoulder and crossed the marble floor toward her target.

Lucas stepped in front of the bank of elevators and pushed the call button. He'd charged into the hotel, intent on going straight to his room, taking a hot shower, and slipping into bed in less than fifteen minutes. Riding the edge of the biggest discovery in the history of mankind, it had been two nights since he'd gotten more than a few hours' sleep. Reluctantly, he had to agree with the commander in chief. If he allowed the reckless schedule to continue, he wouldn't be worth shit come morning.

Their meeting had taken place without a hitch. The president still believed the DIA alone should be in command of the investigation until they decided to call in the military. They also agreed that there was a high probability the aliens had come in peace and, for whatever reason, were biding their time to contact a person of importance. Otherwise, their visitors would have done us in with the flip of a switch on their obviously superior technology when they entered our atmosphere.

If they were intent on doing harm, Earth and all its citizens would already be in the throes of chaos.

Shifting on his feet, he fought a stronger wave of pain. Damn if it didn't feel like his head was going to explode. He needed drugs and a drink, in that order, and the sooner the better. Clasping the handle of his briefcase, he cursed inwardly as he stared at the overhead panel. At this hour of the night, all of the upscale hotel's elevators should be waiting on the ground level. What the hell was taking them so long?

Ready to go to the front desk and complain, he spun on his heels and ran smack into a woman who seemed to appear from thin air. Grabbing her by an elbow, he stared into an angelic face with rose-petal cheeks and dark shining eyes.

"Sorry, I didn't mean to bowl you over. Are you all right?" he asked. *Had they met before?*

"Fine," she answered through lush pink lips.

"I was on my way to talk to the night manager. The cars are taking forever."

She reached out and tried the call button herself. "I'm sure it will only be another few seconds."

Feeling more than a little stupid for being so impatient, Lucas stared straight ahead. Another second passed, and he felt her sidelong glance. What was it about his lobby mate that seemed so familiar? Had they been introduced at one of the political fund-raisers he was continually forced to attend? Probably not, because he'd certainly remember a woman with a face as arresting as hers.

Unable to recall if he'd locked his briefcase, he shifted the attaché case to his left hand. He knew of several factions that would pay plenty for the information he carried. He didn't believe a hotel guest would try to steal his documents, but it was important he be doubly careful these days. He took a bolder look to his right, and the woman smiled at him with open regard, then turned her attention to the overhead panel counting down the elevator's snail-like approach.

Tapping the fingers of his free hand on his thigh, Lucas resisted the urge to speak, though he was fairly certain she would welcome the attention. Without a thought to propriety, his gaze wandered downward from her shoulders, enabling him to admire her impressive breasts and sinfully long legs. When his groin twitched to attention, and he realized where his exhausted mind was headed, he shrugged. This was a ridiculous time to get hit with a serious case of lust.

Finally, the elevator opened its doors, and he stepped aside to let her enter ahead of him. From his vantage point it was impossible not to notice the stretchy black fabric, tight as the skin on a grape, that covered her heart-shaped rear, or the long black hair that cascaded to her shoulders in shining corkscrew curls. When she turned and tilted her head, she tucked a springy strand behind one dainty ear and he caught the glimmer of diamonds adorning her lobes. Wearing black stiletto heels, she almost matched his own six-foot height. He couldn't help but think she was one heck of a package. Watch out, Xena, Warrior Princess.

Their eyes met, and she rested her backside against the mirrored wall. Lucas found his lips curving in what he was certain was more of a grimace than a smile. "What floor?"

"The eighth," she answered in a smoky drawl.

"We're neighbors? I didn't think that suite was oc-cupied."

"It could be," she whispered hesitantly.

He clasped the back of his neck, hoping to hide a wince of pain. "Sorry, I'm not following you."

"I'm thirsty and the bar is closed," she continued as the elevator glided upward. "I was hoping there might be something cool to drink in your room."

He stiffened at the suggestion, though her throaty voice brought his erection to full mast. There were only two apartments on his floor, and he'd thought the other one empty. He'd been a guest there ever since they first sighted the stars, in order to stay close to the tracking team. Of course, she could have registered anytime since he'd begun sleeping on his office sofa.

He raised his gaze from her mesmerizing breasts to her beautiful face. Captured by her storm gray eyes, he was struck with a wave of pain so strong it caused him to clutch at the nape of his neck.

She gave him a come-hither smile, and his gut rolled. Shaking his head, he tried to clear the near-agonizing haze lingering in his brain. All he could think about was getting close enough to touch her, to feel her skin under his fingertips and taste those lush ripe lips.

"I don't mean to be presumptuous, but I was hoping you might ask me to your room," she said, as the elevator climbed.

Bombarded by a dozen reasons why he shouldn't make the invitation, Lucas swayed on his feet. She didn't say another word, just set her mouth into a curving line and waited.

When she followed him into the hall and stopped beside him, he prepared to brush off her request. Then he remembered the last words of advice he'd been given by the president. *You're all work and no play, Lucas. That's not good for a man, even one in the middle of a crisis. Find the time to do something for yourself once in a while.*

Pondering the sage words, he said, "Sure, why not?"

Four

Mira's heart was pounding so loud she felt certain Lucas could hear it. Poised at the very edge of her goal, she cloaked her anxiety with an aura of confidence while he slid a card in the lock, opened the door, and stepped inside. Tucking the frantically blinking bracelet under the edge of her sleeve, she followed him into a sitting area. Without glancing her way, he set his briefcase on a table, then removed his jacket and draped it across a chair.

She placed her tote bag beside the case, while he walked to a waist-high chest holding crystal decanters filled with liquid. "I have bourbon, brandy, scotch." He read from a small silver plate attached to each decanter. "If that's not your poison, the honor bar's fully stocked, including wine, beer, and those little bottles of gin and vodka. I can make just about any kind of drink you want."

Alcohol. She should have known he would assume she wanted the unhealthy brew. The hazardous concoction was still a socially acceptable part of life on Earth, as were cigarettes and a host of drugs that less sensible humans either smoked, swallowed, injected, or inhaled. She'd been informed of their perils by the council and warned not to partake of any of them.

"Water?" she asked, intent on following the advice.

He pivoted toward her, then winced, and she imagined what the rapid movement had done to his head.

"You're joking, right?"

Caught, Mira realized she had to accept the alcohol or risk rousing suspicion. "With a bit of—of—"

"Scotch?"

"Fine." She would sip slowly, take just enough for him to think she was drinking. Millions of humans imbibed more than that every day, and her own physiology was very close to theirs. How bad could her reaction be?

"Ice?"

"Yes, please." She edged the bracelet from her sleeve and quickly snapped the emerald back in place, while he filled two glasses with the requested ingredients.

"I'm surprised you don't have a setup like this in your suite." His expression turned questioning as he passed her a drink. "Or do you?"

She held the offering at her waist. "I don't know. I

just arrived today and spent my time exploring the city instead of the room."

He raised his glass in her direction. "Is your drink okay?"

She brought the amber-colored liquid to her lips. Sensing it would be bitter, she took a small taste and waited for the burning sensation to ease. "It's f-fine."

A muscle flexed in his jaw. "You should know I don't usually pick up strange women or—" Suddenly, he grimaced. "Damn!" Tossing back his drink in one gulp, he set down the empty glass. "Sorry, I can't seem to shake this lousy headache."

"You're in pain?" she asked, feigning surprise. "Have you taken anything for it?"

"Over-the-counter medication." His face paled, and he sucked in a breath. "I may have a different brand in the bathroom. Give me a minute to—"

"Wait." Mira set her drink next to his empty glass and inched to his side. "I mean, let me see if I can help."

He raised a brow. "Are you a doctor?"

"No, but I do practice a type of hands-on healing." She gave a teasing smile. "I believe your peop—some people call it 'New Age mumbo jumbo.' "

"Uh-huh. Listen, I don't mean to belittle the offer, but—"

"Just give me a few seconds. If I can't help, feel free to take your pain reliever."

He straightened. "I guess it couldn't hurt any more than it already does." Glancing around the room, he asked, "Where do you want me to sit? Or should we do it standing?"

Wicked thoughts, thoughts the elders would find shocking, filled Mira's head. From the moment she'd gotten a good look at Lucas Diamond's arresting face, seen the stretch of fabric as his shirt spanned the contours of his muscular back and tapered waist, she'd thought of nothing but the two of them engaged in the sexual act. Warmth bubbled from the pit of her stomach. She wanted to say they could "do it" anywhere he chose, but knew it would sound too forward. Once she took away his pain, they'd be free to investigate places to mate.

"How about if you relax over there." She pointed to a seating area situated in front of a fireplace. "While I sit next to you? That way, you'll be comfortable."

"Might as well make ourselves at home." He crossed the room and sat in the center of the sofa.

Mira settled on the side closest to the implant. He closed his eyes and she admired his chiseled profile, the sharp blade of his nose, and the way his dark hair curled over the collar of his shirt. She knew his age was thirty-three Earth years; if she converted the time frame used on her planet, she was older, though he would never think so. Thanks to medical advancements in her world, her hair was a vibrant near black, her body toned, her skin clear and unlined. If anything had changed for the worse in Lucas's physiology, the implant wouldn't have reacted to the locator, so she knew he was in prime physical condition.

Hesitantly, she touched his neck and skimmed her fingers upward. If she had any doubt of his identity, the pulse of the microchip gave final confirmation. She sent out a quick mental command, and it ceased functioning. In moments, he placed his hands on his thighs and groaned in response to the freeing sensation.

"Is that better?"

"It's damn near a miracle," he answered, his eyelids still shut. "How—what did you do?"

Mira grew bold, threading her fingers through the tendrils at the back of his head. He stiffened, and his hands clenched into fists, but they remained on his thighs. She shifted her gaze to the zipper of his slacks and noted a bulge. Like most of the women on her planet, she'd never seen a fully erect penis, a fact she intended to rectify.

She rested her palm over the rising fabric. "As long as the pain is gone, does it matter?"

Lucas thought he might be losing his mind. What in the hell had just happened? He'd allowed the ache drumming in his brain to lead him somewhere so illogical and potentially dangerous it could jeopardize his job. Inviting a stranger, albeit an attractive and seemingly innocent one, into his hotel room was not his style. In the throes of this latest crisis, it was downright irresponsible.

He had no idea what she'd done, but the pain had disappeared in an instant, leaving behind an unbelievable rainbow of colors swirling in his mind. For better or worse, the stirring in his groin was even more fantastic. The urge to bury himself inside this mystery woman overwhelmed him, and it dawned on him he didn't even know her name. He needed to have his head examined, for a variety of reasons; but first he had to get rid of her.

He touched the hand she'd placed on his zipper. "Listen, I—"

She moved the fingers of her other hand from his nape to his lips. "Don't ask questions. It will ruin everything."

Still fog-brained, he snagged her wrist. "I don't know why you're doing this. Hell, maybe I don't want to know." Turning, he leaned into her, hoping to read her intentions.

Her gray eyes warmed to molten silver as her mouth curved up at the corners. Inching forward, he grew hard as the barrel on a gun when he inhaled her intoxicating scent. "This goes against every rule, every boundary I've ever set for myself. I don't—"

She kissed him then, devouring his mouth like a starving woman. Lucas couldn't breathe, couldn't think, couldn't do anything but feel. Pulling her to him, he splayed his fingers through her silken curls, grabbed at the ebony strands, and tugged her into him, as if he could absorb her through his clothes. When she whimpered her approval, he wanted to pound his chest and shout his ownership to the world.

Reason be hanged, he had a beautiful, willing woman in his room, and she damned sure wanted to show him a good time. Right now, he couldn't imagine a more enjoyable way to obey the order he'd been given by the president.

"Let's move this to a better place," he said when he drew back. Standing, he eased her to her feet, took her hand, and led the way to the bedroom.

Lucas stopped at the side of the bed, grateful a maid had turned down the covers and clicked a nightstand lamp on low. Reaching out, he crushed his visitor in his arms. Mouth to mouth, she opened for him, and he savored her essence. He couldn't get enough of her breasts rubbing against him, the way she fit his body like a tailor-made suit.

He'd never been this desperate to claim a woman for his own and make her scream with completion. To pray she wanted him as much as he wanted her.

Focusing on her face, he unknotted his tie and unbuttoned his shirt. Her silver eyes grew huge as he freed the tab on his slacks and tugged the shirt from his waistband. The pleasure in her eyes made him feel ten feet tall. Though he was a desk jockey, he knew his body was in decent shape. During less stressful times he made a point of visiting a gym three mornings a week, and he was an avid tennis player. Still, he raked his hair with shaking fingers and slowed the pace. She'd made the first move, and he didn't want to act like a frantic high school sophomore.

Her gaze traveled from his chest to his waist. She closed the gap between them and ran her hands over his zipper. "I want you, and it's obvious you want me." She kicked off her heels and peeled out of her form-fitting jumpsuit. "Please, don't stop."

Lucas stared at her barely clothed form, a wet dream come to life. A sheer black bra covered her voluptuous breasts, while matching panties revealed just enough of her feminine charms to make his already engorged shaft quiver with anticipation. He'd never been turned on by pencil-thin or fashionably slim women. He enjoyed feminine curves and softly rounded flesh, ached to be cradled in the sensual cushion of thighs, relished every difference between himself and a generously proportioned female.

And this woman had it all.

Pulling off his shoes, he did a hop and dance, tugged at his socks, and tossed the rest of his clothes aside to let her look her fill. Curiosity replaced determination as she scoured his body, inspecting him as would a connoisseur of fine art. Her gaze began at his shoulders, slid to his chest and stomach, and rested on his rigid penis. A smile twitched her lips as she ran a finger from the base of his shaft, stopping to stroke the drop of fluid at the tip.

"Careful," he warned, his voice a harsh rasp. "Unless you want this to be over before we begin."

As if mesmerized, she continued to caress him. Lucas growled low in his throat. Intent on meeting her torture with a taunt of his own, he unfastened her bra. Ducking his head, he cupped a breast in both hands, and tongued a beaded nipple.

Mira moaned at the exquisite torment. Her knees buckled and she swayed. He caught her and guided her to the mattress. She clutched his head, tangled her fingers in his hair, arched toward him when he scraped his teeth against her sensitized flesh. Nothing in her training had prepared her for this moment.

For this man.

He licked her fevered skin, slid his lips down her rib cage to her navel, then roamed to the apex of her thighs. Digging her heels into the mattress, Mira raised her hips and he slid off her panties. She welcomed his tongue, even as it shocked her when she realized what he was about to do. Spreading her legs wide, he parted her folds and suckled the core of her desire, nibbling until the heat in her belly grew to an inferno. Unable to rein in her reaction, she rocked in time to his movement, every muscle taut as it tremored in surrender.

Releasing a pent-up breath, she keened a wild cry as her body fragmented into a thousand pieces.

Still vibrating from her release, she watched through shuttered lids as Lucas nuzzled her belly, dipped his tongue in her navel, then nipped at the skin on the undersides of her breasts.

Capturing an aching nipple, he drew it deep into his mouth. Tension once again coiled low in her womb. Begging for whatever came next, she clawed at his shoulders. As if reading her mind, he smoothed a hand across her stomach to her quivering mound and filled her with his fingers. Her thighs clenched, and he trailed kisses from her collarbone to her throat, continuing to stroke until she moved with the motion of his hand.

"You're making me crazy. I've never been with a woman so in tune with my body, my every action," he whispered. "Ready for the next step?"

Unable to speak, her inner walls spasmed, and she whimpered a half-sensible response.

He smiled seductively. "That's what I thought." Nestling between her open thighs, he sighed into her mouth. "It's time, sweetheart. Let's get there together."

He entered in one swift thrust. Pain crested and died as he pumped into her sensitized core. The demanding rhythm called to her, encouraging, compelling, until they moved as one.

Lucas used his tongue to mimic his actions, showing her the pace, guiding her to his tempo. When she met his pistoning hips, he moaned his approval. She stiffened beneath him, and he knew she was ready to shatter.

Pleasure washed over him, and he longed to shout her name, but he still didn't know who she was.

In a heartbeat, it didn't matter. She was his for this moment, and they were riding a tumultuous wave of desire. Soaring together, they raced to heaven and met the stars in perfect harmony.

Mira stretched in the darkness. Shifting slightly, she settled against Lucas's muscular thighs and snuggled her bottom into his groin. Sometime during the night, he'd extinguished the light, and the room seemed as colorless as a black hole.

Tucked so close to him that she could feel his heartbeat, she smiled. So this was mating, the act that had every female on her planet talking, the reason they envied her being chosen for this mission. No wonder the Council of Women had demanded the elders find a solution. And how dismal for the citizens of her planet, how sad that their males had lost the urge to partake of this important and fulfilling contact with their women.

She'd been warned by a few of the older members of the council about the dangers of romanticizing the encounter. There was no room in her life for fantasy, not when her world depended on success from each of the nine travelers.

Their planet needed an infusion of healthy male sperm, not a cryogenic version. Each of the men chosen had sold his sperm in college, where it had been tested and found to have an exceptionally high percentage of the Y chromosome. Short of contacting the leaders of Earth and asking for volunteers, there had been no other choice but to match those men to her planet's women and deploy a ship. Soon, after a generation or two of revitalization, the elders would send a message of introduction and seek an alliance. But it couldn't happen until Earthlings were ready to accept that other species existed in the universe.

Overcome by a wave of melancholy, Mira tamped back a tear. She'd been chosen for her bravery, her logical mind, and her expertise on the habits of those who lived on other planets, but doubts about the ethics of what she'd just done assailed her. The man beside her had been giving, trusting, even kind, and she had deceived him. Once she left for home, she would never see him again.

He would never know they'd created a son.

That wasn't supposed to matter, she reminded herself. The first lesson the travelers had learned in their study of humans was to be wary of their chosen target, because it was possible he would be one of the vain and self-absorbed. Swaggering in their masculinity and cavalier in their ability to please women physically, many of the men of this planet were interested in only three things: sporting events, food, and sex. Sex in the basest of terms, of course. Then came television and their control of the remote, drinking beer, and spitting, followed by a love of fast automobiles and faster power tools, and an irrational greed for riches.

The desire to father a son—not out of love of children but to stoke their ego—and commitment to a woman ranked quite a bit farther down the list.

Thane and a few other elders did not admire these humans and failed to acknowledge there was also a group of Earthlings who were kind and compassionate, with a fierce love of freedom and independence. This group demanded honesty on all levels, worked to better the conditions of their fellow humans, and believed in the sanctity of home and family. Unfortunately, the travelers knew not into which category their targets would fall.

Again, she told herself, it didn't matter. She'd taken the first step in meeting her goal: She had mated with Lucas Diamond. Hours needed to pass before she could test herself for pregnancy. If she'd been successful, she would never see him again. If not . . .

Another smile tugged at her lips. If not, she would have to mate with him a second, possibly a third time.

He'd said the suite next to his was unoccupied. This hotel was convenient to a pleasant area of the city, and there were still many things she hoped to see. The people of Earth, their history, and their culture, intrigued her. The ability to investigate the species firsthand would not only help her pass the time, but also further her career. Her findings might give her a better argument when she returned and took her positive stand for Earth before the elders.

Lucas stirred, and she held her breath. Earlier, at the elevators, when she'd attempted to ease into his head, she'd found his mind wary and difficult to explore. Perhaps now, when he was relaxed and at rest . . .

His lips touched her shoulder, and she thought she might stop breathing altogether.

"You asleep?"

"Hmm-mmm."

"Me too," he said in a satisfied tone. "But there's a part of me that's wide-awake and looking for some company." Moving his shaft against her bottom, he brought a hand to her breast and squeezed a rigid nipple. "You interested?"

Mira melted against him. *Interested* was not the proper word. *Hungry* might be better. *Craved* was probably correct. She craved the touch of his hands, the crush of his body as it joined with hers, the feel of his rigid length stroking her insides to a frenzy.

She craved *him.*

Turning, she nipped at his jaw, met his parted lips, and let her tongue taste his.

Skimming her breasts with his palms, Lucas plucked at her distended nipples, ran a hand over her belly to her mound, and parted the already slick folds. Delving inside, he circled the bundle of nerves centered there until she drew her thighs together and rolled to pull him on top of her.

He speared her with his sex, filled her with his desire, and began to move against her. Now that she understood the primal action, her response was automatic, her longing to dance to his rhythm as natural as her next breath. This journey, she told herself, would be as exciting and magical as the first.

He clutched her to his chest, and Mira molded herself to his body, cradled his head in her palms, and matched the frantic gyration, giving herself to him with abandon. As one, they achieved synchronization. He let out a guttural cry, and she allowed herself to fly over the edge at the exact moment he stiffened above her. Rising from the swell of her breasts, he kissed her throat, then her lips. Soon, he relaxed and exhaled his contentment.

When certain he'd fallen asleep, she waited a few minutes before easing from his arms and slipping from the bed. After gathering her clothes, she inched through the darkness, left the room, and closed the door. Light seeped into the sitting area, enabling her to pinpoint her tote bag and a mirror over the bar. She turned on a table lamp and gazed at her reflection. Her face appeared abraded, and she remembered the roughness of Lucas's beard as it rasped against her skin.

Tilting her chin, she spotted a mark and recalled the way he'd sucked and nipped at her flesh. Brushing her tangled hair, she smelled him on her hands, her arms, all over her body. She didn't doubt that anyone who saw her right then would know exactly the type of activity she'd been engaged in for the past few hours.

She longed to cleanse herself, but worried the sound of running water would wake him. She had no wish for a confrontation with her target, especially when she was too exhausted safely to answer questions or explain why she'd invited herself into his domain. Instinct told her that a fully cognizant Lucas Diamond could be a very dangerous man.

Mira moved to retrieve her tote bag and spied the case he'd clutched when they'd first met. She'd taken an oath to do anything to ensure her mission. Besides, she was curious. He'd given the impression that the hotel wasn't his residence, so where did he live? Did he have a family? What was his profession? If she lost track of him, where could he be found?

Who was Lucas Diamond?

She slid the tabs and raised the lid, telling herself the actions were justified. Peering inside, she noted the efficient organization of rulers, pens, and sharpened pencils lining the outer sleeve of the top half, while a notebook and several tablets occupied the leather pocket. Stacked in the main compartment were pale-colored folders, each labeled clearly in thick dark print.

She tugged at the chip in her earlobe, intent on understanding every word she read, then peaked into the file marked SEARCH GRID. Inside, she found a map of Washington, DC, with an overlay upon which had been drawn boxes, each with a number in the center. Setting the folder aside, she opened the second labeled TEST RESULTS. Her breath hitched when she saw the words at the top of the first page: *Rock Creek Park*.

The next sheet made her tremble.

The next had her stomach roiling with disbelief.

Fighting the tremor of fear bubbling through her veins, she opened a file marked DIA. Division of Interstellar Activity was typed at the top of the initial page. First came day-by-day information on a cluster of stars the agency had tracked, along with dated paragraphs of meetings with the president of the United States. Next she read a sheet on Montana, one of the nine states where a star, now officially classified as a UFO, had landed, and its exact touchdown coordinates.

Stifling a gasp, she slipped through the papers one at a time, recalling the travelers who'd been sent to the states named: Minnesota, Xia's destination; Texas, Zara's; Arizona, Clea's; Virginia, Rila's . . .

At the bottom of each sheet were the names of investigators who had been assigned there, along with a plan to intercept the alien they hoped to capture.

Heartsick, Mira was loath to read more, but knew she must. Her sisters were in danger, and there was nothing she could do to warn them. Of course, each of them had known the possibility of peril existed. It was the reason that she, as the expert in Earth customs and information, had schooled them in the best way to talk and act to avoid detection. They had come prepared to succeed, though well aware of failure.

But the threat was so much more a reality, when seen in print.

Steeling herself, she found the final sheet labeled ROCK CREEK PARK. There, described in great detail, were the actions of the DIA on the night her pod had landed. Scent hounds, trained alien hunters, vehicles with specially equipped lights and recorders, a team of scientists who extracted soil and water samples for testing . . . Each step was clearly defined.

And at the end, written in a bold hand with clear sweeping letters, was the signature of the leader of the mission.

Lucas Diamond.

Five

Lucas woke in a daze and came slowly to his senses. A wave of tranquility unlike anything he'd ever experienced clogged his throat with threatened tears. His headache was a distant memory, and he couldn't recall the last time he'd experienced such a peaceful night's rest.

Normally, he fell asleep to a cacophony of ideas, plans, or worries over one kind of crisis or another battling for attention in his subconscious. When he awoke, the same thoughts pounded inside his skull until he worked them off in the gym.

In time, he'd come to believe the mental overload was his rational mind's way of coping, stuffing itself so full of minutiae it wouldn't have space to recall the horror of a thirteen-week-old son's death or a near-devastating divorce. Several years had passed since those life-altering events, as had the weeks of agony and months of guilt that followed, but Lucas had never forgotten.

He couldn't.

Most days, he'd take a quick shower, dress and eat, then speed from his Chevy Chase town house to the DIA. When there were reports of a valid sighting, or they were tracking something of merit, he spent the night on his office couch. It was rare for him to get five hours of unbroken rest, yet at this moment his mind, his very soul, felt at ease, even though he knew there was a huge discovery hovering, as well as a ton of work awaiting him at headquarters.

The creek's unusual test results, his meeting with the commander in chief, and the punishing ache at the base of his head were all cause for a lousy night's slumber.

What had been different about last evening?

Even as he asked the question, bits and pieces of the answer solidified. A memory of the beautiful woman who had accompanied him to his suite returned in vivid detail. After Madam X invited herself into his room and cured his headache, they'd fallen into bed like sex-crazed teenagers.

In typical male fashion, he'd awakened with a hard-on, but he usually never had any particular woman in mind. At present, he envisioned silver eyes and a lush pink mouth waiting to be kissed. He rolled to view the opposite side of the bed, then winced at the sunlight streaming into the room. Dappling the pillow next to him, it brought perfect clarity to the situation. As he'd suspected, his mystery date was gone, the only reminder of her presence an intoxicating aroma that still scented the air with passion.

Damn, but she'd been incredible. She'd outsexed every woman he'd ever been with, even his ex, and Tina had been an inventive and eager lover. Unfortunately, sexual compatibility hadn't been enough to keep their marriage going. Having Kevin had brought them closer, but losing him had ripped them apart, which only proved the weakness of their marital infrastructure. Lucas always thought that if he and Tina had loved each other more, they would have overcome the blow and faced the tragedy together. It had been Tina's choice to leave him to explore her options, and quickly involved herself with another man.

The telephone rang, and he glanced at the clock on the nightstand. Cursing, he picked up the receiver. "I know what time it is, Peggy." He imagined her flap of surprise. "I'll be there by nine."

"Well." She made a production of clearing her throat. "This is refreshing. I'm usually the mind reader, not you."

"I overslept." He swung his legs over the edge of the mattress. "It happens."

"You must have been exhausted, because it hasn't *happened* since I've known you." She chuckled. "I just wanted to give you a bit of good news. Rigosi found something. And Pruitt's team is bringing in the tin can man and the woman who heard voices for an oral swabbing."

"What about the teenagers?"

"No luck yet."

Lucas straightened. "Convince the man and woman to sign a waiver and make sure it covers the DNA test, as well as a promise to keep everything confidential. Scare the pants off them if you have to."

"Got it. Anything else?"

"What did Rigosi find?"

Peggy hesitated. "Um, it's difficult to explain. You'll have to see for yourself."

"Great, I love being kept in the dark."

"Trust me," she answered, in an amused tone. "It's not something that's easy to describe."

He ended the call and stretched as he assessed the bedroom's disarray. His tie and shirt were on the floor in a heap alongside his socks and shoes, while his slacks were crumpled at the bottom of the bed. God only knew where his boxers had disappeared to.

His gaze slid to the bedsheets, and Lucas did a double take. Pulling back the covers, he found a rusty stain no larger than a stick of gum. Holy hell, had he been that rough? He shook his head as he recalled the two, or was it three vigorous bouts of sex he and Madam X had shared. They'd definitely gone at it hot and heavy—a couple of wrist clamps, lots of teeth, even a series of wrestling holds—but nothing that would have drawn blood. Unless . . .

She'd been tight, but he remembered her body's resistance as slight, his initial penetration smooth. She'd cried out so many times he'd lost count. Surely he was experienced enough to recognize a shout of denial over one of encouragement. He'd never had sex with a virgin, so he had nothing for comparison, but—

The next fact hit him upside the head with the force of a baseball bat. He hadn't used a condom. And not having any in the room or on his person was a piss poor excuse for his lack of good judgment.

Thoughts of unwanted pregnancy, HIV, and a host of other sexually transmitted diseases reared their ugly heads while he bent to retrieve his clothes. He'd been a total idiot. And so had she. What moron in today's world had sex with a stranger and didn't use a condom? Modern women, he'd heard, even carried them in their purses. Madam X might have been a virgin—he was still doubtful on that score—but she'd been the aggressor. Why the hell hadn't she thought of it . . . before things had spiraled out of control?

Frustrated, he stomped to the bathroom and unzipped his shaving kit. There wasn't a damn thing he could do about the lack of a condom, but how was he supposed to get the truth about the spot on the bed linens?

Excuse me, Madam X, but was that stain on my sheet what I think it was?

He squinted into the mirror to study his stubbled jaw and was met instead with a detailed impression of her arresting face. Huge gray eyes fringed in sooty lashes, a strong nose, prominent cheekbones, and a wide, kiss-me-now mouth, all backfilled by skin the color of fresh cream stared at him in return. Frame the entire delectable picture in ebony hair that had felt like spun silk between his fingers, and the vision was complete.

One virgin with the power to seduce the devil himself.

The problem was, none of it made any sense. How could a beautiful woman over the age of twenty-five, and she was at least that, be untouched in this century?

And why had she chosen him to be the first?

Was it a coincidence that she'd been on the way to her room at the same moment he'd walked to the elevators, or was there some nefarious plan in motion?

Had the encounter been a whim or something more?

His thoughts swung to Everett Randall, major in the United States Army and a total pain in the ass. The man had a tenacious curiosity about all things extraterrestrial, and his bulldog nose was out of joint at being ordered to stand clear. Was Madam X part of a scheme orchestrated by Randall? Did he hope to use the night of indulgence to smear Lucas's good name? Or was the woman a ploy to keep him so enamored he'd ease up on the UFO investigation, thus opening the door for the major's interference?

If she was truly an innocent, would she have disappeared?

While he showered and dressed, Lucas told himself that whatever the reason for their tryst, he couldn't worry about it now. In the outer hallway, he cast a side-long glance at the door to the second suite on the floor. If he wasn't running late, he'd walk over and knock until she answered, provided, of course, she actually occupied the room. Too bad he had no time to check it out, just as he had no time to play sexual roulette with a vamp pretending to be an innocent who got her rocks off by seducing strangers.

Downstairs, he grabbed a cup of coffee from the complimentary stand and scanned the lobby, noting the lone clerk at the desk. Okay, so he had five minutes—what could it hurt to spend them learning his supposed neighbor's name? Dragging his manners out of mothballs, he strode to the counter.

"Mr. Diamond." The female attendant smiled warmly. "How can I help you?"

"I was wondering about the suite next to mine," he began. "Is it occupied?"

"Is something wrong with your room?" she asked, her expression one of concern. "If so, I'm sure we can take care of it without your having to move."

"My room is fine, thanks. But I was told the other suite on my floor was empty, and this morning I thought I heard the television."

She tapped on her keyboard, stared at the screen, then met his gaze. "The room has a guest, though it didn't when you checked in. Do you want me to speak with them about keeping the sound down or—"

"No, no, I was just curious." Lucas mentally crossed his fingers and focused on her name tag. "Tell me, Ms.

Jones, do you think I could have the occupant's name?"

Ms. Jones furrowed her brow. "I'm sorry, but it's against hotel policy to reveal that information."

"Even if it's a matter of government security?" he pushed. Not that he planned to get a court order, but a little side muscle might coerce her into breaking the rules.

"No. I mean—I'm not sure." She worried her lower lip. "I could speak with the front desk manager and check on what sort of protocol you'd need to follow."

"Don't go to any bother. I'll see what I can do at my end," Lucas said affably. All right, so maybe Madam X hadn't been lying about staying next door. That still didn't answer why she'd decided to ride the elevator at the precise moment he had. Or how she'd cured his headache. Or why she'd practically jumped his bones once they were alone. "Have a nice day," he muttered as he turned to exit the building.

Met with brilliant morning sunshine, Lucas headed toward the Treasury. The president was on his way to Bucharest, which left him in complete charge of the current crisis. He had to contend with the army, the media, and the members of his team without losing his cool. Luckily, he had permission to call Martin and tell him he was on the payroll again.

That, at least, was one bright spot in his day.

Mira raised an eyelid, then peered at the bedside clock and groaned. When she'd left Lucas, she'd been in a panic. Well aware she was in danger, she'd swallowed her fear and gone downstairs to check into the room next to his. Since it had been near 5:00 A.M., the clerk had given a single bleary glance at the computer screen before he'd taken an impression of her purloined card and instructed a bellman to escort her to the suite. She'd used the shower and fallen into bed without a thought to her next move.

Now that she was rested, she needed food, which would enable her to think more clearly about her predicament. Standing, she walked to the desk in the sitting room and looked over a menu. After ordering her meal, she returned to the bedroom and dressed. Sorting her clothing, she stowed her apparel and toiletries. If she ever had cause to entertain Lucas there, it was important she give the impression of a tourist new to the city who planned on a short stay.

Back in the open area, she turned on the television and searched for a news program, hoping there was no mention of a UFO sighting in DC or any other part of the country. Thirty minutes later her food arrived, and she ate while listening to various topics. When nothing caught her attention, she decided to stroll the sidewalk and contemplate strategy.

Mira rode the elevator to the ground level and walked across the lobby. Smiling at a young man sitting behind the bellman's desk, she sauntered into the street and assessed her surroundings. With little more to do than sightsee, she found a bench and took a seat.

Recalling the truth of what Lucas did for a living,

she realized she was in danger. It was best she avoid the area around the Treasury Building and contact him only when he arrived at the hotel. He was a clever man; if he noticed her lurking, he might think she'd been stalking him. Eventually, his curiosity would be aroused, especially since she'd revealed so little of herself. Though there was no way to connect her to the alien landings, she had to be extremely careful.

Again, she thought of her fellow travelers. Strangers when they'd first arrived at Project Rejuvenation, they'd become sisters united in a common goal: the continuation of their race. Clea was well versed in mental telepathy; Zara, the healer of the group; Nita, who had an affinity for communicating with animals; Rila, an empath and deep thinker. Sera, Xia, Mena, Kyla—each of them was unique in her own way, and each fully intended to succeed.

She bolstered her spirits with the knowledge that of the nine, only she had been matched to a human who lived in a densely populated area. If the other travelers stuck to the plan, they should be safe. She was the one, as Thane had pointed out, who would be in the most precarious position. She hadn't given much thought to his concern until she'd inspected Lucas's briefcase, and now saw that her situation was so much worse than precarious it was almost laughable.

What, she wondered, would Thane have done, had he known of her target's profession?

Gazing at the warming sun, she allowed herself a

few heartbeats of fancy. Mating with Lucas Diamond had been worth every moment of insecurity, each second of apprehension, every niggle of fear. They'd done things she'd never dreamed possible, touched and tasted in places that still brought her insides to a simmer. No one had prepared her for the emotions swirling in her brain, feelings that caused her breath to catch in her throat and her skin to tingle.

Sex, in all its thrilling glory, had consumed her, yet during the act she had thought about pleasing Lucas more than pleasing herself. What did such a desire signify?

Glancing at her bracelet, she resisted the urge to test for pregnancy. Her body required a number of Earth hours to give the proper response. More time would have to pass before she knew for certain if their joining had been a success. Heat flooded her chest when a traitorous voice deep inside rooted for failure. She had never failed at anything, yet the idea of coupling with Lucas again and again was too tempting to deny.

She couldn't help ponder what the next time they were together would bring.

Intent on her musings, she was startled by a man's voice. To her consternation, a stranger sat beside her. Tucking a strand of hair behind her ear, she gave him a polite smile. "Excuse me?"

"I asked if you had the time." He eyed her bracelet. "But I see you aren't wearing a watch, so I guess you don't know. Impressive bit of jewelry that. Are the stones real?"

Mira had been warned to guard her earrings and bracelet well. Her sole link to the mother ship, the baubles were her only form of protection and the means of finding out if she were pregnant. Earthlings, she'd been told, often stole stones such as these, something she could not allow to happen.

"No," she lied with a shake of her head.

"You sure?" He squinted against the sunlight. "I've got a pretty good eye for diamonds, and the ones in your ears look real to me. Ditto those rubies and emeralds." He reached out a weathered hand. "Mind if I take a closer look?"

Recalling the evasive measures she'd been taught in training, she drew back, held her palm to her waist, and scanned the street. Spotting a sign that might help her avoid further interrogation, she stood and gave another smile. "It's been nice talking with you, but I have to run. I'm meeting a friend, and I don't want to be late."

The stranger rose to his feet as well. Tall, with sad brown eyes and a day's growth of whiskers, he wore a pair of faded pants, a stained shirt, and an extremely ugly tie. "Sorry, I didn't mean to impose."

Mira hurried to the corner and waited for the light to change. The visitors' center beckoned, and she decided to take advantage of one of the available tours. Crossing with the light, she refused to glance over her shoulder or acknowledge the stranger in any way, but she felt his laser stare long after she went inside.

* * *

"What the hell is that?" Lucas glared at his desktop. For the past several hours he'd been staring at a plastic bag holding a teaspoon-sized lump of something that resembled barely set gelatin.

"Damned if I know. I'd just about given up finding anything concrete when I bent to repair a broken shoelace at the edge of the creek," explained Rigosi, propping himself on a corner of the desk. "This was stuck to the underside of a rock. If we'd had any more rain and the water had risen, it would have been washed away."

"Was this all of it?" Lucas asked.

"Except for what I sent to the lab. The same technician who ran the first battery of tests is taking care of this one," Rigosi added. "I didn't think it's wise we have too many folks discussing the results."

Lucas held the bag to the light, then peeled it open and stuck his nose inside, as he'd done several times that day. "Doesn't have an odor." He used the eraser end of a pencil to lift a small amount from the bag. "Any ideas?"

Martin Maddox took that moment to round the corner. "Lucas. Rigosi." He shook hands with both men. When he saw the bag, he froze. "What do you have there?"

"Martin, good to have you back," said Rigosi. "As to your question, I don't know. But it was found at the landing site. I've sent a sample to the lab for analysis."

Lucas checked his watch, noting it had taken his ex-superior less time than usual to make it there from his cabin in the hills of West Virginia. He must have broken every speed limit on the road to arrive before sundown.

Martin leaned forward and peered at the tip of Lucas's pencil. "Reminds me of what I coughed up last time I had a chest cold." Ignoring Rigosi's snort, he held out his palm. "Can I take a closer look?"

Lucas passed him the pencil, then cringed when he caught the corners of Martin's mouth twitch. "Jeez, are you out of your mind?"

The older man stuck his tongue on the globule and rolled his eyes. "Hmmm. Tastes like chicken," he said in a semiserious tone.

"Christ, you're makin' me sick," crowed Rigosi, his face gone pale. "I'm outta here. Let me know when you get the results."

Lucas waited for the investigator to leave before he spoke. "You are certifiable," he hissed. "We have no idea if that stuff is poisonous."

Grinning, Martin handed him the pencil. "Quit bellyaching. I'm not dead yet. Taste it for yourself."

"I'll wait for the lab report, thanks." Lucas scraped the gunk onto the inside of the plastic, tossed the pencil in the trash, and sealed the bag as if handling a national treasure. Frowning, he gave Martin another once-over. "You sure you're feeling all right?"

Martin gave a rusty-sounding laugh as he took a seat. "Hell, yes. Where's your sense of adventure, son?"

"I lost it when I saw you swallow," Lucas said. "Tell the truth. What did it taste like?"

"Not a damned thing. Perfect medium for a landing pod, if you ask me."

"A what?"

"Landing pod." Martin rested his elbows on his knees. "I had time to think on the ride down."

And it's a damned good thing, thought Lucas, heaving a breath. Thanks to Madam X, he'd found it difficult to form a coherent thought since he'd arrived at the office. "Care to clue me in on your idea?"

"I've been working on the information you gave me. According to your theory, the landing device was small, probably a one-seater. Rigosi and an entire team of dogs and men couldn't find any trace of a ship, yet you have viable touchdown coordinates. The first series of tests found minute amounts of a plasmalike substance basic to sustaining life. My guess is that's what you have in the bag, and, now that I've seen it, I think it's the remains of the creature's transportation."

Lucas eyed the slimy goo sitting in the middle of his desk, trying to see it as anything other than what it looked like—a glob of congealed egg white. "I'm not following."

"Try to imagine a mother ship, something so large there's no way it could enter our atmosphere and set down without calling attention to itself."

"All right, I'm there."

"Now imagine that same ship carrying nine individual miniships, let's call them pods. They shoot from the mother ship in a group, entering the atmosphere at the same speed with the same rate of intensity."

"The way the group of nine stars acted when we first saw them on the tracking screen."

"Correct. Now, envision those nine pods separating and heading for their destination. What self-respecting alien would leave the evidence of its arrival lying around for the army or some hick farmer to find?"

"But if they were made to self-destruct, wouldn't that do damage to the alien housed inside?"

"Not if the pod had the consistency of Silly Putty or a fairly viscous gel designed to absorb impact. The passenger steers the craft on its designated course while it plows through the atmosphere and makes a rubber ball sort of landing. Didn't you say it was raining cats and dogs the night of touchdown?"

"Here, yes. I'm not sure about the other sites." Lucas realized he had yet to show Maddox the report on the DNA. He opened a folder and passed the lab results across the desk.

Martin's eyes grew wide as he scanned the page. Finally, he gave a low whistle. "That caps it, then. My guess is, each craft landed in a body of water or in an area of precipitation. The aliens exited their ships and walked away, while the pods dissolved in the water or the rain. That's why there's been no evidence of a craft, yet that goo was found in the creek."

Lucas leaned back in his chair to contemplate the theory. If Martin was correct, it was a logical answer to why they had yet to locate a capsule, saucer, or suspicious debris of any kind. It also gave plausibility to the reason for the humanoid DNA they'd detected in Rock Creek.

He ran a hand through his hair. "I'm embarrassed I didn't think of it myself. I'm supposed to be the brains of this operation." He picked up the phone and pressed an office extension. "Janice, call the National Weather Service. Get me a report on the weather conditions at each site the night of the landing. If there wasn't rain, call the team captains and see if you can get a handle on the terrain they suspect their touchdown to have taken place."

Lucas hung up and steepled his fingers. "You want to know what I'm thinking?"

"I'm sure you're going to tell me."

"We've been visited by a race so closely resembling man, it's interchangeable."

Martin raised a brow. "If that's the case, we need to go at this from another angle. Instead of looking for the alien who landed here, we try to figure out why. Let the teams in the boondocks find their suspects, while we seek the method behind their madness."

"And allow an extraterrestrial to wander the streets of the nation's capital at will?"

"I'm not saying we stop the search. Your men can continue their investigation, while you and I concentrate on the reason why. We suspect they're friendly but frightened, and we're fairly certain they aren't going to attack us, or they already would have. The president is out of the country, so he's safe. It's going to be a hell of a lot easier for the outlying teams to find a needle in a handful of hay than here, where'd we'd we have to sift through an entire stack."

The phone rang, and Lucas answered. The information the assistant gave him came as no surprise. "Janice just confirmed that it rained at six of the sites. Since we know what it was doing here, I guess we don't need the news from Arizona or southern Virginia." He leaned back in his chair. "So, what do we do next?"

"You have to cover your bases," said Martin, folding his arms. "The fact that our visitors are able to lose themselves in the crowd only strengthens your other belief—they look and act completely human."

Lucas ran a hand over his jaw. "I can't seem to shake the feeling that whatever our alien is here for is specific to DC. Why else would it risk coming to such a populated area?"

"It makes sense they each have a mission or a goal, so let's figure out what makes Washington so special." Martin gazed at a picture of the current president hanging behind Lucas's desk. "What if the one who landed here is supposed to meet the movers and shakers of our world? The US is considered Earth's superpower, so it came to set up a talk with our leader. If that's the case, things will stay quiet as a tomb until the boss gets back from those peace talks."

"I'll buy meeting the president of the United States as a goal for our alien, but what about the others? Eight of them touched down in areas so sparsely populated there aren't enough bodies to fill a movie theater."

A sharp knock kept Lucas from taking the question further as Peggy stuck her head around the door.

"It's late. Janice went home, and I'm planning to do the same. I advise both of you to get some rest."

"There's still no information or updates on suspects in the other locations?" asked Lucas.

Peggy raised her gaze to the ceiling. "Martin, please remind our exalted director that some of our field operatives have been in place for a mere forty-eight hours. They're still establishing their cover and investigating the territory. He doesn't seem to listen when I relay the message."

"I'll try, but you know what a hard-ass the boy is," said Martin, grinning.

Lucas stood, tamping back a smile. "Okay, I get the point. I'm impatient, I'm pushy, and I'm driven." He shrugged. "In general, I'm a pain in the—"

"I'd say you summed it up rather nicely," intoned Peggy, her expression amused. "See you both at 0600."

After following her out the door with his eyes, Martin's face flushed red.

"You feeling up to par?" asked Lucas.

"Hmm? Oh, yeah. Fine. Just a little anxious is all. And not only about this alien thing."

"Something about Peggy?"

"You might say so. I've . . . um . . . been thinking a lot about her since her husband died."

Lucas smiled. "Care to fill me in on your thoughts?"

"Do you think it's too soon for her to be dating?"

"She went out with a congressional rep last week," answered Lucas, holding back a laugh.

"She what?"

"She's dating, pal. So if I were you, I'd get on the ball and make my play. Hell, half the people on staff were aware of your interest in the woman when you worked together. One of the things I've admired about both of you was your ability to keep things professional while she was married. It goes to character."

"Don't be fooled," said Martin, snorting. "It goes to being a workaholic and failing to see what's really important in life until it's too damned late. I should have made my move on the lady when we first met and courted her properly. By the time I was bright enough to realize I had feelings for her, Peggy was engaged to Joe, the lucky stiff."

Lucas glanced around his office, took in the dual computer terminals, interstellar maps crowded with pushpins, shelves overflowing with data. "You think a relationship with a woman is more important than our work here?"

"Damn straight. Proving aliens exist is what we do for a living, but it shouldn't be our life. I've come to realize there are times when a person needs to do his duty to his country, and times when he needs to be selfish, think about himself." Martin gathered his belongings as he stood. "If I hadn't let myself get buried in this damned UFO obsession, I'd have a half dozen grandchildren by now and a good woman to keep me warm when the snow starts to fall."

"I'm impressed," Lucas commented. "That's almost poetic."

"Don't you mean *pathetic?*" Martin arched a brow. "Take it from an old fool who's only recently come to grips with what life is all about. Love makes this world go round, Lucas. Not money or fame or honor to country, and certainly not the far-off galaxies in the heavens. And now that you've told me about Peggy and the dating, I plan to grab my chance at happiness."

A vague recollection of the way Lucas felt the first time he'd held his newborn son tugged at the edge of his mind. It had been the single moment in his life when his entire heart was engaged, and he'd experienced what Martin described. Uneasy with the emotional direction of the conversation, he tried to change the subject.

"What's pathetic is that cabin of yours. Did you ever get the generator to work and install running water?"

"It's all taken care of. So tell me, what's going on in your personal life? Seeing anyone?" Martin asked, continuing his rant.

Lucas expelled a breath. Knowing his mentor, the man would chip away at the topic until Lucas gave a satisfactory response. He tucked a stack of folders inside his briefcase, intending to stay mum, but the words slipped out of their own volition. "I'm not sure."

"Now there's an interesting answer."

They walked to the elevator in silence. Though Lucas knew Martin was waiting for an explanation, he didn't feel like confessing he'd spent the whole of the previous night having sex with a woman whose name he didn't even know.

"It's complicated," he finally muttered as they rode to the ground floor. "I doubt it will go anywhere."

"Do I know her?"

They stepped into the lobby and headed for the exit. "Not likely. I think she's a tourist."

"You *think* she's a tourist?"

Lucas hoped to hell he wasn't red-faced. "She's staying at my hotel."

"Then she's staying at *our* hotel," Martin said with a chuckle. "I checked in at lunchtime."

"You're at the Hay-Adams?"

"Why not? It's close to the office, and I thought you might be there. If one of us gets a brainstorm at 3:00 A.M., we can meet and discuss it."

The only person Lucas had hoped to associate with in the middle of the night was his supposed neighbor. But if and when he saw Madam X again, there would be no more playing the take-me-I'm-yours game unless he had some answers. They walked to the Hay-Adams in silence. Lucas followed his ex-boss through the hotel doors, his mind racing a hundred miles an hour.

Why had the woman been in the lobby at the precise moment he'd been going to his room? What had led her to become the aggressor? Why had she encouraged him to have unprotected sex? Had she truly been a virgin? Why had she left without a note or a word of good-bye?

What the hell was her name?

Martin took a seat in the bar area near a window. Lucas sat across from him and gazed into the dimly lit street. Buses carrying the remainder of the day's commuters trundled by while taxis dodged pedestrians still walking the street, both a reminder of the problem at hand. He spotted a solitary jogger, an older man on a bicycle; a nattily dressed suit type strolled past, carrying an umbrella and briefcase.

Any one of them could be their alien.

"How about we get a bite to eat?" asked Martin.

"A drink is all I have time for. I didn't get much sleep last night, and I have some paperwork to go over for tomorrow's breakfast meeting."

"Do I have to remind you that you need to stay rested and fed to keep on top of things?"

"It's not necessary. Peggy and the commander in chief harp on it daily." Lucas gave his order to a hovering waiter. "Besides, there's always room service."

Six

*M*ira paced the suite, unable to do more than think about her day. After touring a museum in the afternoon, she'd walked the streets and pondered her situation. The beautiful weather had brought to mind her home and its lovely temperate climate. There was no icy precipitation or snow, no hail, no hurricanes or tornadoes to hamper travelers, destroy buildings, or ruin crops. She'd read the *Washington Post* while sitting on a bench along the Mall and considered the upheaval many countries here were experiencing. Unlike Earth, her planet was united in all things. Long ago, her world had gone through the same chaos, come to terms, and found a peaceful solution.

It was then, with life so settled and serene, her planet began to experiment fully with genetics, as Earth was doing now. For generations, the scientists manipulated DNA and cloned their progeny in hopes of creating a perfect species. Too late, they realized the damage they'd done. The small number of men who were still capable of having sex were sterile, the rest impotent. In order to ensure future existence, they needed an infusion of fresh DNA, and this world was the only viable place to find it.

After returning to the hotel, she'd bathed and dressed in one of the sheer snippets of lingerie she'd been sold, then donned slacks and a comfortable shirt. The evening news had no mention of her arrival or that of her fellow travelers, which gave her courage. If she could keep Lucas interested in her long enough, he might lose interest in the landing, thus allowing her and her eight sisters to meet their goal and depart in anonymity.

At the soft *ping* of the elevator, Mira's pulse sped to a racer's pace. She inhaled a deep breath. She had waited the entire day for this single moment, and now it was at hand.

Lucas was here.

A smile tugged at the corners of her lips. She could take the next step. She was not pregnant, which meant she needed to have sex with Lucas again. Circumstances told her she was either incredibly lucky to be able to share in another mating or doomed to fail. Since failure wasn't an option, she accepted the additional opportunity she'd been given: a chance to experience passion with him again.

She went to the mirror above a chest holding liquor

bottles. Running shaky fingers through her hair, she aligned the curling tendrils and straightened her clothes. Lucas had been at his job well over twelve hours. Had he found out more about the landings? About her?

Aware there were still forty-eight hours left in her fertile cycle, she also knew that if she didn't conceive, her body would rest for seven days, and she would then be able to try again. Lucas and his men were searching for her, so she had to take advantage of every moment they were together.

After a final glance at her reflection, she walked to the door. Just as she reached for the knob, a knock startled her. Peering through the small hole, she saw Lucas, dressed in a white shirt with rolled-up sleeves. Save for a muscle tensing his jawline, his face seemed set in granite.

Had he somehow learned she'd examined the contents of his briefcase? Was he angry that she'd disappeared from his bed without a good-bye? The idea he might be seeking her out for a repeat of last night danced through her veins as she swung the door open.

Lucas gave Madam X a nod when she opened the door. So she did have the suite next to his. Relieved she hadn't lied, he took her in from head to toe. He'd forgotten what the sight of his mystery date's long silky curls, heart-shaped face, and lush mouth did to his libido. Reading the look of anticipation in her wide eyes, he reminded himself he was there for answers—not to get embroiled in another game.

"I was hoping you'd be . . . free."

She stepped aside, inviting him to enter with a sweep of her arm. "I'd planned to stay in tonight."

He followed her into the living area, a mirror image of his own suite. She stopped at the sideboard and surveyed the crystal decanters. Suddenly parched, Lucas stood beside her and poured a healthy amount of scotch into a tumbler. Not normally a drinker, he'd swallowed more alcohol in the past twenty-four hours than he had all month. Irritated that the woman seemed to drive him to it, he splashed an inch in a glass for her, then added water from a bottle on the chest.

She accepted the drink with a nuance of hesitation. He raised his glass, and she mimicked his actions. Together, they brought the liquid to their lips and sipped. He stared at her mouth, and her face flushed a soft pink.

"Would you like to join me—on the sofa?"

Lucas's penis throbbed to life at the suggestion. Gripping the tumbler, he shrugged. "Sure, why not."

She carried her glass to the seating area and settled in the middle of the couch. Recalling all that had taken place on the comfy piece of furniture in his own room, he opted for a side chair, close enough to read her facial expressions but with enough distance to retain his "hands-off" policy.

"I'm—"

"I—"

"You go—"

"No, you—"

They stumbled over their words, until he realized she was as nervous as he was. "Ladies first. I insist."

"Did you have a good day?"

She sat with her hands folded primly, and he almost laughed out loud. Though her mannerisms were that of a school principal, he wasn't fooled. Underneath the tailored slacks and demure shirt was the body of a living, breathing goddess with the sexual appetite of a seductress. What kind of game was she playing now?

"I spent it at work. How about you?"

"I took a tour of a museum, then spent the afternoon wandering a few of the buildings and monuments open to the public."

Lucas relaxed in the chair, hoping to project a man-of-the-world attitude. "Meet any friends?"

"Friends? Um . . . no. I don't know anyone here."

"You know me."

"Yes, but—"

"You don't know my name? Funny, I was thinking the same about you. I'm Lucas Diamond, by the way."

"I—I'm Margaret. Margaret Weston," she responded. Her cheeks flushed again. "I guess we forgot to exchange names last night."

"I guess we did," he drawled, stretching out the words. She didn't look like a Margaret or any variant of the old-fashioned name. "So, what do I call you? Marge, Margo—?"

"Mira. Please, call me Mira."

He raised a brow. "Unusual. Then again, I can't

help thinking everything about you is unusual. Take the way we met, for example . . ." He let the sentence hang. "I can't remember the last time I was accosted in a hotel elevator by a strange woman."

Her eyes flashed annoyance. "Accosted. Is that what you think I did?"

He gave a lazy smile. "What would you call it? I was minding my own business when you initiated a conversation and invited yourself to my room. Then you practically threw yourself at me. I'd say the word fits the description of how things got started fairly well."

Her fingers turned white around her drink. "I offered to cure your headache, if I remember correctly, and you accepted."

"Oh, you did that, too. I was hoping you'd explain how."

"I told you—I have a gift. It's nothing."

"And what we did afterward? Was that nothing, as well?"

She set the glass on the coffee table with a resounding *thwack*. "You're a grown man. You could have said no."

Interesting. She'd rationalized the act and apportioned blame accordingly. He'd already told himself he'd been a fool—he could have ushered her out, no harm–no foul. He was willing to accept half the blame for what they'd done, but she didn't need to know that just then.

He stood, hoping to ruffle her composure. "You were a virgin."

"How did you—?"

Lucas dropped onto the cushion next to her and leaned forward, looking to intimidate. "I'm not stupid, Mira. I saw the sheets."

She held a hand to her throat. "Oh."

Her smoky-sweet scent surrounded him, and he drew back. No way was he going to fall under her spell again. "We didn't use a condom."

She worried her lower lip. "It wasn't necessary. I don't have a disease."

"But you know nothing about me. What if I do?" he challenged.

"Do you?" she queried in return.

He squelched a bark of laughter. One thing was certain, she was quick on the uptake. Her sassy retorts reminded him of how exciting this type of sparring between a man and a woman could be. How important it was to test the waters for that special glimmer of compatibility that might lead to something more personal. Though he had no doubt the spark was there, ready to burst into flames, this was not the time or place to put the theory into practice.

"I believe there's another reason for wearing one. An important one," he threw back at her, trying to stay on track.

"That reason is not a consideration," she answered in a quiet voice.

Lucas glanced from her suddenly pale face to the fingers knotted in her lap. A wave of pity washed over him. Was there something in her past, something she couldn't bring herself to speak of, that had caused her to remain untouched until last night?

Like most men, he knew little about the female reproductive system other than what it took to get a woman pregnant—or prevent it. Aside from an expensive-looking bracelet and the diamond studs in her ears, she wore no jewelry, so he assumed she was single. He couldn't imagine why an unmarried female might try to conceive the way she had. These days, sperm banks were doing a booming business. He'd helped bolster their supply himself a decade ago, when he'd needed help paying for college.

A more ridiculous scenario played in his mind. Had she just left a convent or awakened from a coma, said "the hell with it" and decided to have sex with a stranger in order to play some weird game of catch up with society?

If so, why had she chosen him?

Her eyes glittered wetly, and he feared tears. Tina had turned the waterworks on and off at will, but something told him this was not the case with Mira. He hadn't meant to bully her, but he did want to show her he wouldn't be manipulated.

"How about we chalk up the entire experience to a mistake? Blame it on the late hour and loneliness; that way, we won't owe each other an explanation."

Her chin rose a notch. "I didn't think what we did

needed explaining. I'd been told—I thought sex between two healthy adults was a natural progression if there was an attraction."

"It is, provided the adults have things in common and share mutual respect. We don't know each other well enough to say that's true."

Her eyes narrowed and her brows rose. "You're here now, and so am I," she argued. "I doubt either of us has had dinner. If we ate together, we could do all those things and explore the possibilities."

"If this were any other time in my life—"

"Do you have plans?"

"I have paperwork to go over, a report to study. I'm supposed to be preparing for an early-morning meeting—"

"And sharing a few moments with me would ruin your night?"

Lucas stood, unwilling to admit that a few more hours with her would probably drive him crazy with frustration. "I'm sorry I came on so strong, but I'm in the middle of something critical at work. I don't think this is the right—I just can't get involved with anyone at this point in my life."

He went to the door, intent on escaping before she changed his mind.

"Lucas?"

When he turned, she was so close he had to grab her by the elbows to keep her upright. She stepped into his space, and his erection reminded him that he was the liar of the century. Seconds passed as she gazed at him, as if studying every emotion he felt certain was written on his face.

The urge to kiss her, to toss her over his shoulder and carry her to bed, was overpowering. From the moment he'd entered her suite, he had a gut feeling it would be dangerous to get close to her. He had to get away before he did something stupid, like touch her more intimately.

Backing up a step, he shook his head. "We have to end this before it gets complicated."

Mira stared at the closed door for a long moment and considered whether she should use her mental powers to call Lucas back. When she heard his door slam, she decided it was too late. Her talent didn't work through walls, and she suspected he would be a difficult subject. Dejected, she returned to the sofa and plopped onto the center cushion.

Lucas had walked—no—he'd practically run from her suite. But why?

Confusion bubbled up from inside, mixing with uncertainty. Bending forward, she rested her elbows on her knees and cradled her head in her palms. Unlike Earthlings, emotion did not rule the lives of her people unless they willed it. She was a logical being, and therefore capable of finding a logical solution to this current dilemma.

She mulled over the past few minutes. She and Lucas had sat face-to-face, enabling her to admire the intelligence in his eyes, as well as his dark wavy hair, broad shoulders, and large capable hands. He'd worn a stern expression to go with his gruff attitude, yet he'd been polite. The sight of long fingers curving around his glass had brought back memories of a night filled with tender strokes and intimate touches.

His questions had been a bit rude, but not overly so. It was obvious from the tenor of his deep, probing voice that he was annoyed she hadn't told him her name. And he was definitely concerned about the status of her virginity, as well as his error in not using preventative measures to avoid conception.

Was it any one of those things that had him so angry, or a combination of the three?

When she'd shown displeasure with his questioning, he'd adopted a forgiving attitude and headed for the door. She'd followed him with the hope of changing his mind, but it was only after they touched that he'd acted flustered . . . nervous . . . unsure.

The memory of that single joining of skin warmed her from the inside out. Her stomach trembled, recalling the way he'd cupped her elbows and let his fingers wander to her forearms. The words had died in her throat as she'd stared into his eyes. A heartbeat passed before she'd caught a glimmer of longing hovering in their compelling depths.

He had leaned so near she'd felt his breath on her cheeks, and she'd thought he might kiss her. Then he'd pulled back and told her their friendship had to end. Fumbling for the door, he had disappeared, leaving her irritated and . . . and . . .

Mira tugged at her ear, trying to find a way to best describe her feeling in order to translate her reaction into human terms, but the only word that continued to repeat was *wanting*. She smiled. Of course she *wanted* him. He was supposed to be the father of her child.

Feeling a bit more in control, she smoothed her hands down the front of her shirt, pleased at the logic of the word. If he suspected she had anything to do with the alien landing, he would have questioned her. Lucas didn't appear to be a cowardly man. Surely she could convince him to change his mind?

Failure was not an option, Mira told herself a second time. Squaring her shoulders, she readied for confrontation. She would see Lucas Diamond again, and she would be in control.

"You met the woman you saw Diamond talking to in the hotel lobby last night?"

"I did, and she seems perfectly ordinary. Attractive, polite, with a body that would stop traffic. She acted a bit skittish at first, but I don't blame her, considering I wasn't exactly dressed to impress."

"Then you have her information?"

The caller fiddled with his tie, an interesting blend of oranges and reds on faux-satin fabric. They'd never been formally introduced, but he'd done enough work for Major Everett Randall to know he was a somebody. His pay arrived in a plain brown envelope at a PO box in Silver Spring, Maryland, and the money was good no matter who it came from.

"Yeah, my bellman buddy copied the info from her credit card, and the rest was easy. Her name is Margaret Weston. Lives in McLean, in one of those gated, upper-crust neighborhoods where the homes look like libraries or courthouses. The report says she's married to a lobbyist, a good reason for Diamond to be so secretive about their meeting." He rattled on without stopping for a breath. "My informant says she has the suite next to Diamond's. With no other rooms on their floor, nobody would see her enter his. That way, when they did the nasty, no one could accuse them of shacking up together because she still had her own space."

"You're certain she's Margaret Weston? The woman's description matches that of the subject?" asked the moneyman.

"Close enough. Tall, dark brown hair, gray eyes—"

"What about her age?"

"Um . . . says here she's forty-five."

"Diamond is barely thirty-three. You saw her up close. Did she appear middle-aged to you?"

"How the heck should I know?" He would never confess the woman he'd met hadn't appeared to be a day over twenty-one. "Lots of guys go for older women, and there are plenty of ladies getting nipped and tucked these days. They can look twenty again, no sweat."

"Still, I find the disparity . . . unsettling. Where are they now?"

"The woman's been in her room since five. Diamond arrived about a half hour ago, had a drink with an older guy—he's staying here, too, by the way—and went upstairs."

"That would be Martin Maddox. Did they leave the bar together?"

"Nope. The old fellow stayed and ordered dinner."

"So Diamond and the woman, this Margaret Weston, could be together as we speak?"

"Could be. You want me to check?"

The major made a rude noise. "What do you propose to do? Knock on their doors?"

"I could have my bellman buddy deliver flowers to her room, or food to his. Tell them it's compliments of the house or—"

"Don't be stupid. Diamond won't fall for it, and he's the one I have to focus on." Randall exhaled a breath. "Let me use my connections to further investigate Mrs. Weston. You continue with your assignment. Just remember to keep detailed records of who she meets and what she does, and do not, under any circumstances, call attention to yourself. The two of you have already had one accidental meeting. Another might make her wary."

"Gotcha. I tail the woman when she leaves the building, write down what she does, who she sees and talks to, then I report back to you."

"That's all—for now."

Seven

Lucas stormed into his suite and slammed the door. He deserved a hit upside the head with a baseball bat— for several reasons. First, he should have skipped the excuses and made it crystal clear when he left Mira Weston there was zilch possibility of their having an affair. Then he should have let her bounce off his chest and fall flat on her backside when she'd all but run into him.

Instead, he'd almost kissed her—which would have led to God knows where if his common sense hadn't kicked in. Obviously the tension of the UFO landings and his stunted social life were conspiring against him. Between listening to Martin expound on his "love makes the world go round" theory, and the memory of what he and Mira had done, it was no wonder his sex drive had shifted into high gear.

He stomped to the bedroom, unknotted his tie, and flung it at the armoire, where it crumpled onto a stack of clean shirts. Mira's wide eyes and subtly defiant attitude flashed in front of him, and he muttered a curse. Even while arguing, she held an odd appeal that caught him by surprise and made him wonder what she was thinking. Worse, her open attempt to lure him back to bed was so flattering it bordered on the erotic. He'd spent less than fifteen minutes with her, and his erection was still at full mast. He couldn't remember when he'd last wanted a woman as much as he desired her.

To his consternation, thoughts of Mira had crept into his mind at odd moments throughout the day. Aside from the weeks after his son's death, he hadn't once allowed his personal problems—more specifically his divorce—to interfere with his job. The current UFO investigation could take from a week to a year. Fat chance he'd be able to have a relationship with her or any woman while things were so unsettled. Meeting her couldn't have come at a more inopportune time.

Oh, hell, what was he thinking? She probably lived halfway across the country. Which was the reason that as much as he was drawn to her, making a clean break of their encounter was only sensible.

Midway in the process of undoing buttons, he heard a knock. Since he'd made it clear to his neighbor he was no longer interested, he assumed it was his ex-boss, here to discuss another side to the missing alien theory or give him a second lecture on life, love, and the pursuit of happiness.

"Hang on!" He sprinted into the foyer and opened the door as he spoke. "What's the problem? Can't fall asleep?"

"Well, actually," said Mira, her expression amused. "No, I can't."

Lucas sucked in a breath. The woman really needed to get a handle on accepting rejection. She breezed past him, and he locked on to her swaying hips. His insides twisted when she sauntered to the sofa and settled in as if she belonged there.

Now what?

Best-case scenario, she was a woman who didn't take no for an answer, because he didn't want to deal with a nutcase or a stalker. Walking to the seating area, he dropped into a side chair and opted for a casual pose. The air between them crackled with sexual tension, a phenomenon Lucas decided to ignore as he studied her. Just minutes ago she'd been pale and weepy. Now she appeared calm, with an air of steely resolve in her silver eyes. Copying his relaxed posture, she seemed to be checking him out as well.

Lucas frowned. "I thought I made my feelings known. This isn't a good idea."

"I heard what you said."

"Then which of the words didn't you understand?" he continued. "Because I was pretty much to the point."

"You were." She flirted with a smile. "But in your haste to express yourself, you neglected to allow me to present my side. An oversight on your part, I'm sure."

"I thought your *side* was self-explanatory," he quipped, hating the fact that she was right.

"I also hoped to set the record straight, in case I gave the wrong impression. I'm not a stalker or a woman with . . . issues."

Great. She was a mind reader, and he had little patience for dealing with one of those right then. "Just because you don't resemble the typical garden variety stalker doesn't mean you're home free. I've heard they come in all shapes and sizes, and most of them appear normal, too."

"Normal can mean different things to different people," she sparred, still grinning.

"What are you? Some kind of shrink?"

"Not exactly, but I have studied human behavior. You might say it's my specialty."

"And what did you come up with where we're concerned?"

"For one thing, I don't think this . . . attraction we have for each other is normal, yet you're trying to pretend it is. Don't insult me by denying you feel the chemistry bubbling between us."

Lucas raised a brow. "I feel it, all right. But that doesn't make it safe to act on. And it damned well isn't convenient."

Her mouth twitched mischief. "You don't appear to be a man who does things because they're safe or convenient. In fact, I'd guess you're the type who enjoys a bit of mystery, maybe even a hint of danger in his life."

As she spoke, she ran a hand over the floral-printed sofa pillow at her side, and damn if Lucas didn't feel the heat of her fingers tripping up his chest. Glancing down, he gripped the chair arms when he realized his shirt was still unbuttoned. The last thing he wanted was to act like a prude while engaged in a battle of wills with such a smooth and clever talker.

"It won't work, Mira."

"I thought things *worked* fairly well last night." She stood and quickly covered the few feet that separated them. "You do remember last night, don't you? And the things we did with and to each other . . . several times."

Drawn by the light flickering in Lucas's dark eyes, Mira grew bold. When he moved to stand, she sat on his thighs and anchored him in place. Setting her palms on his cheeks, she leaned in and kissed him, moving her lips in blatant invitation.

Lucas growled into her open mouth, and she threaded her fingers through his hair, holding him captive with her hands. Then he took command of the kiss, overwhelming her with desire as his tongue stroked a primal call. Her heart hammered in expectation, waiting . . . yearning . . . aching for what came next.

She sucked at his full lower lip, trying to devour him sip by sip. Then he drew away. "This is crazy. We have to stop."

She snuggled into his chest. "Why?"

"Because I don't know you. Because things shouldn't be this simple. Because—"

Mira reached for his zipper, pulled it down in one drawn-out movement, and fondled his engorged flesh. "Let me show you how simple it can be."

Groaning, he inched his hands to her rib cage, moving so slowly she moaned in frustration. He flicked his thumbs over her aroused nipples, and a whimper caught in her throat. "I want to feel you sliding naked across my skin. Please."

Lucas gazed into her eyes as if searching deep inside her core, and Mira held her breath. Seconds passed, then he gave a lazy smile. Standing, he lifted her up, walked to his bedroom, and set her down next to his bed.

"Damned if I know why, but I can't seem to say no to you and make it stick."

"Then don't."

He sighed in resignation, and she stepped back to remove her clothes. Lucas matched her actions with enthusiasm, hopping on one foot, then the other, as he stripped off his shirt, shoes, and pants.

His teeth flashed white in the darkness. "You sure you aren't a stalker?"

"Positive," she said, aware he would consider it a lie if he knew her true identity.

He whipped aside the covers with one hand and pulled her close, kissing her like a drowning man taking his last breath. Tumbling onto the mattress, they rolled to the middle and began to feast. He licked at her breasts, and she trembled. Writhing against him, she tasted all the places she'd missed the night before. His salty-sweet skin teased her senses, making her hungry for more.

He bit gently on a nipple and drew it deep into his mouth. At her moan of approval, he slid a hand over her navel, moved lower to fondle the damp curls at the apex of her thighs. Mira parted her legs, and he found her hidden center. Using two fingers, he stroked in rhythm to her surging hips until she cried in surrender.

Gasping, she ran her palm down his shaft and cupped him from beneath. Skin to skin, they fought a raw, sensual battle, until she sat victorious on top of him.

Lucas grasped her hips and guided her onto his turgid shaft. The breath hissed from between his teeth as, inch by torturous inch, he filled her completely. Then he reared up and cradled her in his arms, rocking in place until she matched his mounting thrusts. Fused from pelvis to chest, they rose and fell in synchronization, as if born for this single incredible joining.

He nuzzled his lips against her neck, driving faster, higher, harder into her heat. Every nerve in her body vibrated when he spasmed inside of her and propelled them into the void. Mira's muscles stiffened as she hung suspended, lost in a star-filled moment of perfect harmony.

Together, they sighed their completion and fell slowly back to earth.

* * *

Mira woke in darkness and checked the clock glowing on the nightstand. It was past midnight, and she remembered that Lucas had an early-morning meeting to attend. Sensing that the topic of discussion would most likely be her and her fellow travelers sent a ripple of fear creeping up her spine.

Though the idea was terrifying, she had to accept it. She was Lucas Diamond's quarry, as much as he'd been hers. In seducing him, she had done her duty, just as he was doing his in leading the search to find her. He was sworn to uphold his mission, as she was hers.

Her eyes adjusted to the dim streetlight filtering through the window, and she saw that he'd crushed a pillow in his arms and held it to his chest. At rest, with a relaxed and sated expression on his handsome face, he appeared no older than a boy. She imagined the weight he carried on his shoulders, the enormous responsibility of heading an investigation that might change the course of his planet. People in charge of his government were depending on him but, thanks to her and the wiles of her fellow travelers, he would fail. Generations from now, when Project Rejuvenation was proven a success, they might meet again, and she could explain the reason for her actions. For the time being, these moments were all they would share.

Mira moved to the edge of the mattress and stood. Come morning, Lucas would be angry with her a second time, but she had to leave. She didn't want to answer what she was sure would be more questions, and she'd come to detest the falsehoods she'd been forced to tell, even though there had been a reason.

Thinking to make things easier for him, she closed her eyes and linked with his mind, now fully open to her through sleep. It would be easy to probe his subconscious, learn his secrets, and find out what he knew of her sister travelers, but there had already been too much subterfuge between them.

Instead, she planted a reminder that he rise automatically in order to ready himself for his appointment. She'd brought enough upheaval to his life. She refused to be the cause of trouble at his workplace.

She tiptoed through the room, gathering her clothes. In less than twenty-four hours, she would know if their joining had been successful. If they'd created a child, she would leave and find a safe haven at the appointed pickup site to wait out her time. If not, she had one more night in her current cycle to conceive.

She left his suite and opened the door to her room. The travelers had been warned there would most probably be dishonesty between them and their targets, but each had understood it was for the greater good. The elders had insisted the lies would come easily provided the women kept the goal foremost in their minds.

A feeling of dread welled from the pit of Mira's stomach. How foolish those words had been. Her people were an honest species who had built their present world on open communication among all their brethren. So far, the humans she'd dealt with had treated her kindly. Perhaps the elders had been wrong about them. Perhaps they would have understood the dilemma, helped with the rejuvenation of her race, and joined in a dialogue of friendship.

Considering Lucas's position in the government, he might even be one of their emissaries when that time came, just as she hoped to represent her world. Then they could work together, and he would see her not as a scheming interloper, but a woman with brains as well as commitment, a woman who wanted nothing more than happiness for her people.

Focusing on her mission, she drew comfort from the knowledge that she would have a child to love and care for when she was home.

What, she wondered, would Lucas have?

Eight

Lucas accepted the Styrofoam cup of coffee his administrative assistant handed him and sipped the bracing brew. Black and sweet, the steaming liquid trickled into his stomach and filtered caffeine to his foggy brain, bringing him a much-needed sense of clarity.

"You look rested," Janice observed, in her usual cheerful manner. "Better than I've seen you since this incident started."

"Thanks . . . I think," said Lucas, assessing the attendees as Janice walked from chair to chair to make certain everyone had what they needed before the meeting began.

Peggy sat to his right, Martin his left, a united front prepared to face the small group still in DC. Ringing the table from Peggy's right sat Rigosi, Elise Rodriguez, and a crew of dedicated professionals. Each was a team captain with a pair of underlings to command, but it wasn't nearly enough manpower to do this job justice.

Lucas rubbed the bridge of his nose as Peggy straightened a sheaf of papers. He smiled inwardly at her deceptive demeanor and motherly appearance. Her irreverent sense of humor and efficient attitude hid an intelligent and perceptive woman, one of the reasons he depended on her in a crisis.

Peggy would do the talking while he and Martin listened and pondered the next step. It also gave them both the luxury of reading the team members. Though their jobs were highly classified, this was still a place of business for people of varied personalities and principles. It was often better to learn of their concerns in private.

Taking another swallow of coffee, Lucas conceded there was a second reason for his decision to observe, and it had no place in this meeting or even in the building. Thank God Martin was a master at reading faces and body language, because Lucas was too distracted to trust his own judgment at the moment.

That morning, he'd awakened alone. Again.

Perversely, instead of being furious, he'd been accepting of Mira's absence, almost as if his brain had expected it. But that didn't mean he had to like it. It was obvious she enjoyed his company, not to mention their activity between the sheets, so what was it about him—or her—that kept Mira Weston from sleeping beside him throughout the night? And why had he felt so crestfallen when he'd found her gone?

"Ladies and gentlemen." Peggy called the meeting to order. "First on the agenda, Rigosi will bring us up to date on his team's search of Rock Creek Park."

Rigosi, the most talkative of the bunch, gave them the particulars of his findings, then regaled them with Martin's daring move at tasting the goo. Which led him to explain the lab analysis of the gelatinous substances they'd received from each of the eight sites.

"Question is," said Elise Rodriguez, one of two women in the group, "do we tell the other team captains what this stuff is? Now that it's dissolved in a storm or the water in which it was found, does it matter?"

"It might add to their understanding of the situation," Martin explained. "Lucas. What do you think?"

Lucas rested his gaze on the center of the table. "In order to keep the playing field level, I expect everyone on this assignment to have the same information." He went on to explain the bouncing-pod scenario, and exactly what they thought the goo had been used for. "Any questions?"

"You're saying this alien life-form had a way of using its mind—its intelligence—to guide a ship made of common everyday chemical compounds?" The comment came from Pruitt, new man on the team. "That's pretty incredible, sir."

"I agree. But it supports the rest of our theory. Now that we know the substances from each site are identical, Peggy's going to send field leaders a list of the chemicals that make up the goo. But before we continue, there's something else you need to know." He glanced at Martin, who nodded. "The results on the water revealed information that has us even more disturbed."

A hush fell over the room. "We believe the aliens are humanoid in appearance, possibly to the extent that it will be impossible to tell them apart from one of us without a complete DNA scan."

The pronouncement started a chain reaction of four-letter words. Lucas allowed his charges to grumble for a few moments before he filled them in on the reasoning. After answering a handful of questions, he instructed Peggy to move on.

"Okay, let's hear what the rest of you have in the way of information."

One by one, the captains gave an accounting of the little they'd discovered. Frowning, Peggy passed packets around the table. "Janice duplicated everything we received from the others. We haven't heard from our operatives in Minnesota, South Dakota, Montana, and Idaho, but because of their isolated locations we're not surprised. Arizona and the Michigan peninsula have had better luck—claim they're checking a few viable leads. The team on Virginia's eastern shore say they have one suspect, but they're waiting to attend some meeting run by a group of senior citizens before they fill us in. It seems a group of retirees had the stars in sight the same time we did, bombarded the

NASA station at Wallops with calls, and decided to run their own investigation."

Guffaws rang out around the table. "Serves the boys at Wallops right," commented a man who'd been in the division for twenty years. "Might give them something to do besides tracking weather balloons."

"I wouldn't knock our coworkers, considering we're batting zero." Peggy's statement held a note of chastisement that had the participants hanging their heads.

Rigosi tossed a paper clip on the table in disgust. "Hell, we have about a million people to search and a thousand public buildings to comb. Now that we're sure our target looks like any John Doe on the street, it'll be impossible to find him."

After a knock on the door, Janice entered the room. Peggy turned, and the assistant handed her a note. "The Texas team just called. I took down what they said word for word."

Peggy read the note and her face paled. "Well, it seems there's been an interesting development in Texas. They've come up with one viable suspect. And it's a woman."

Lucas's heart skipped a beat. She passed him the note, but he didn't bother reading it. How could he have been so stupid? They'd been searching for a man or a manlike creature, but not once had he thought the aliens would resemble the female form.

"They're sure?" he asked Janice, who was lingering in the doorway.

"Yes, sir. Frank told me himself. He wanted the others to be aware, in case they neglected checking women in their area."

"Great. Maybe NOW will offer them free membership," suggested Elise, her smile grim.

Griggs pushed from the table. "Well, hell. The idea of sifting through 49 percent of the population was tough enough. We'll never manage it now."

"What about the army?" asked Harden, his expression blank. "I know we have the upper hand on this sighting, but we might be able to use them to set up some kind of screening system—or something." He glanced around the table. "I don't see how we can do it alone."

Harden had never been high on Lucas's list of favorites. It figured he would bring up a suggestion that might involve Major Randall. "No military, at least not yet," he ordered, his tone harsh. "The last thing we need is some self-important GI Joe detaining, arresting or—God forbid—shooting innocent civilians." He rested his fists on the table. "Peggy, how many more bodies do we have available?"

"Five—ten if you count those on the tracking monitors."

"We can't afford to lose tracking power, but each of you can add one more to your team and return to your assigned grids. We'll meet here again at the same time tomorrow morning, unless there's a lead. Then we follow the usual drill."

The room emptied amid wry quips and angry observations. Lucas imagined what was going through each operative's mind. Like Griggs said, it was bad enough having to concentrate on the male population—now they had to include the females. It wouldn't be that difficult to broaden the hunt in the eight sparsely populated areas, but in DC it would be as tough as searching for a grain of black sand on a pristine white beach. The grain was there, right in front of your eyes, but owing to sheer numbers you'd never find it.

The door closed, and Martin drummed his fingers on the table. "Okay, now everybody knows what we know." He gazed at Lucas. "You going to call Texas, or shall I?"

"You do the honors. And make sure they give you details. I want to know what makes them think their alien is a woman, no matter how small the clue. Peggy, you continue trying to reach the teams we have yet to hear from. When you do, inform them of this female alien theory."

"Not to be nosy," prodded Martin, standing, "but what will you be doing?"

"Thinking."

Peggy circled the table, clearing coffee cups and picking up debris. When Lucas spoke, she smiled. "As if no one else working this project can?"

"Sorry, I didn't mean it as an insult," said Lucas. "I know you're both giving 100 percent."

"Thanks for the vote of confidence," said Martin. Peggy left the room and closed the door behind her. "Anyone you have doubts about?"

"I thought that was supposed to be your job," Lucas goaded.

"I didn't get a good read on anybody, but when Harden mentioned the military he was sweating."

"Do you think he's sleeping with Randall?"

Martin's smile stretched wide. "Nice way to put it."

"You know what I mean."

"Yeah, I know. And like I told you a few days ago, I don't trust him."

"You have connections. How about putting someone on it?"

He continued to grin. "Me?"

"Why not you? If I issue the request, it'll look as if I don't trust my own men. Coming from you—a crazy old retired guy calling up a favor from a friend—it'll be natural." Lucas sighed. "Besides, I need a background check, too, on someone unrelated to the office."

Martin raised his eyebrows. "You looking into someone I need to know about?"

Am I? Lucas had nothing to go on but gut instinct. Now that he knew there was at least one female suspect, there could be more. And one of them might have landed here.

"Sort of. It's just a hunch, and I doubt it will amount to anything, but I need to be sure."

"Okay." Martin headed for the door. "Someone should call within thirty minutes."

"Thirty minutes? Holy hell, Maddox, is there anything you can't do?"

"Leap tall buildings in a single bound?" quipped Martin as he strutted from the room.

Lucas leaned back and gazed at the ceiling. A wave of nausea swept over him at the idea they were searching for women. Rodriguez and Manderly wouldn't hesitate to take down one of their own, ditto Edith Hammer. But what about his men here and in the field? He and Martin and the rest of them had conducted plenty of talks on what an alien life-form might look like. They'd joked about little gray men, slime-dripping, three-eyed monsters, and ET doppelgängers, but he doubted any of them had ever believed an extraterrestrial would resemble the human race, let alone a woman.

He'd seen to it a check was run on Tina the morning after their second date. The few women he'd dated since his divorce, including a senator's daughter, had also received a thorough investigation. It would be irresponsible of him not to follow through, especially with what he'd just learned.

At the soft rap on the conference room door, he lowered his head.

"Lucas?" Janice brought in his handset. "There's a man on the line who says you're waiting for his call. Said to tell you he knows Martin."

He waited for her to leave before raising the phone to his ear. "Hello . . . that's correct . . . I want a background check, and I want it classified priority one. All I have is a name and a current address—the Hay-Adams."

He expelled a breath. "Her name is Margaret Weston."

The informant's left eye twitched, a nervous habit that popped up in times of stress. From the moment he'd answer his cell phone, he had the sinking feeling this conversation was headed for trouble.

"The woman in the Hay-Adams is an imposter," Randall began. "Margaret Weston is in her home as we speak, preparing to entertain guests for an evening of bridge."

At the sound of the major's strangled tone, he unknotted his tie. "Can't be. The bellman worked off a copy of her credit card. I secured the information through a reputable party. Your source has to be wrong."

"Credit cards can be stolen."

Since he'd once run an identity theft ring to earn extra cash for the start-up of his current business, he knew it was possible. He just couldn't imagine the woman he'd been tailing capable of such a dishonest act. "You sure she's not Weston?"

"My source is never wrong." A heartbeat passed before Randall's disgruntled voice continued. "Remember who you're talking to. I have channels at my disposal you can't even begin to realize. Thanks to your bungling, I'm forced to revise my direction in this matter."

"Hey, I resent that," the henchman answered. He

cleared his throat, ignoring the pointed silence. "So, who is she?"

"It's still unclear, but I have several parties working on it. It's imperative I find out why she's meeting clandestinely with Diamond at this particular time. To do so, I think it best we revert to Plan B."

"Plan B? Today?"

"Yes, today."

"But the day's practically over. I don't know if I can scare up the manpower this late—"

"I'll supply the personnel. All you have to do is verify when the subject leaves the hotel and what direction she's taken, then phone this number—" He rattled off ten digits. "They'll take care of the rest."

"But how—"

"You don't need to know. Simply call when our pigeon has flown the coop."

"What if she's with Diamond?"

"In light of his current responsibilities, I highly doubt he would be so stupid as to be seen with her in public, even though they've spent the last two nights together."

The statement aroused his curiosity, forcing the informant to ask, "So what does this Diamond guy do, anyway?"

"None of your business."

Dumb question. "That still don't mean they can't meet on the street, like it was an accident or something."

"If that is the case—well, let's just say it will enable me to take care of both birds with one shot."

"Hey, I don't like what I'm hearing. Maybe I should walk right now, 'cause it sounds to me as if someone's gonna get hurt. I don't have a problem doing a little computer hacking or tailgating, but I never signed on for anything that would get me ten-to-twenty." *Or the electric chair.*

"It's a bit late to start having pangs of guilt, don't you think? Simply tell the person who answers that number when the woman next leaves the Hay-Adams, and your work will be done. Once things are under control, your fee will be sent to the usual address. Understand?"

The informant fingered his loosened shirt collar. He didn't want to be part of a job that got anyone killed, especially a babe who seemed as innocent and refined as Margaret Weston, or whatever her name was.

"You're sure all I got to do is call the number?"

"Positive. Now get moving."

When Mira left Lucas's suite that morning, she'd hung the DO NOT DISTURB sign on her door and programmed herself to wake after a decent interval. Now fully aware, she was unable to concentrate on anything except her next meal and finding out if she was pregnant. She doubted Lucas would arrive anytime soon, and it would be several hours before she could take the test, so she ordered food from room service, turned on the television, and skipped from news program to news program.

Relieved there were still no reports of an alien or

UFO sighting anywhere in the United States, she ate while she read the *Washington Post,* a periodical the hotel delivered to her door each day. It was always possible the paper had a source the rest of the media weren't able to access. After scanning the headlines in each section, she sat back and breathed a sigh of relief.

She was safe.

She walked to the window to admire the view. The setting sun glowed warmly in a pale blue sky, bathing the formidable marble-and-stone buildings in an attractive luminescent glow. Washington, DC was old when measured in Earth time, but compared to her culture the capital of this country was barely past its infancy. Generations ago, the cities on her planet had looked very much like this one, until a momentous conflagration destroyed all but the most fortified of strongholds.

It was then the remaining elders held a summit with the last surviving leaders and decided on a plan to force their myriad nations to unite. Desperate for peace, they haggled and made concessions, turned from the amassing of weapons, and installed a new world order. The scientists were ordered to concentrate on two distinct avenues of research: exploring other galaxies and investigating a way to reinvent their people so they were perfect in both mind and body.

A vast amount of time passed, during which the original elders died and others were elected. The council refined their planet until it surpassed everyone's imagination. Her people found the idea of propagating an exceptional race fascinating and urged the scientists to continue their efforts to create a superior species.

That she was on Earth and capable of this mission proved their foray into space travel had been a success. Mira glanced at her bracelet, a beautiful and ingenious testament to ninents of their mental growth. Their single failure had been that of manipulating the DNA code. No one had realized the danger waiting to strike until it was living among them. Her people had learned so much, but in the learning had lost more.

Now they were a dying race.

The necessity of lying to Lucas saddened her. From what Mira understood of humans, he was one of a minority who believed in the existence of life on other planets. More than that, he was assigned to capture any of those beings unfortunate enough to land on Earth. If his superiors found he'd allowed an alien to slip through his fingers . . .

She sighed, unhappy to admit her second worry was more personal, and therefore more troublesome. She was confident they would conceive a child. When that happened, Lucas would reside with her forever in the guise of his son.

She tried to focus on her goal, but memories of Lucas and what he was coming to mean to her blurred the line she'd been ordered never to cross. His penetrating stare, his wry wit and teasing laughter, his smooth capable hands and clever fingers stroking her skin, came flooding back in a wave of longing. When she closed her eyes, she swore she felt his mouth skimming her body, warming her blood and her heart.

A shiver of warning rippled through her veins, reminding her such wayward thoughts would lead nowhere. She had to do something constructive to pass the time instead of dreaming about an intimacy that could never be.

A second glance out the window convinced her the weather was glorious, just right for a stroll. Minutes later, she passed the bell stand and pushed through the hotel's revolving door. Intent on avoiding Lucas's place of work, she crossed the street and walked in the opposite direction until she found a store selling souvenirs, packaged food, and a variety of publications.

Next to the shelf of newspapers stood a wire rack holding smaller periodicals with grainy photos enhancing their cover pages. She noted the *Daily Reporter, National Enquirer, Star Magazine*. Peering at each one, she gave a quiet gasp when she spotted the bottom corner of the *Weekly World News*. A box, boldly outlined in red, enclosed a single sentence: BIZARRE RITUAL IN MONTANA BLAMED ON ALIENS.

Mira paid for the paper, shoved it into her tote bag, and headed outside, intent on finding a quiet bench where she could peruse the article. She didn't notice the black sedan that pulled to the curb next to her until a man climbed out and stood at her side.

"Margaret Weston?"

She held a hand to her throat. "I'm—I—"

The stranger, broad of body with a square face and severe haircut, grabbed her elbow. "Please come with me."

Her heart jumped. How did he know her name? What did he want? Had Lucas somehow found out who she was and sent this person to collect her?

She tried to read his thoughts, but was unable to concentrate. She jerked away and took a step of retreat. "Excuse me, but I don't know you."

"That doesn't matter." His voice turned threatening. "Come along quietly, and you won't be hurt."

"Are you arresting me?"

Growling his frustration, he reached for her a second time, but she dodged his grasping fingers and set out at a frantic pace. She'd learned the rules of this country well; if he were someone of authority, he would have shown his credentials. Refusing to panic, she trotted toward the hotel and zeroed in on a police car parked across the street.

Her mind filled with possibilities. If the person followed, she would assess the danger and act on it. If not, she would go to her suite and take the pregnancy test before deciding her next move, even though it might be too early for a competent reading. A negative or unclear result would force her to wait for Lucas in order to be intimate with him one final time. But because of the man who had just accosted her, she would still need to leave.

She stopped at the official vehicle and smiled through the window. "Excuse me, Officer."

The patrolman stared at her. "Can I help you?"

"I was wondering, could you—could you recommend a good restaurant, something nearby that's not too expensive?"

"There are plenty around," the man said, his expression polite but disinterested. "I'm sure the hotel you're staying at can give you a list."

"Guess I should have thought of that myself. Thanks."

"Not a problem."

Mira straightened and walked to the corner to check the opposite street. There was no sign of the stranger or his car.

Nine

Lucas read for a third time the typed pages that had arrived by special messenger less than fifteen minutes ago. He tried to make sense of it, but the information still boggled his mind. Other than a list of data, it had no marks to identify the source or which agency had run the search, but it seemed thorough and professional.

He stared at the unfamiliar black-and-white photo copied from a Virginia driver's license, then gave the accompanying paperwork another scan. Margaret Weston was a five-foot-six inch, forty-four-year-old female with dark brown hair and gray eyes who lived in McLean with her husband Harold and a pair of poodles named Mickey and Minnie. A registered Republican, she drove a Jaguar, played bridge, and belonged to a variety of charitable and civic organizations. In her spare time, she worked as an interior designer at a well-established firm, but thanks to her husband's position as a respected lobbyist, didn't need the money.

And that afternoon Mrs. Weston had filed a report with her bank stating she'd misplaced her debit card sometime in the past few days. She was also disputing a large cash withdrawal and charges made three days ago at a high-priced boutique.

A knot formed in the pit of Lucas's stomach. He had choices, but none of them were palatable. If he barged into Mira's suite and accused her of being a fraud, there was a good chance he'd kick in her flight response, which would leave him looking like a grade-A fool when he went to the authorities. If he asked her about the possibility of identity theft and she had a plausible excuse, he'd also look stupid.

Either way he doubted he'd ever see her again.

He raised his head at the knock on his office door.

Martin stepped inside. "You have the report?"

Lucas nodded. "Your friend is fast."

"He's just an acquaintance who knows how to get things done. You can't work in this town half your life and not collect a few of that sort." Martin took a seat. "Does it tell you what you wanted to know?"

Snorting, Lucas slid the papers across the desk. "Hardly."

Martin's eyebrows rose as he scanned the data. "I take it this is the woman we discussed the other night? The one you thought was a tourist?"

"According to that document, she isn't a tourist. And she isn't the woman I've been seeing."

"Sorry, I'm not following."

Lucas leaned back in his chair. "I believe the enclosed information is true of Margaret Weston, a forty-four-year-old married woman from McLean. There's just one problem. My friend is about twenty-five, a lot better-looking, and from the sound of it she's guilty of credit card fraud." He frowned. "I have no choice but to confront her."

"Guess so." Martin glanced at his watch. "Think she's still awake?"

Lucas recalled how late it had been when he'd gone to Mira's room the previous night and found her waiting. Realizing he'd never seen her in the light of day, he mentally shook his head. For all he knew, the woman was a damned vampire.

"If she's still in town, she'll be up."

"Maybe you should stay out of it—go straight to the police and turn her in. Better still, let the hotel do it. They'll be contacted soon, if they haven't been already. That way you won't look like the bad guy."

Though the first idea wasn't palatable, he knew it was the most responsible. Except he'd have to explain to the authorities how he and Mira had met and admit he'd been duped into playing some sort of sexual game with a stranger. Before he let that happen, he wanted to hear from her own mouth the reason why she'd approached him at the elevator.

"I don't have the time to file an offense report or get involved," Lucas said, knowing it was a plausible excuse. "Did you reach the team in Texas?"

"That's why I'm here. I finally tracked down Frank, who's not as sure as Chuck about their suspect. Either way, the details are sketchy. The woman they're watching is young and new to town. She helped a local boy with a medical problem, and she's close-mouthed about her background. She also seems out of place. The area is Hicksville, USA, just like the others. She's working in a rinky-dink diner, yet she's got class, wears expensive jewelry—"

Lucas straightened as the knot in his stomach tightened. "What kind of jewelry?"

"Frank mentioned a gem-studded bracelet— diamonds, rubies, emeralds. He's no expert, but he thinks they're real. She also wears a diamond big as a pea in each earlobe. They don't have much else past a gut feeling about her."

"Do you have a description?"

"She's a blond, tall and full-figured, with curves in all the right places. There's some man in the town, father of the kid she helped, who seems interested in her—"

"Did they give his name?"

"Nope, but I can get it." Martin scratched his jaw. "You think that's important?"

Lucas had no idea. His imagination had taken hold and set his brain running wild. The scenario he was concocting was so crazy, so unbelievable—

"Does he—do they—" He stumbled over the words. It was useless worrying about what was going on fifteen hundred miles away, when the answer to everything might be sitting three blocks from here. He checked his watch and saw that it was near midnight. "Forget what I said. I'll work it out."

His mind buzzed with the bizarre stories he'd read on alien abduction in a few of the more outrageous reports. If the facts had been correct, he might very well have a starring role in the next version. Torn between what he hoped to be true and fearing what would happen if it was, he made a decision.

"If I'm not here for tomorrow's meeting, I want you to come looking for—scratch that—if I don't call you in an hour, come to my suite. If I'm not there, check the room next door. If it's empty—" He lowered his gaze to the report. "I expect you and Peggy to follow up on the female alien theory and handle things if I disappear."

"Disappear?" Martin grinned. "You plan on taking a vacation with the woman?"

"No, but I am going to confront her."

"And you think it will be so traumatic you won't make it in to work?" He shook his head and stood. "Talk to your supposed credit card thief and let me know what happened in the morning. In fact, I'm heading for the hotel right now. I could come with you."

"No." Lucas fairly shouted the word. He felt foolish enough without being made a fool in front of Martin. "I still have a few things to clear up here. I'll take care of it myself as soon as I get there."

Martin raised both eyebrows. "Is something else bothering you? Something you're not telling me?"

"I have a lot to think about. The woman is just the tip of the iceberg. Think we'll get full briefings from our operatives tomorrow?"

"I'd say yes. They're in their fourth day, so they should have something we can chew on." His expression conflicted, he edged to the door. "You know I'll back you a hundred percent, even if you have a hunch that makes no sense."

Lucas nodded, too keyed up to voice what he was thinking. "Thanks. I'll let you know."

As the ex-director's footsteps faded, his thoughts turned back to when he'd changed his career path. Eight years ago, he'd entrusted his passion for the unknown to Martin Maddox. If not for his mentor, Lucas wouldn't be where he was, only moments from the possibility of fulfilling his dream. He owed the man so much, yet couldn't bring himself to share this latest idea.

If he was wrong, he'd look like an idiot. Either way, he had to go head-to-head with a woman he'd begun to care about.

Shocked by the surreal thought, he pushed it to the farthest reaches of his mind, but that didn't calm his nerves. An inner sense told him that after tonight, his life would be changed forever.

Leaning sideways, he unlocked his bottom desk drawer. He hadn't wanted Martin to see what he kept there, but something told him it was time he put the handcuffs and revolver—two pieces of hardware he hadn't needed since his stint in the Secret Service—to good use.

He slipped the cuffs in his jacket pocket and the gun and an extra ammo clip into his briefcase, and left for the hotel.

At the *ding* of the elevator, Mira woke from the foyer floor and struggled to her feet. The moment she'd returned to the hotel, she'd stuffed her tote bag with a change of clothes and a few essentials. Then she'd taken the pregnancy test.

The negative result of the test, combined with the men who had tried to abduct her, had shredded her composure until she thought she might scream.

If not for that disappointment, she would have left immediately, never to see Lucas again. The fact that someone beside him knew her by sight and wanted to take her away terrified her, but she couldn't lose this final chance to conceive a child before she ran. She'd decided to await his arrival here and fallen asleep.

She peered out the peephole and saw him standing with his eyes riveted on her door. With his jaw clenched, he seemed absorbed in thought as he stepped toward her suite. She slipped her tote bag into the entry closet and waited for his knock.

When it came, she opened the door and smiled a greeting. "I've been waiting for you."

He walked past her, and she followed him into the

sitting room. Turning, he set his briefcase on a side table and undid the locks, but didn't raise the lid. She held her breath, positive he was going to pull out the papers he'd amassed on her landing. Instead, he propped himself against the back of the sofa and gazed at her through brooding eyes.

"What did you do today?"

"Do? Not much." She sidled toward him, refusing to glance at the briefcase. "I missed you."

"Did you?"

When Mira focused on the front of his shirt and began to undo the buttons, he caught both her wrists in one hand and held them against his chest. The forceful gesture was not meant to be endearing.

"We need to talk."

She bit her lower lip. His wary expression seemed cast in stone. "Can't it wait until after—"

"After what? You seduce me again?"

She detected anger in his tone, and it frightened her. "I thought we already had this talk, and agreed to disagree."

"First, tell me your name."

"I already told you, it's Margaret. Margaret Weston."

"Where do you live?"

"For the moment, here," she answered, hoping to make him smile. "Does it matter?"

"Humor me. Give me an address or the name of a city—even a state—some simple fact about you that I can verify as true."

Mira knew then that something had happened to make him suspicious of not just her actions but *her*. She had to mate with him one more time, then she could leave this place, find shelter, and think.

"We can talk later. Let's go to bed first."

"As tempting as the idea sounds, it won't work, not this time. If you won't tell me where you're from, tell me your birth date and year."

"Why?"

"Are you married?"

"No."

"Running from the law?"

"I'm not a criminal." She tried to pull away, but he tightened his grip. "You're hurting me."

He sighed. Fumbling in his pants pocket with his free hand, he brought out a set of metal rings. When Mira realized what they were, she tugged free of his fingers. Crossing her arms behind her back, she took a step of retreat. Was Lucas going to make her his prisoner? Was he arresting her for the theft of Margaret Weston's credit card?

Did he know who she was?

She thought fleetingly of using one of her energy stones, then decided she might need them all to make her escape. Meeting Lucas's stare, she knew the intense concentration needed to give a proper suggestion would take too long. The best she could hope for was a minute's head start and the possibility of leaving him with no memory of their time together.

She yanked on her earlobe, and gave a silent command.

Stop! Don't move! Forget the past three days! Forget me!

Pivoting on her heels, she raced to the closet, picked up her tote bag, and ran from the suite.

Seconds passed as Lucas, his brain suddenly fogged, watched the woman leave. Who was she? What was her name?

Unable to take a step, his eyes darted around the room. *Hotel.* The word clicked in his mind. Not his room . . . Mira's.

Blearily, he came to his senses. What the hell had just happened? He rotated his shoulders to unloosen taut muscles, then glanced at his hand. Why was he holding handcuffs?

Go after her, his brain commanded, breaking through the haze. *Don't let her get away.*

He stuffed the handcuffs in his pocket, got to the door before he remembered his gun, and ran back to remove it from the briefcase. In the foyer, he noted the elevator's descent, found the fire exit, and took the stairs two at a time, his mind clearing with every step.

He'd been an idiot for not putting the pieces together sooner. He deserved to be fired for his inability to control his raging hormones. He'd almost blown the biggest find of the century for nothing more than a few nights of horizontal recreation.

At the lobby level, he noted the elevator was already climbing upward from the parking garage, so he raced back to the stairs. Slamming open the garage door, he stopped in his tracks. Scanning the dimly lit space, he spotted Mira in the distance, walking briskly toward the exit.

Before he could move, he heard the squeal of tires. A midsize black sedan, its high beams blinding, swung around the corner and screeched to a halt at her side. Two men jumped out, grabbed her arms and pinned her to the car.

Drawing his gun, Lucas took off at a sprint and rounded a row of parked vehicles in a crouch, hoping to intercept the trio from the rear. He couldn't risk firing, but he could intimidate.

"Stop!" He aimed the weapon. "Let her go! Now!"

Ignoring his command, the men tried to wrestle Mira into the car. Instead of giving in or crying out, she kicked free like a martial arts expert, whirled, and dived for cover, impressing Lucas with her strength and agility.

He used the distraction to get closer and attacked from behind. One swift whack with the butt of his revolver had the first thug on the cement. The shorter, stockier man turned and plowed a fist in his gut. He lost his grip on the gun, stumbled, and came up swinging. Three punches later, the second man was stretched out next to his pal.

Bending down, Lucas retrieved his weapon, then turned both men over and scrutinized their faces. Though they were dressed in civilian garb, he'd dealt with enough military to know an enlisted man when he saw one. Searching their suit pockets, he found nothing.

He rose to his feet and panned the garage. *Where the hell was she?*

At the sound of a scuffling noise he duckwalked toward a far row of cars, sneaked up on his quarry, and wrapped an arm around her waist. "Going somewhere?"

Mira struggled, her heart beating against his forearm in triple time. He hauled her upward in a punishing grip, and she rammed an elbow in his ribs. Inhaling a painful gasp, he asked, "Is that anyway to treat your savior?"

Her shoulders sagged, her body went limp. Had she fainted? He loosened his arm, and she took off running. Cursing, Lucas zigzagged between vehicles to gain ground, vowing never again to underestimate her. When he was close enough to hear her panicked breathing, he tackled her to the ground. She thrashed beneath him, and damn if the squirming didn't bring his arousal to life. Too bad for her he was smarter now. No more would he be swayed by a hot body and even hotter sex.

She expelled a gasp of air and stilled. Willing his erection to take a hike, he grunted out a whisper. "Swear you won't run, and I'll let you up."

A moment passed before Mira nodded. He came to his feet, his free hand still clasping her upper arm. Slowly, she rose to her knees, collecting her tote bag as she stood. He hauled her against his side and dragged her along until he found the vehicle he was looking for. Good thing Martin had decided to stay at the same hotel.

Clutching her tightly, he tucked the gun in his waistband and bent toward the Humvee's rear wheel well. When he found his prize, he gave a silent prayer of thanks to whatever angel was watching over him. The ex-director hadn't changed the hiding spot of his spare key.

Dragging her to the driver's side, Lucas thrust her none too gently into the vehicle and tapped on the childproof locks. "Climb over," he ordered, "and get situated." He slid behind the wheel and slammed the door, then started the engine.

At this hour the garage was deserted. He steered past the black sedan and drove for the exit. Pulling down the visor, he found the parking ticket and passed it to the sleepy-eyed attendant along with a twenty-dollar bill. "Do me a favor and add the charges to my tab."

He held the wheel in a death grip as he swung the Hummer into the street. "Put on your seat belt."

Mira obeyed without a word.

He didn't have a clue what question to ask first. Who were those men? Why were they after her? Where did she come from? Was she an alien? If so, why had she and the others traveled to Earth? Where had she planned to go when she left the hotel?

Why had she seduced him?

Lucas gave a sidelong glance and caught her staring

through narrowed eyes. He doubted he'd ever heard a grain of truth from her lips, so why would she be honest with him now? He was a patient man, but her belligerent manner pissed him off.

This was his country, dammit. His job. His dream. She had no right to use him and run away.

She sighed loud and long. "Where are you taking me?"

He fought the urge to gloat. Just because he had her in custody didn't mean he'd won. Somebody knew who—or what—she was, and they wanted in. Now.

"I'll make a deal with you. A question for a question."

She gave a strangled laugh. "I suppose you want to go first?"

"Don't sound so superior. I'd say I earned that right about five minutes ago."

"You have a weapon, and I'm your prisoner. What am I supposed to say?"

"How about you begin by promising not to lie?"

Her silence told Lucas he had a fifty-fifty chance of getting the truth. There was so much he wanted to know, but only one sentence formed on his lips.

"Just who the hell are you?"

Mira didn't answer. There was nothing she could say that would protect her identity and appease his need to know at the same time. She'd recognized one of the men in the garage from the kidnapping attempt on the street, so she was certain the two incidents were linked. Since the only human she'd interacted with on a personal level was Lucas, he had to be the key. But how were they connected?

She stared at her bracelet. Lucas was in control of their vehicle, and they seemed to be leaving the city. She could implant another suggestion, tell him to stop the car and let her out, but from the easy time he'd had slipping free of her last mental order that might not work. And it would be unwise if they were being followed. Better to deal with a man she knew than run from strangers.

So what if he believed her a thief or thought she was an alien? She merely had to keep him guessing until they were intimate one more time. Though she was on the last day of her first cycle, there was still a slim possibility she might conceive. If she failed, there would be other trips to this planet, other men. Did it matter that once she left Earth, she would never see Lucas again?

Sighing, Mira hardened her resolve.

"I'm waiting for an answer. I think I deserve the truth after saving your bacon back there, don't you?"

His annoyed tone pulled her to attention. *Saving your bacon?* She itched to use her translator chip to interpret the odd saying, but couldn't afford to call attention to any more of her abilities in his presence.

"How do I know you're not in league with those men in the garage?" she asked, knowing full well he wasn't.

He snorted. "Sweetheart, if I was working with them, you'd already be on a plane heading for a cozy little hideaway in the desert. I assume you've heard of Area 51?"

Mira swallowed a gasp. The place he spoke of was legend in the universe. Years ago, humans had captured the crew of a downed ship that had come to Earth on a peaceful, information-gathering mission. The government had hidden the craft in an underground facility so isolated they were able to deny its existence. Rumor had it they'd dissected and destroyed the passengers, and were still studying the craft in hopes of learning its secrets. The story only reinforced the reason alien species were fearful of making direct contact with the people of this planet.

"To update your information, Area 51 is the place we Earthlings take aliens to perform our dastardly experiments. There are dozens like you in cold storage, just waiting to be sliced and diced," he said wryly, as if amused by his own wit.

"You're delusional," she responded, hoping bravado would mask her horror. "Aliens don't exist."

"No?" He shrugged. "Then I guess that mind control thing you zapped me with up in the room was your half-assed version of the Vulcan mind-meld."

When she didn't answer, he cleared his throat. "Is that why you and the others are here? To have sex with us poor pathetic humans, then play mental games to find out what makes us tick?"

"I have no idea what you're talking about."

His eyes never left the road. "All right, have it your way. We'll go at this from another angle." Merging onto a highway, Lucas kept the vehicle in the slow lane. "Who are you? And don't tell me Margaret Weston, because the woman reported the credit card you used at the Hay-Adams as stolen."

"How do you know that?"

"I ordered a background check run on the credit card."

The statement stabbed at Mira's heart. She knew Lucas was an intelligent man with an important position in his government, but she thought he might have developed some nugget of feeling for her, as she had for him. It hurt to know she meant so little to him that he'd pried into her nonexistent life.

"You had me investigated? After what we did—the time we spent together? That's insulting."

"I asked for answers, and you refused to give them. Under the circumstances, I had no other choice."

"What circumstances?"

He shifted in his seat. "My job, for one thing. I have to be careful who I associate with. And you and I did a hell of a lot more than shake hands and exchange business cards."

"You have a profession that interferes with your personal life?" she asked, pretending she knew nothing of his career.

"I'll tell you about it after you show some honesty." He gazed at her, then back at the road. "Is Mira your real name?"

"Yes."

"Truth?"

"Yes. And I've just answered two questions. I believe it's my turn."

His bark of laughter bounced off the interior of the huge vehicle. "You're a piece of work." He sighed. "Okay, shoot."

"Where are we going?"

He had to question her, but where? If she was an alien, and there was a covert group looking to make big money on her capture, he had a duty to keep her safe . . . and Peggy and Martin, too. He named the first place that came to mind, then realized it made perfect sense.

"To Martin's house—but it's more of a cabin. Last time I visited, it was a bit on the rustic side."

"Who is Martin?"

"My ex-boss. You'd like him, and I know he'd like you. He's waited a long time to meet an alien."

She decided to ignore any reference he made to aliens and space travel. "Very funny. And this cabin is where?"

"In the mountains of West Virginia. It sits on top of a hill, uses a generator for power, has some sort of complicated water and plumbing system, and there's a high-powered telescope so he can stargaze. That's how he knew you and your friends were on the way here."

"Fine, wake me when we get there." Determined to continue the charade, Mira curled up against the door, clutched the tote bag to her chest, and closed her eyes.

Lucas clenched his jaw. Damn but she was stubborn. And so good at playing the innocent he almost believed she didn't know what he was talking about. *Almost.* But he'd caught her subtle intake of breath when he mentioned Area 51. She might not be aware of what he did for a living, but she had to know he meant business.

His gaze sidled to the right and quickly returned to the highway. She looked so freakin' normal. So beautiful. So human. What if he was wrong? What if she'd double-crossed an identity theft ring, and the men in the garage had been sent to bring her to their boss. It was certainly a more feasible scenario than believing she was from another planet.

But he hadn't imagined his momentary memory lapse in the hotel room, or the way his brain had lost touch with reality. If she hadn't orchestrated the incident, who or what had?

He stopped to pay the toll on the expressway and slid a second glance in her direction. The jewels on her wrist glittered in the overhead lights, reminding him of what the team in Texas had revealed. Their prime suspect wore a bracelet very much like Mira's, as well as the diamond studs winking in her earlobes. It wasn't much, but it was all he had to go on.

His fingers tightened on the steering wheel. How many coincidences could he overlook?

He took the exit for I-81 south. It had been over a year since he'd last gone to Martin's cabin, and he'd made the drive in daylight. Getting there from memory would be tricky, but at least he'd had the good sense to borrow Maddox's Hummer. The men who'd tried to snatch her were professionals. There was a good chance they'd hidden a tracking device on his vehicle sometime over the past forty-eight hours. The switch had probably bought them a few day's grace.

He wracked his brain until he came up with two other possible scenarios. It was obvious they had a leak in the department. It was also a given that Randall hated him and would do anything to undermine his authority. Was Mira in danger because the major had found out she'd slept with him? Did he think that capturing her would take him off the trail of the alien?

Or had the office traitor described the suspect in Texas to the major, who had, when he'd heard about Mira and her jewelry, guessed at her identity and ordered her to be picked up?

Lucas hunched his shoulders and told himself his sleuthing was futile. Randall wasn't the only one who'd sell his soul to get an alien. He knew of several tabloid journalists who were trawling for a scoop, and a half dozen covert groups that hoped to beat his organization to the punch and rake in the glory. And the money that would come if they had a real-live alien in their possession.

Mira's eyes were closed, but her breathing told him she was still awake. He thought back to the garage and the way she'd fought to free herself. She was tough, clever, and so damned exasperating he wanted to pull off the road and shake her until she told him the truth. She made him doubt his sanity, brought out his protective instincts, and had him thinking in circles—

definitely not the reactions he thought he'd have when confronted by a creature from another world.

His stomach growled, and he checked the dashboard clock. Damn, but time really did fly when you were having fun. "You hungry?"

"Does it matter?" she muttered, her eyelids twitching.

"It's close to 4:00 A.M., and I didn't have dinner. There's a truck stop a couple of miles ahead with twenty-four-hour service. We can talk before we head into the mountains."

"No thanks. I'll pass."

"Sorry, that's not an option. Where I go, you go, and vice versa." Lucas hit a straight stretch of road and set the cruise control to the speed limit. Virginia troopers were rampant in this section of the state, and they lived to hammer speeders. Though he had government ID, the last thing he wanted was to call attention to himself.

He angled his head, hoping to make the next statement crystal clear. "Someone is out to kidnap you, and only you know the reason why. I want to help you, but I can't until you tell me the truth. The sooner you do that, the better things will be for both of us."

Ten

*M*artin locked gazes with Peggy. After the many years they'd worked together, he recognized the worry in her suddenly solemn blue eyes. She was fighting panic. And frankly, so was he. It was 8:00 A.M., two hours past the appointed morning briefing, and there was no sign of Lucas.

"I should have known something was wrong last night when he asked me to call him an hour after I left here," he said, circling the conference room. He'd just returned from the Hay-Adams, where it had taken fifteen minutes of intense persuasion to convince the manager to let him into Lucas's room. He'd practically had to phone the president to get access to Margaret Weston's suite. "I could tell he had something on his mind."

"Of course he did. We all do," said Peggy, her smile brittle. "What did you find at the hotel?"

"Not much. His room looked normal, but his briefcase was sitting wide open in the woman's suite."

"Lucas?" Peggy's expression brightened. "And a woman?"

"I guess I'd better start at the beginning. Yesterday morning, after our meeting, Lucas asked me to use my connections to run a background check on a woman he'd met in his hotel."

"She must be pretty special. He hasn't shown an interest in anyone since he stopped dating that senator's daughter, and even that wasn't serious."

"I get the feeling this relationship could have been," confided Martin. "Until he got the check. Lucas was upset, and rightly so. Seemed very disappointed when he found out she'd used a stolen credit card to book the hotel. Told me he was going to confront her about it when he got to her room." He set the leather case on the table. "He forgot his cell phone and all his paperwork, so I know he left in a hurry. What has me puzzled is why he'd unlock the damned thing in front of a stranger he suspected of being a thief."

"Maybe she forced him into it?"

"Force Lucas? I doubt it. When he got the report, he was adamant about his next move."

Peggy pulled out a chair and dropped into it. "Talk about inconvenient. I can't imagine how he could handle that and this alien invasion at the same time. He's had to wade through a lot of crap in his life."

"More than his share. Funny thing was, I could tell he had a hunch about her, something that really got him to thinking." Martin stared at the ceiling. "We spoke about the stolen card, then we discussed the report, which explained why his female friend couldn't be Margaret Weston. After that, he asked if I'd received any information on the suspect from Texas."

"The woman Frank and Chuck are tracking."

"Correct. I relayed everything Frank told me, including the fact that she'd shown some interest in a local man. I described her, the type of jewelry she wore . . . Lucas gave me an odd look, almost as if he had an 'ah-ha' moment. That's when he asked me to call his room an hour later."

"Did you?"

Instead of kicking himself, Martin ran a hand through his hair. "No."

"Because—?"

"Because he didn't give a concrete reason, just made some comment about the two of us following through on the theory that our aliens might be women, and if he disappeared—"

Martin stopped breathing for a second. As the pieces fell into place, he took a seat across the table from Peggy. Trembling, he swiped a palm over his face. Could he be any bigger idiot?

"Martin, what's wrong?" Peggy leaned forward. "You're white as a sheet."

He raised his head and stared at her. No. It couldn't be. It didn't make sense. But it was the only thing that did. "I know this is going to sound crazy, but I think Lucas has been abducted by an alien."

Mira woke to the patter of rain beating an angry-sounding symphony on the Hummer roof. Raising one eyelid, she noted the rhythmic movement of wiper blades slapping across the fog-covered windshield. Water poured from a murky gray sky that gave no clue of the time, though the clock read midmorning. Thunder rumbled, accompanied moments later by a brilliant flash of light.

Maneuvering upright, she took in the furiously swaying trees looming from both sides of the road. "Where are we?"

"Almost to the cabin," said Lucas, his voice grim. He fiddled with a knob and a gust of air blew across the windshield, dissipating the misty film. "I think."

"You think?" She peered through the pelting rain. "You said you'd been here before."

He jerked the steering wheel hard to the right to avoid a large branch partially blocking what appeared to be little more than a wide path. "I have—twice. But it was daylight, the weather was great, and I had written directions. Like I said, this place is isolated."

"Why does your friend—Martin is it?—why does he live here if it's so remote?"

He waited to speak until a boom of thunder abated. "He had a demanding job. When he retired, he wanted to get away from everything and everybody. Now that you've arrived, he'll probably move back to DC."

Ignoring his last comment, Mira hung on to the seat belt as the vehicle bucked ahead. Lucas was persistent. And he meant what he said about keeping her near. They'd sat side by side in a booth at the diner. After breakfast, he'd followed her into the single-stall ladies' room and stood at the door while she took care of personal business. When she came out, he'd grabbed one of her hands, stepped into the stall, and suggested she close her eyes. It seemed some human males had no sense of modesty.

They'd been the only customers in the restaurant, and all they'd received in the way of comment had been a wide-eyed stare from the waitress when they left the restroom together. She had fallen asleep in her seat before they'd driven from the diner parking lot.

Now, with the rain coming down so hard she could barely see, Mira watched Lucas lean into the wheel and clutch it as if willing the vehicle to stay on the path. They crested a rise accompanied by another shattering flash and boom, and he seemed to relax slightly.

"This is it."

"This?" Mira squinted through the driving water, dismayed to find that her superior sight was no help in the murky storm. "All I see is a bridge. That is a bridge, isn't it?"

"Yep. Once we cross the stream, we go another fifty yards straight up." The car crept toward the edge of the one-lane wooden span. "Hold your breath. I'm thinking the faster the better."

He gunned the engine, and she automatically sucked in a lungful of air. Glancing out the side window as they bumped over the rickety-sounding slats, she viewed the torrent flowing beneath them, more a raging river than a stream. Water had risen to the top of the bank, only inches from the braces of the bridge. If the rain kept up . . .

She exhaled as the Hummer landed on the other side and began to climb. Rain washed over the vehicle in sheets. "How can you see where you're going?"

"By only focusing about five feet in front of us. Believe me, it's not easy," Lucas muttered, his knuckles white around the steering wheel.

Lightning strobed the sky, illuminating a barely passable road. The vehicle seemed to shudder with every roll of thunder, until Mira wondered if the ground itself would open up and swallow them. She hadn't been this frightened of the elements since she'd entered the Earth's atmosphere and guided her pod to a safe landing. In front of them, a bolt of lightning struck a huge pine. His face twisted in determination, Lucas stared straight ahead. The engine raced as he pressed against the wheel, and they shot forward.

She screamed when an earsplitting crash sounded behind them. "What are you doing!"

"Trying to get to safety." A half minute later, he muttered a curse. "No wonder Martin bought a Hummer. It was either that or a helicopter."

Mira chewed on her lower lip. It felt as if the car

was standing on end, propelled by its rear tires alone. Seconds passed, then the slanted ground eased to an incline, and finally leveled to an even surface. As they neared the base of a mountain, the vehicle lumbered to a stop in front of what she assumed was their shelter.

Painted a soft buff color and surrounded by towering hills, the cabin seemed nestled in the rock itself, as if its designer had carved a niche and set the cottage-like house in a place of honor. With a covered front porch that ran the width of the building and a bright red door, it appeared welcoming and safe.

"We're here," said Lucas. The childproof locks clicked off, and he slid out his door. "Careful where you step. The ground is probably like a sponge."

She gazed at her white canvas shoes, the ones she'd worn to walk the city. She had nothing to protect her from a downpour, but the cabin was just a few feet away. Sighing, she swiveled in her seat, stepped out gingerly, and sank in the soggy earth.

"I told you to be careful," said Lucas, standing in front of her. His expression unreadable, he swiped the water from his face, reached around her, and slammed her door shut.

Before Mira realized it, he scooped her into his arms. Grunting, he carried her to the cabin and set her under the overhang. Eye to eye, they stared at each other while the water and wind surrounded them. Mira's heart thudded as heat pooled low in her belly. She gazed at his mouth, swore his lips softened, and licked at her own. For all the animosity that lay between them, she couldn't deny that Lucas still made her dizzy with desire.

A roll of thunder brought her to her senses. Blinking, she moved aside to let him pass. Without a word, he joined her on the porch and opened the door. Then he slipped off his equally muddy shoes and aligned them next to the mat.

She took the hint and set her shoes beside his. "Your friend doesn't believe in locks?"

He shrugged. "Think about the ride we just took. I doubt he entertains many traveling salesmen up here. Get comfortable. I'll be along in a minute."

Mira gave him a half smile and disappeared from view.

Lucas shook his head. What the hell was he thinking? He gathered an armful of wood from a rack as he cursed himself for a fool. Consorting with a criminal in his line of work was stupid. And if the woman was an alien—

He jumped as lightning flashed, then gazed at the teeming rain and the river creeping up the banks. They were going to be stuck there for quite a while, which was both good and bad. They'd be safe from whoever was trying to kidnap Mira, while he had time to question her, get to the bottom of things, and figure out their next move.

Unfortunately, being with her kept him away from the action in Washington. He'd left his cell phone in his briefcase, and Martin probably had taken his to town, so they had no means of communication.

In his head, he knew Martin and Peggy would pick up the slack and take over. Lucas had no doubt the ex-director would check out the hotel suites, as he'd asked. Martin didn't know about the kidnappers, but he would remember the talk they'd had. He was a logical man. Eventually, he'd put the pieces together. He only wished he could be in the room when the truth dawned.

He stopped at the door and sighed. Whenever he was close to Mira, she always knocked the wind from his sails. Judging by his body's reaction when he'd carried her to the porch, he still wanted her physically. Never in a million years did he think he'd be involved with a thief. How in the hell was he supposed to handle his attraction to her if she was an alien?

Stiffening his spine, he pushed inside and kicked the door shut. After dumping the wood next to the fireplace, he took in the cozy room. Where had she disappeared to?

The toilet flushed, and he released the breath he'd been holding. Mira stood in the doorway, a hesitant smile on her dewy face. Her gaze lighted on the surprisingly modern kitchen, moved to the spacious living area with its large bow window. Rustic oak tables and comfortable-looking furniture sat on wide-planked floors covered with colorful area rugs. There were no curtains, but Martin had arranged his fishing rods on either side of the window and mounted a few old lanterns and a creel on an overhead shelf.

Lucas glanced at the end wall, filled with framed photos his old boss had collected over forty-odd years of fieldwork. He'd bring Mira to the picture gallery later, when he told her who he was, and keep a careful eye on her reaction.

"This is charming," she began, walking to the kitchen. "I'm hungry. Do you think he'd mind if we—"

"Made ourselves at home? I doubt it." Lucas went to the refrigerator and took out a carton of milk. "Due date's good." He set it on the counter and rummaged in the bins. "Cheese, ham, tomatoes . . . Martin must have left in a hurry." He removed a jar of mayonnaise, one of mustard, a couple of apples. Then he checked the freezer. "We can have steak or salmon for dinner. He's even got some frozen vegetables in here."

He found two bottles of beer, popped the top on one and set it on the counter, then opened the other. Mira was already assembling sandwiches. He propped a hip against a cabinet.

"I'll take mustard on my bread."

"Fine."

She read the labels, then selected a container, and Lucas felt the knot that had taken root in his stomach tighten. What normal American citizen didn't know the difference between mustard and mayo? He watched as she laid on the cheese and tomato, but hesitated at adding the meat.

"Just a couple," he encouraged. "What's there has to last a few days."

As if handling a dead insect, she picked up a slice of ham between two fingers and set it on the bread. "I . . . um . . . I don't eat meat."

Lucas thought back to the only meal they'd shared, breakfast at the diner. She'd had hot oatmeal, fruit, and toast. "So you're a vegetarian?" he stated with a chuckle. "That's a relief."

She added a second piece of ham to the sandwich, slapped on another slice of bread, and shoved the plate toward him. "Why is that so amusing?"

"It means you're not a cannibal."

"A canni—" She tugged at an earlobe, and her mouth curled into a grin. "Very funny."

She assembled a sandwich of mustard, cheese, and the last of the tomato, wrapped the leftovers, and pushed past him to store everything in the refrigerator. Averting her gaze, she carried her plate to a table situated under a window that overlooked the front porch and began to eat.

Lucas brought his lunch over and both bottles of Coors and joined her. They ate in silence. When she got up to fill a glass with milk, he realized she hadn't touched her beer. Come to think of it, he didn't remember her finishing any of the scotch he'd offered her either.

"So, your species doesn't eat meat, and they don't drink alcohol."

She thinned her lips as she returned to her chair.

"What other earthly vices do you avoid? And don't say sex, because I know that's a lie."

Her cheeks flushed pink as she continued to eat in silence. After swallowing the last of her sandwich, Mira downed the entire glass of milk in one long drink. Then she stood and carried both plates to the sink.

Lucas couldn't resist. Standing, he crossed behind her and placed his hands on either side of her hips, caging her between his arms. Leaning against her, he nuzzled the soft skin at the nape of her neck. She trembled, and his erection sprang to life as the blood seeped straight to the area behind his zipper.

Bad idea, jerk.

He retreated as if burned, and she turned.

"I'm tired." Her smile warmed him to an inferno.

"Yeah, it's been a long day."

"So, maybe we should go to bed?"

Uh-huh, sure. "Maybe we should."

Lucas led the way, knowing she would follow. In the back foyer, he ignored the smaller guest room with its twin beds, and opened the door to the master suite, which he knew held a king-size bed.

Mira sat on the edge of the mattress and stared at him. Lucas removed his suit jacket, walked to a chair in the corner, and hung it on the backrest, then dug in the side pocket. Returning to the bed, he plopped down next to her and set his gun on the nightstand.

She raised a hand and cupped his jaw.

Ordering his brain to function rationally for ten more seconds, he met her heated gaze. "You ready for a nap?"

"It wasn't a nap I was thinking of."

He clasped her arm and snapped on a handcuff, then attached the other cuff to his own wrist. "Too bad, sweetheart, because that's all you're going to get."

Mira woke to absolute darkness and the sound of the cabin creaking in the gusting wind. Gone was the violence of the lightning and thunder, but the storm still lingered, wielding its power over the helpless earth. Rain beat a steady, natural rhythm that brought her both comfort and a subtle memory of all that had passed.

Curled on her side with no view of a clock, Mira guessed it was the middle of the night. She and Lucas had been so exhausted, he'd spooned his front to her back and fallen asleep with his arms around her waist just seconds after they'd adjusted the handcuffs.

She'd had a more difficult time.

In shock after Lucas snapped the metal ring on her wrist, she'd refused to cower. But her huffs of indignation, angry glares, and attempted arguments had done nothing to change his mind. He told her he'd rest easier knowing they couldn't be separated. Once she heard his slow, even breathing, she'd accepted that she was well and truly caught and resigned herself to her plight.

She'd drifted to sleep with a host of unanswered questions dancing in her brain. What connection did the men in the garage have to Lucas? What did Lucas intend to do with her here in the wilderness with no means of communication? Were her fellow travelers also under suspicion? Already captured? Had they at least managed what she had so far failed to do, and become pregnant?

Now that Lucas thought she was either a thief or an alien, further deception would be impossible. She had a mental power that unnerved him. He knew she'd lied about her identity, suspected she had ulterior motives in their midnight meetings, and wondered, as did she, who had tried to kidnap her and for what reason. Though it was obvious he didn't trust her, it was evident she'd become too important and intriguing a commodity to release.

Mira considered the resources at her disposal. She couldn't utilize an energy stone until she tried one final time to conceive. She also had Thane's transmitter, but she had to escape from Lucas before making use of it. None of her so-called weapons would hurt him, but if he found her with them, it would validate his suspicions. He would have no choice but to bring her to his superiors, something she hoped to avert.

Searching her heart, she admitted she bore Lucas no ill will. His quasi threats were nothing more than a ploy to manipulate her into a confession. He had been honorable, even heroic in the garage, thereby bolstering her view of humans and their sometimes dubious intentions. She enjoyed his sense of humor, was often amused by his irreverent remarks about aliens. More importantly, he had taught her passion, something she never would have experienced on her planet.

There had to be a way to achieve her goal and get to the mother ship without causing him pain, even while she attempted to make him understand her turmoil.

Lost in contemplation, Mira stilled when Lucas clutched her to his chest and tightened his grip around her middle. It was obvious from the prodding of his erection that he wanted her, or at least his body did. She'd touched his mind once before in sleep. Perhaps she could gain entrance to his thoughts while he was at rest, convince him to make love to her and give her a last chance to get pregnant.

Softening in his arms, she sighed into the darkness and nestled against his chest.

He moaned, nuzzling his face into her neck.

She thrust her bottom against his front, sliding up and down his rapidly swelling shaft.

Love me, Lucas. Take me and fulfill us both.

He gave a murmur of protest, but it wasn't enough to deter her. Nor were the handcuffs. Mira inched a hand beneath the fabric of her shirt and undid the front clasp of her bra, then moved his hands from her waist to her breasts. Pressing her backside against him, she writhed in enticement, unashamed of her mounting desire.

Lucas groaned as he plucked her nipples to aching points. His lips found her earlobe and drew it into his mouth. She shivered under the onslaught, and maneuvered her body and their arms until she faced him. Undoing his zipper, she filled her free hand with his throbbing penis, thrilled when it hardened to stone in her palm.

He shifted his hips in encouragement. It was difficult, but she managed to remove enough of his clothing to free him for her hands. Fusing her mouth to his, she shimmied out of her jeans. Stripping off her T-shirt, she broke contact to let the garment slide over her head and shoulder and onto their joined wrists.

Her fingers caressed the hair curling on his chest, molded to the muscles of his shoulders and arms and felt them tighten under her palms. Bending down, she licked a pebbled nipple, ran her lips to his collarbone, his throat, over his jaw to his mouth. When he opened for her, she thrust her tongue into the warm moist cavern, showing him what they both desired.

She lowered herself onto his shaft, letting him fill her completely. Impaled fully, she sat up and began to rise and fall, matching his rapid movements with abandon.

He tugged her forward and bit at her nipple, sucking until she screamed with pleasure. When he found her other breast, Mira wrapped her arm around his head, threaded her fingers through his hair, and rocked, setting her pace to his. Mouths mating, bodies quivering, they rode the crest of their climax as one being while the moaning wind joined with the roar in her brain. Light swirled and exploded behind her eyelids, propelling her to a place she hadn't known existed in the universe.

Finally, trembling from her release, she melted against him, absorbed his heartbeat, and knew instinctively that she had attained her goal.

Together, they had created a new life.

Seconds passed as an intense quiet filled the room. Mira rolled away, but didn't go far before she felt a tug on her wrist. Lucas muttered words of contentment, dragged her to his chest, and draped her over him like a blanket. Then he imprisoned her between his thighs, proving in one possessive action that she belonged to him.

She exhaled in frustration. Emotions welled from somewhere deep in her core, and the tears began to flow until they matched the torrent flooding the mountains and surrounding woods. When Lucas found out where she came from, knew what she was, he would hate her. When she left, he would despise her for eternity.

In moments, she acknowledged her fate. Lucas Diamond was the father of her child. He made her angry; he made her cry with joy and weep with frustration. And he made her burn with a passion she'd never thought to experience.

He was the only man she would ever love.

Sniffling, she stifled a sob. The longer she remained on Earth, the harder it would be to return home. She had to leave before she did something stupid, like confess the feelings in her heart. He would accept nothing less than the truth about who she was. Once captured, she would never be set free.

Her head ached at the idea of betraying her world. If they found out she loved a human, her people would brand her a traitor and shun or banish her. She was one of the chosen nine. One of the perfect.

The one who would not fail.

Lucas turned on his side and clutched her near. Lulled by the sound of the wind and rain, Mira fell asleep in his arms.

Eleven

Martin sat across the conference table from Peggy and shuffled through the stack of papers he'd compiled during his day of snooping. They'd divided the current crisis into two segments. She would handle the ongoing investigation, while he searched for Lucas. So far, he had hunches up the wazoo, but nothing concrete. Every scenario he concocted sounded like a comic book caper so fantastic even Peggy would be skeptical.

"Okay, let's go over the facts I managed to dig up," he began. "I contacted Lucas's sister, and she met me at his town house. The place was deserted, and I doubt he's been there since this mess started."

"Have his parents heard from him?" Peggy's expression turned sour. "His ex-wife?"

"Debbie hasn't spoken to Lucas in weeks, ditto his

mom and dad. I couldn't get an answer at Tina's house, so I called her husband's office. His secretary informed me the happy couple is in Mexico celebrating the fact that she's pregnant."

"Oh, God, do you suppose Lucas found out?" Peggy's eyes glistened with unshed tears. "Maybe the idea was too much for him, and he had to get away or—"

"I doubt it. Unless he said something to you?"

She shrugged. "No, it's just that I remember how devastated he was when he lost Kevin."

Martin tossed her a half smile. "There is one thing. His car is still at the Hay-Adams, but my Hummer is missing."

She frowned. "Lucas took your car from the hotel?"

"That's my guess."

"Because . . ."

Martin sat back in the chair. "Think about it. We know there are covert groups who'd like to get their hands on one of these aliens. What if Lucas captured this alien who's been impersonating Margaret Weston, and on the way out of the hotel they got waylaid by someone? The boy has good instincts. He'd know a setup if he smelled it."

"So he'd steal *your* car?"

"If he thought to make an inconspicuous getaway. Someone could have had both him and the woman under surveillance—tagged his vehicle, too. I'll have a friend go over his for bugs, and if they find one, well, it would prove my theory. Lucas and I think alike. If he read this the same as me, he'll recall my Hummer is so new nobody in town would recognize it."

"Do you still keep an extra key attached to the underside of the wheel well with one of those magnetic thingies?"

Martin huffed out a breath. "Jeez, does everyone in DC know about that?"

"Remember that list of quirks Lucas and I compiled for your retirement roast?" she asked, grinning. "That was supposed to be oddity number two, but we decided it wasn't a bright idea to let the world know where you keep a spare key. If your car ever got stolen, you'd blame us for spilling the beans."

"Smart move."

"But it came in handy if Lucas used it to escape." Peggy thumped the eraser end of her pencil on the table. "So, where do you think they went?"

"Someplace he'd feel safe. He has a boat docked in Annapolis. Janice is calling the marina now to see if there's been any activity on his cruiser." Feeling positive about his deductions, Martin asked, "What about you? Find out any more from our men in the field?"

"Yes, and it supports the information we received from Texas. North Dakota, Arizona, and Virginia are all reporting a woman as their prime suspect. Looks as if our aliens sent a group of females. Pretty clever, if you ask me."

"Anyone close to bringing in a suspect for questioning?"

"Idaho might be. Frank and Chuck have been un-reachable, as have Edith and her team. And that's not everything. The president phoned a little while ago from Bucharest, looking for our missing director."

"What did you tell him?"

Peggy sighed. "I stretched the truth, said Lucas was out of the office following a lead."

"You lied to the commander in chief?" He raised a brow. "I never thought you'd be so devious."

"It was only half a lie. Lucas *is* out of the office, we suspect he's with this Weston woman, and she's the best lead we have right now."

A knock kept them from speaking further. Janice stuck her head around the doorjamb. "I called the ma-rina. Lucas's boat is still in its slip, and no one's seen him for weeks." She stepped into the room and closed the door. "I know I shouldn't ask, but is there a prob-lem, I mean beyond the alien landing?"

"Sort of." Martin signaled Peggy to take over.

Peggy gave the assistant a motherly smile. "What we're about to repeat goes to your oath of confidential-ity, Janice. Swear to us that what we say will not leave this room."

The girl's face went pale. "Of course."

"We're only telling people Lucas is tracking a lead. Martin and I think he's missing."

"Missing?"

"Unaccounted for, though we've checked the usual places. Now that you've reached the marina and been told he's not there, we have no idea where he might be."

Janice opened and closed her mouth. "But why?"

"If we knew that, we wouldn't be so worried," said Martin. "Do us a favor and keep your eyes and ears open. If you hear any office chatter, report back to one of us."

"Because someone at DIA might be involved in his disappearance?"

"That's a strong possibility," confided Peggy. "You need to be our eyes and ears while we continue with the job at hand. In the meantime, maybe you could think back to anything Lucas ever said about taking some time off. Besides his boat, did he mention going anywhere out of the ordinary? Someplace remote where he found peace and quiet?"

Janice gave Martin a smile. "The only vacation I remember him taking was the couple of trips he made to your cabin. He always told me how much he liked it there, even though he thought it was the ass end of the earth." Her grin turned apologetic. "Sorry, but that's what he called it."

Martin knitted his brow. Then he snapped to a stand, grabbed Janice and kissed her on the forehead. "You, my child, are an angel. Take the rest of the day off, pick that little boy of yours up early from day care, and go for a walk in the park." He removed his billfold and pulled out a hundred-dollar bill. "Take your husband to dinner. It's on me."

After scooting her out the door, he turned to Peggy. "Bingo."

* * *

Distracted by the sound of running water, Lucas stood at the counter and added a couple of scoops of premium roast to the hopper of Martin's state-of-the-art coffeemaker. He'd awakened fifteen minutes ago to find Mira ready to rise and insisting he release her from the handcuff. He'd groggily agreed, and together they'd stumbled from the bed to the chair holding his jacket, where he'd retrieved his keys and set her free. She'd raced into the bathroom and slammed the door. Only then had he realized they were both buck naked.

Scanning the room, he'd taken in the disheveled sheet and blankets, their clothing strewn across the floor, and gotten a sick feeling in the pit of his stomach. His memory was fuzzy on the details, but by the time he heard the toilet flush and the shower run, he'd come to a disturbing conclusion.

Sometime during the night, he and Mira had engaged in consensual but not exactly coherent sex. And the act had so disturbed her she couldn't wait to wash the feel of him from her skin. The idea added to his frustration, not only with Mira, but the entire situation.

A few evenings ago she'd been the seducer, and he a willing participant in her game. Then he'd accosted her in the hotel and accused her of credit card theft along with being an alien. After that, he'd kidnapped her, exactly as those men in the garage had tried to do, and forced her to sleep at his side. He didn't remember pushing her to have sex, but he might have. Was it any wonder she didn't want a thing to do with him?

The shower stopped and he set the coffeemaker to

brew. Moments later, Mira bustled into the kitchen barefoot, with her gaze firmly on the floor, and headed straight out the door. Dressed in women's wear he knew she didn't find in any of Martin's dressers, she didn't even bother to say good morning, a sure sign she wasn't ready to talk to him.

Lucas sidled to the window. Where, he wondered, had she gotten the change of clothes? Had she been packed and prepared to leave when he'd come to her room? If so, why?

He made an internal vow to not mention what had transpired between them in the bedroom, picked up the handcuffs from the counter, and stepped onto the porch. Gazing past her, he checked out the scenery. Only moments ago, the sun had begun to rise over the mountains to the east, spilling golden light across the path that led from the stream, now a river flowing halfway up the incline. The bridge itself had disappeared sometime during the night, destroyed, he imagined, by the raging wind and water.

Propping his backside against the porch post, he waited until she stopped pacing and walked to the railing. "Good morning. How was the shower?"

Mira hung her head and concentrated on her fingers, which appeared to be wrapped tightly around the rough-hewn wood.

"I'll make breakfast, but I need about fifteen minutes in the bathroom first."

She nodded and her damp hair fell over her pale cheeks, shielding her face from view.

He held out the cuffs. "We can do this inside or out here. Whichever you prefer."

"And if I give my word that I won't run away?" she asked, her voice quiet but steady.

Lucas sighed. "You're asking a hell of a lot, you know that, don't you?"

A gust of wind caught wayward strands of her corkscrew ringlets and sent them trailing in the breeze. "I doubt I can ford a river, and I have no idea where we are. I'd be a fool to leave without assistance."

He gazed at the swollen stream, the woods thick with trees and shining with puddles, and silently agreed she made sense. But it still didn't mean he could trust her.

"If I don't cuff you, I want a promise in return."

"I thought as much."

Cringing at the hopelessness of her tone, Lucas almost tugged her into his arms, then remembered how Mira had struggled to get away from him earlier. She didn't want any part of him, and he didn't blame her. This was America, the country where people were supposed to be innocent until proven guilty. Yes, she'd used Margaret Weston's credit card, but what if she had a perfectly good explanation for doing so, only she wasn't at liberty to tell it?

As for being an alien, well, he'd given it some thought and been hard-pressed to come up with a law that condemned a foreign being from another planet as a felon. One of the main reasons the DIA existed was to befriend extraterrestrial visitors, not make them enemies. Maybe if he gave her another chance . . .

"Answers," he prompted. "Promise me answers."

"I'm sorry." She whispered the words. "It's the one thing I can't do."

Lucas swiped a hand over his face, working to control his temper. So much for being a nice guy and giving her the benefit of the doubt. He grabbed her arm and pulled her into the cabin. Assessing the kitchen, he dragged a chair to the stove and sat her down, then snapped a cuff on her wrist and hooked the other to the handle on the oven door. Standing back, he surveyed his handiwork. Unless she had a screwdriver or blowtorch up her sleeve, no way could she get free.

He poured a glass of milk and smacked it onto the counter, ignoring the liquid that sloshed over the side. "This will have to do until I get back."

He stomped into the bathroom and jerked open the medicine cabinet, where he found toothpaste, shaving cream, disposable razors, and a host of over-the-counter products for everything from insomnia to warts. Checking under the sink, he located a couple of extra toothbrushes, unwrapped one, and used it while he considered the more personal mess he was in.

How the hell had he allowed himself to have sex with her again? They'd been exhausted, and she'd been furious when he'd used the restraints. He remembered tucking her against him in bed, but that was the only way he could ensure them a good night's rest. What was it that linked them so closely they had to screw each other's brains out whenever they were alone? Had she pulled that mind-meld thing on him again, as she'd done in the hotel, or was it a simple matter of animal attraction?

And why was it that no matter how angry or suspicious she made him, he was drawn to her? What kind of power did Mira hold over him that brought out his protective instincts, as well as his lust?

Shaving methodically, he concentrated on the practical side of the problem and reviewed a mental list of questions he planned to press as soon as they sat down to eat. He didn't give a rat's ass about the credit card fraud, and the men in the garage were puzzling, but not paramount to the situation. There were only two things that stood out like blood on new-fallen snow, and everything depended on her answers.

Was she an alien? And why had she seduced him?

The questions beat in his brain as he turned the water on hot, jumped in the shower, and began to scrub. When he'd first come on board with Martin, he'd believed with his heart, mind, and soul that there were intelligent life-forms on other planets, and someday he'd be lucky enough to meet them. Over the years, he'd had his hopes dashed so many times he'd become a cynic, a man who needed proof positive. Why was he being hostile to Mira, when there was a chance she could lead them to an alien alliance and restore his dream?

Because she used you, pal, echoed a voice that sounded very much like his ego.

But why? Did the eight other sites around the country each have a female alien befriending and having sex with one particular male? If he were in DC he'd have had Peggy run a screening, ask the teams if they suspected their female was doing the same. Unfortunately, that tactic would have to wait.

For the moment, he was stuck in the middle of nowhere with a woman he didn't trust. And every instinct told him he had to protect her at all costs, because alien or not, they were connected. He only wished he knew how.

When Mira heard water run in the bathroom, she raised her gaze to the boxy, metal appliance on the counter and tugged on her earlobe. *A toaster, made to cook bread and heat various thin, flat edibles.*

Staring into its reflective side, she studied her once ordinary gray eyes. Eyes that now seemed to glow as if lit from within. Coupled with the fact that she'd awakened with her stomach weak and heaving, much as it had done when she'd been hurtling through Earth's atmosphere in her traveling pod, the unusual shift in their color left no doubt in her mind.

She was pregnant.

At first, she hadn't believed what she'd seen in the mirror. Then she'd put her bodily changes into perspective. There had been a few discussions on what might happen to the travelers when they conceived, but since no woman of her species had ever become pregnant by a human male, it was fanciful speculation. Now she knew.

Still gazing at her silver-colored eyes, she smiled, softly at first, then with gleeful abandon. She had not failed her people. All she had to do was continue playing Lucas's game of twenty questions until she was able to escape and use one of the emeralds to call for an emergency pickup by the mother ship.

If he asked about the disparity in her eye color, she would insist he was mistaken. Hadn't she heard it said that Earthmen paid little attention to the physical details of the women in their lives? There were so many things Lucas had on his mind where she was concerned, he probably wouldn't even notice.

She raised the glass of milk to her lips and consumed every drop. Holding a hand to her belly, she cradled it as if protecting the life inside. She was going to be a mother with a son to love and nurture. A child she would raise with an open mind and a joyous heart, unlike the way Thane had raised her.

Mine, she thought.

And Lucas's, her brain corrected.

Immediately, the vision of a boy with curling dark hair, bright brown eyes, and a disarmingly mischievous grin came to mind.

Her people had no use for the odd words—curses—humans used when annoyed, but just then there were several she thought appropriate to her situation. She recalled what she'd been told of Earth males and their progeny. Many ignored their children; some were so dishonorable they refused to claim the ones they'd created, even as they continued to make more. Perhaps Lucas would be that type?

The ridiculous thought made her exhale a breath. Lucas would never shirk his responsibilities, especially if he had feelings for the woman who gave birth to his child. He didn't think much of her at the moment, and would detest her if he ever found out what she was and why she was there.

How would he react if he knew she carried his child?

Lost in thought, she was suddenly surrounded by Lucas's clean, masculine scent. Mira held her breath as he unlocked the handcuff, and she made a point of rubbing her wrist, afraid if she lifted her head he would notice her eyes. Now that she'd accepted her feelings for him, it was going to be difficult to stay focused and treat him impersonally. If he knew how much she cared, he might find a way to use it against her.

He walked to the refrigerator and removed eggs, bread, and milk, then rummaged in a cupboard and brought out a small jar of what she guessed was seasoning. After setting everything on the counter, he opened a lower cabinet, found a pan, and placed it on the stove top.

"Sorry I took so long, but I've got a couple of inches on Martin, so it was tough finding clothes that fit." He glanced at his shoes, leather boots with thick soles and heavy laces. "Lucky for me he has oversized feet."

She sighed and moved her chair closer to the table when she saw the plaid shirt stretch across his broad shoulders and muscular frame.

He cracked eggs into a bowl and added milk, then poured the mixture into the pan, slid bread in the toaster, and filled a cup with coffee. Turning, he propped his backside against the counter and gave her a level gaze. "Hungry?"

Mira clasped a knee with both hands and stared at her entwined fingers. Her stomach had calmed with the soothing shower, and she was starving. "Yes."

"You didn't say, but I assumed since you drank milk and ate cheese that you ate dairy and eggs."

His consideration of her dietary needs threw her off guard. Why was he acting kind when he didn't trust her? "It's just animal flesh we—I avoid. There's a saying . . . nothing with a heartbeat. Maybe you've heard of it?"

He grinned. "I have now."

"Where did you learn to cook?"

"My mother made sure my sister and I knew our way around a kitchen, and it paid off when I got my own place during college. After my divorce, it didn't take long to get reacquainted with a stove. I make a decent omelet, grill a mean steak, and my skill with a microwave is darn near professional." He went back to the eggs and stirred in a bit of the seasoning. "This is just about ready."

So he had been married. A flicker of something akin to jealousy stabbed at Mira's heart. She longed to ask about his past. Did he and his former wife have children? If so, where were they? If he'd vowed to spend the rest of his life with a special woman, why had they separated? Did he love her still?

Lucas loaded their plates with food, then moved to the toaster and spread butter on the bread. Opening a drawer, he took out forks and carried everything to the table. "I gather there's no man in your life," he said in a wry tone. "At least not anyone you care to sleep with."

Ignoring the comment, she folded two paper napkins and pushed one toward him. "When do you think we'll leave here?"

"I'm not sure." He scooped eggs onto his fork. "Maybe never."

"You can't mean that?" she gasped. Then she caught his subtle smile and guessed he was joking. Or was he?

"Think about it?" He sipped his coffee. "This place is a perfect hideaway. Martin's probably figured out where I am by now, but I bet all hell's broken loose with my disappearance. Who knows if he'll find the time to come to our rescue. I don't have my cell, and there's no phone here. The bridge is gone, and we can't cross the stream until the water level drops to normal, which means it'll be near impossible for anybody to get in." He cocked a brow. "Why? Is there someplace special you're supposed to be? Like on a rendezvous with your mother ship?"

Mira kept her head down and concentrated on her breakfast. The meal tasted creamy, spicy, and delicious.

"I wasn't able to check them out fully in the garage, but the men who attacked you looked borderline mercenary, so I suspect they have connections with the military. As an alien, they're the last group you want to tangle with."

She knew all about the United States military. They'd taken a harsh line toward every effort of friendship species from other galaxies had made in the past hundred Earth years, and each encounter had ended in tragedy for the visitors. Since it didn't sound as if Lucas had any respect for them, she wondered to which branch of the government his department reported.

"I don't know who those men were, but I have no intention of *tangling* with your—the military." She bit into her toast and chewed thoughtfully. "I want to go home. If I apologize for doing whatever it is you think I've done, can't you set me free? Then you can return to your office and forget you ever met me."

His laughter echoed in the room. "Sweetheart, that will never happen. At least, not unless you start giving sensible answers to my questions. If I decide you're telling the truth, I'll consider it. Until then . . ."

Lucas carried his empty dish to the counter and filled the sink with water. Mira's stomach began to roll, and she shoved her half-laden plate away. She assumed her pregnancy was the reason for her quirky appetite, but being held a prisoner didn't sit well, either. She had to go somewhere private to think.

"May I go outside? I'd like some fresh air."

"And you'll stay near the cabin?"

"Yes."

He shrugged. "All right, but don't wander too close to the river. The wet grass is slippery. If you slide down the bank and fall in, I can't promise I'll be there to save you. Again."

On the porch, Mira held back a scream of frustration. She glanced at the encroaching forest, the rain-soaked grass, and washed-out bridge. The man was insufferable when he was right.

She hated that her body was still drawn to him, that she continued to think impossible thoughts about him, that her heart still beat with love for Lucas, even after they'd created a new life. She'd fulfilled her mission. Her job there was done. All she had to do was get away.

But that was the last thing she wanted to do.

Twelve

*L*ucas smiled when Mira huffed and stomped from the cabin. He had to admit, she was one cool cookie. He'd goaded her ten ways to Sunday and she hadn't taken the bait—hadn't even bothered to look him in the eye. If the aliens they were hunting resembled the people of Earth as closely as he suspected, there was a good chance they had emotions, feelings, and needs similar to a human's. Even if Mira wasn't an alien, it stood to reason she had a soft spot for something— maybe her family or friends? It sure as hell wasn't past lovers.

He went to the window and found her standing at the railing, gazing at the magnificent view. The stream still ran at a sprinter's pace, but the water seemed a few inches lower. The sun, a shining golden ball, glittered off the droplets and puddles that covered the surrounding vegetation and ground. Mountains in the distance formed a picture-postcard scene of green, purple, blue, and every color in between. Where did Mira come from? What was the weather like on her planet? Was she weighing the similarities between her home and Earth?

An eagle cried as it stretched wings overhead. Moments later, a second bird circled, and together the two swooped low over the forest. Gliding and soaring, they performed a breathtaking air show better than any he'd ever seen by the famed Blue Angels. Were they a bonded pair? He'd read that certain species of animals mated for life. Did eagles? Did anyone in today's modern world?

Sitting across from Mira at breakfast had kept him on his toes, especially when bits and pieces of what they'd done in bed decided to take an encore in his brain. Warm skin, hot kisses, and trembling body parts combined to create a memorable fantasy. He recalled the dreamlike quality of their coupling, his fevered moans and her ragged whispers of encouragement . . . her shapely body and the way it molded perfectly to his . . . the climax that had left him breathless and longing for more.

The previous night, Mira had connected with a part of him he'd buried deep under layers of resentment and despair. He'd given up on finding a partner who could reach him there. How ironic that the one woman who could might be an alien.

Damn, but he wished he knew for sure.

If she was a thief, how was he supposed to justify to the president his having a relationship with a felon? If he turned her in and she was convicted, he'd be on the hot seat when word got out about the way they'd met. And it would be just as bad if he let her go. The police might bring him up on charges of aiding and abetting, and she'd be on the run from those thugs with no one to cover her back.

Mira's shoulders rose and fell as if their current problem and a hundred more weighed her down, but Lucas hardened his resolve. He ran a hand through his hair, then walked outside. Hit by a gust of wind, he sucked in a lungful of frigid mountain air. She had her arms wrapped across her chest, and he realized she wore nothing but a thin T-shirt and khaki slacks. Ducking into the cabin, he found a windbreaker hanging from a hook on the door and brought it onto the porch. He stepped behind her and draped the garment over her, telling himself he'd do as much for a stranger.

She clutched the jacket close. Curling tendrils of her hair danced in the heady breeze. "Thank you."

"Don't mention it." He took a half step back, though his fingers itched to sift through the spiraling ebony strands. They stood in silence, their bodies so close he caught her smoky-sweet scent on the wind. "What are you looking at?" he asked, following her gaze.

"Animals." She tugged at an earlobe. "Deer, to the

right in that stand of trees. I think it's a doe and her fawn."

Lucas squinted until he caught a shifting of color and shape, and recognized the dark figures to be just that. Considering the dense vegetation and shadowy interior of the forest, Mira had the eyesight of a jungle cat.

"Do you have that type of animal where you come from?"

She stiffened and dropped her head to stare at her clenched fingers.

Against his better judgment, Lucas turned her in his arms. "If I give my word that I'll do whatever I can to keep you safe, will you tell me the truth?"

Her eyelids lowered, she concentrated on the buttons of his shirt. Enfolding her in his arms, he rested his forehead against hers, noting her shiver. So far, he'd shouted and threatened, but he had yet to do anything physical that would make her afraid.

"Sooner or later you're going to have to trust someone, Mira, and right now I seem to be the only one offering for the position."

When she didn't answer, he drew back and cupped her chin, lifting her head. A long moment passed, then she peered at him for a quick second.

Uncertain of what he'd seen, Lucas blinked.

A single teardrop slipped from beneath one of Mira's water-spiked lashes and rolled down her pale cheek before she locked on to his stare. Absorbing the silvery sheen of her eyes, a curiously striking, lightly polished pewter, Lucas could only gaze in bewilderment.

He'd aced training for the White House security detail, and undergone intensive testing when he'd been hired for the DIA. He'd taken hits on a personal level, too, losing a child and wife within a year. He'd always thought himself a survivor, unflappable in the face of danger or impossible odds.

But now, focused on Mira's uniquely colored eyes, he knew he was in trouble—real trouble—for the first time in his life. And he hadn't a clue what to do about it. Almost speechless, he used a thumb to brush away her trailing tears while he gathered his thoughts.

"Sorry." Mira sniffed. "I don't usually cry. It's just that I'm not used to evading kidnappers or being a prisoner or having someone accuse me of the things you say I did."

He cocked his head and gave her face a thorough inspection. Her eyes glowed with a curious inner light that startled but intrigued him at the same time. "It's not the tears that have me worried."

"Then why are you staring?" she asked in an innocent voice. "Do I have dirt on my nose?"

Lucas's suspicious nature was a personality trait that had served him well over the course of his career in the White House as well as his stint in the DIA. He'd heard every story imaginable as a field operative under Martin, and learned to tell the difference between a lie and a sincere belief through careful questioning guided by gut instinct. He'd met and interrogated people who were difficult to read, but Mira was the first who had him thoroughly stumped. Though he'd run the gamut from accusatory to demanding to sensible, none of it had gotten him very far.

If the military and Randall were involved, they'd stop at nothing to make her talk, which was one of the reasons the president had given the green light to the DIA and put them solely in charge of this current mission. In a normal situation, he'd put the subject in his office and opt to play good cop–bad cop. Just his luck, he was alone without Martin or Peggy to take their part, and the subject in question was Mira. What else could he do to force the issue?

"Have you looked in the mirror this morning?"

"I'm a fright, I know." She ran a hand through her tangled curls. "I couldn't find a hairbrush, and there weren't any cosmetics in the bathroom. I hope your friend Martin won't mind that I opened a new toothbrush and used his shampoo and—"

"I'm not talking about your lack of makeup or disheveled hair. It's your eyes." He narrowed his gaze. "I don't remember their color being so—so—"

"Boring? I guess gray is drab, not like green or blue. Even brown can be more exciting." She stepped back and scanned the forest. "Our voices must have carried on the wind. The deer have gone."

Instead of falling for her ploy, he spun her in his direction. "Mira, stop. This game is getting old."

"Game?" Her silver eyes darted first to his chest, then the fingers he had wrapped around her upper arms. "You've handcuffed me, kidnapped me, driven me miles into a mountain wilderness, and now you're hurting me. If this is your idea of a game, it's sick."

Lucas released her, and she rubbed where his hands had been. "You're right. It's gone way past that. Tell me what's happened to your eyes."

The body parts in question opened wide. "Happened? I don't know what you mean."

"Stop acting as if I'm stupid. What the hell is going on?"

She had the decency to blush but still didn't answer.

"All right, how about this. What say we both come clean? I'll even take the first step and tell you about myself," he said, hoping to appeal to her sense of honor.

"I know all I need to where you're concerned," she snapped, tilting her chin.

He met her haughty gaze, and she quickly lowered her eyelids. "Please let me go. Turn your back or walk into the cabin, and I'll disappear from your life as if I'd never been in it. You can go to Washington and make up whatever story suits your needs. Tell them I had friends who overpowered you and helped me get away. Invent anything that will make me a criminal and exonerate you."

"You already are a criminal," he answered. "Credit card fraud, remember?"

"Oh, yes. The great identity theft scandal. Fine, how much money do you think I owe the woman? I'll find a way to repay her."

"Then you admit you're not Margaret Weston, and you stole her credit card?"

"Can't we say 'borrowed'? I planned to replace the money."

He leaned a hip against the railing and gestured toward her ears. "And just how were you going to manage that? Sell one of those rocks?"

"Rocks!" Her eyes flared molten steel. "These are jewels. Genuine diamonds."

"Really?" He gave a whistle of approval. "Take one off and let me have a look at it."

She put a hand over each ear, as if to protect the gems, and he grabbed the wrist that sported her bracelet. "What about one of these? Each stone is about two carats. I hear good-quality rubies are going for more than diamonds these days."

Mira whipped her hand back. "Don't touch me or anything I'm wearing."

"Don't touch you?" He crowded closer, pressing his body against hers in an effort to intimidate. If he was going to take the bad cop route, he might as well make every move enjoyable. "Funny, that's not what I remember you saying last night, or any of the other nights we spent together. If I recall correctly, you begged me to touch you." He ran a finger down her cheek. "Here."

He grazed her collarbone with his knuckles. "And here." Sliding his hand to her chest, he molded her ample breast with his palm. "And definitely here."

She stepped back, but he kept a tight grip on her upper arm with one hand while he continued the sensual assault. He found her nipple and rolled it between his fingers. "Remember how I licked this little bud, then bit down until you screamed? I can do that again, sweetheart. Just say the word."

"No—I—"

"Or maybe you want me to use my tongue somewhere else?" He reached between her legs and cupped her through her slacks. "You begged me not to stop the last time I tasted you here."

Mira squeezed her thighs together, capturing his hand.

"What's wrong. Can't stand a dose of your own medicine?" he whispered darkly. "It's okay for you to seduce me, but when the tables are turned you're not willing to play?"

Lucas moved until he loomed over her, then pushed his straining erection against the front of her slacks. "I'm ready for you, and we both know you're always ready for me. We can do the deed right here, right now."

"This won't get you what you want. I won't talk."

Mira's eyes closed, and another tear escaped, but he was in too deep to stop. "How do you know what I want?"

"Isn't it obvious? You're doing this to coerce me. You want to know where I come from, who I—"

"Honey, at this moment that's the furthest thing from my mind." He bent forward and ran his mouth over hers. She sucked in a breath, and he bit her trembling lower lip. "Open for me, let me come inside."

Mira shook her head, and he rumbled out a laugh, then trailed his mouth to her satiny throat, lingering to ply his tongue over her rapidly beating pulse point. Moving downward, he found her breast. The jacket fell off her shoulders, and her nipple jutted into his lips. Circling it with his tongue, he wet the cotton fabric.

Her knees buckled, and he caught her in his arms. Slipping his hand under her shirt, he undid the clasp of her bra and plucked the hardened bud to rigid attention. Alien or not, and bad cop be damned, he had to taste her. Raising the fabric, he exposed her swollen, cherry pink nipple to the cool air. Caressing her breast, Lucas scraped with his teeth, primed to take her here on the porch or against the cabin wall, whatever was quickest.

She whimpered and threaded her fingers through his hair, holding him close.

He undid the button on her slacks and tugged at the zipper, then slid his hand under the edge of her panties and found her hot wet center.

Mira moaned when he pushed two fingers inside her. "Please . . . no."

The feeble protest registered from afar.

"Lucas . . . stop."

He pulled his hand away, drew back, and found her liquid silver eyes awash in tears. Stabbed by guilt, he stifled a curse. He hadn't meant to take the charade to this dangerous a level. Hell, he'd never had a woman ask him to stop before, but he was coherent enough to realize that no meant no. Easing her to her feet, he pulled down her shirt until she was covered.

She brushed at her damp cheeks, then did up her zipper and button while he chided himself for being an idiot.

"I'm sorry," he muttered. "I didn't mean to let things go that far."

Mira inhaled a breath, but the tears continued to flow. Lucas had been crude and demanding, and so potently masculine in his possession of her she'd almost lost her common sense. It was wrong of her to continue to lead him on when she planned to disappear from his life. Each time they made love, her heart ached a little more, knowing they could never be together. Yet she'd almost agreed to have sex with him there on the porch or anywhere he chose, just as long as he came inside of her and brought her to fulfillment.

The thought that he wanted her even when he knew she was a liar was a powerful lure. They had made a baby together, so it was natural they had a connection. They couldn't trust or be honest with each other, but their sexual compatibility was undeniable. Now he was apologizing, while she couldn't seem to stop weeping. How ridiculous.

"I understand," she said, sniffling.

She gazed at him, and he frowned. "Then how come you're still crying?"

"I don't know." She could only assume the tears

were a combination of her mind's reaction to her pregnancy and all the physical and mental stress she'd been under. "I—I—"

He pulled her near and hugged her tight. "Guess things have gotten crazy, huh?"

She nodded, comforted by the protection his strong, solid body offered. Moments passed while they stood locked in each other's arms. Finally, Lucas pulled away.

"I think it's time we drove the Humvee to a safe place. Then there's something in the living room you need to see."

"Where are we taking the Hummer?"

He scanned first the left, then the right side of the area leading away from the cabin. "I'm not sure; somewhere near enough that we can get to it, yet hidden from view. I don't like the idea of letting it sit in the open. The Hummer's olive drab, so it won't need much in the way of camouflage. I thought I'd park it at the edge of the woods and cover it with some of the branches the wind took down. If we hustle, we'll reach it without a problem."

"And go where?" Mira asked, unhappy with Lucas's plan. She couldn't imagine any area in the United States where she'd be able to hide if the military came after them.

"Back to Washington. The president is due home in a day or two, and the sooner we get to him, the better. Once Martin figures everything out, he'll make that appointment, and we'll have the upper hand. You'll be given immunity—"

"Your belief in this Martin person is commendable." She lowered her eyelids. "I'm not admitting to anything, but do you honestly think your leader would be willing to give immunity to a visitor from another solar system?"

"Martin's a very persuasive guy with a serious reputation in this business, and the president is the commander in chief, which means he can do just about anything he wants. Unfortunately, here in the middle of nowhere, it's every man for himself. That's why we have to return to DC." He took a step closer. "I'm concentrating on the military, but you may have been targeted by an arms dealer who hopes to sell you and the information you possess to the highest bidder. Or maybe a group of scientists who want to study your physiology, or a billionaire with the crazy idea he can add you to his collection of oddities. I'll have a better handle on things if I hear a chopper."

Mira searched her memory chip for a definition of the strange word. "A helicopter? You think they'd go that far?"

Lucas pinned her with a laserlike gaze. "You'd be surprised what lengths certain people would go to for the opportunity to capture and question an alien."

She tucked strands of flyaway hair behind her ears as she studied his fierce expression. "I don't even know why we're discussing this. I'm not an—"

"Before you say something that isn't true, you need to know there's one thing in your favor." He clasped her hands in his. "Whoever those men are, they won't harm you. You're far too valuable a prize."

The touch of Lucas's fingers did more to allay her fears than did his words. She recalled the location of his office, hidden in the basement of a heavily guarded building; the documents she'd found in his briefcase, each folder stamped CLASSIFIED. It was obvious he was in charge of interrogating alien life-forms, and someone in his government had given the project top security. From the sound of it, he'd dealt with men like her would-be kidnappers before.

She now realized he meant every word he'd been saying. He might not trust her, or know exactly *what* she was, but he wasn't going to let anything untoward happen to her, not here and not if they returned to Washington. His job was to make contact with an alien—not cause it harm.

She sighed, accepting the idea that an arm of the military had learned of her existence. The possibility of her capture and that of the other travelers had been discussed openly with the Council of Women and the elders. Each of the nine had vowed to die for their world if necessary, but she no longer had only herself to think of.

To her knowledge, Earth had no laws or protocol in place regarding the safekeeping of extraterrestrials. If a group of military renegades caught her, they could hold her by force, as if she were an animal, and bring her to a center for questioning or experimentation.

Eventually, they might put her on display to be gawked at as humans did a creature in a zoo. And when they found out she was pregnant, they would take her child and do the same to him.

In a protective gesture, Mira moved a hand to her stomach. No one was going to take her baby from her. *No one.* Raising her head, she met Lucas's sharp-eyed stare. He smiled, as if he suspected she was close to telling him the truth.

"You ready to take a drive, then a walk back here?"

"I think I'd enjoy it," she admitted. Anything to be close to him and spend more time with him before she left.

"You're sure?" He released her hands. "Because I won't cuff you to the stove if you want to stay here."

"You wouldn't?"

"Were you hoping to escape?"

"I thought about it . . . but . . . no." She offered a sincere smile. She imagined Lucas had just taken a huge step in gaining her confidence. It was daylight, and until she came up with a better idea, she didn't have any choice but to put herself in his care.

His grin stretched wide. "Okay, come along. Just be prepared for a messy walk. The ground is saturated."

"Give me a minute. I have to put on shoes."

Thirteen

*M*ira darted into the cabin while Lucas slogged to the car and climbed in the driver's seat. He'd been certain that after his bad cop routine a few minutes ago, she'd never want to be close to him again, but they'd just held a sensible conversation in which she actually appeared to trust him. Though Mira hadn't confessed she was an alien, she hadn't protested when he warned her not to lie. How much longer would it be before she admitted what she was and why she was here?

His stomach rolled at the thought. As a kid, he'd dreamed of the first time he might meet a being from another star system. Over the years, he'd taken all manner of ribbing from classmates and family members whenever he'd expounded on his theory of extra-terrestrial life. After a while, he'd learned to keep his hopes and aspirations locked away in order to stop the jibes and jokes uttered at his expense. Instead, he'd trained himself to project a wait-and-see attitude while he erected a wall of secrecy around his personal and business affairs.

He, Martin, and Peggy had prepared to greet little green men or the "grays"—slightly built, gray-skinned beings with huge eyes and tentacle-like fingers. He was certain his coworkers would agree that a beautiful woman with curling ebony hair and a laugh as bright as morning sunshine was the last thing they'd expected to meet in their first alien encounter.

And now, with the dream so close to realization, all Lucas could think was how to keep Mira for himself.

From the moment he'd met her, she'd turned his world upside down. She infuriated him, confused him . . . fascinated him. And tempted him on a level he'd never thought he could be tempted. It didn't really matter if she wasn't an alien; she had become his to protect and care for. It would make his life and hers so much easier if she wasn't from another planet, but if she was . . .

He smiled, still willing to believe the dream had come true. It was going to be a challenge to bring her to the Oval Office and introduce her to the president while skirting the story of how they'd met, but there was no way he could tell the big boss that he'd let himself be seduced within five minutes of seeing her. The idea dredged up a wave of unanswered questions.

As far as he could tell, Mira's physiology was identical to a female human's, yet he knew there were anomalies in her DNA. He was also aware of the subtle mind-enhancing abilities she possessed. What possible reason could an alien life-form have for engaging in sex with a human? If she'd come to experiment on an Earth male, either in a mental or physical capacity, why had she chosen him?

Where did she come from? How far had she traveled to reach Earth? If her pod was destroyed, as he and Martin suspected, how did she plan to return to her world? He believed she and the others had come in peace, but for what purpose?

The cabin door slammed, and Mira bounded down the stairs. Besides donning shoes, she'd slipped on the windbreaker, rolled up the sleeves, and zipped it to her chin, but it didn't conceal her lush feminine form. She met his gaze through the windshield and tossed him a brilliant smile. Her eyes shone like silver coins in the sunlight, a glaring reminder of their change. Was living in the Earth's foreign atmosphere harming her physical makeup?

She walked to the passenger side, opened the door, and slid into the seat. "I'm ready."

"Sure you're feeling all right?" Lucas asked, his gaze centered on her luminous eyes. "You're not sick or anything?"

"Sick? Why would you think that?"

"Your eyes, Mira. You have yet to tell me the reason for their change."

She pressed the control button and lowered her window. "I love the way the air smells after a storm, don't you?"

Lucas sighed as he backed away from the porch and steered toward a stand of trees. It was going to be a long afternoon.

Back from their mission, Mira removed her muddy shoes and set them to dry beside the welcome mat, then stood on the porch and shook water droplets from the windbreaker. After entering the cabin, she hung the damp garment on a hook behind the door. The vehicle wasn't far, but covering it with downed branches had taken a while, and the walk back had been slow but interesting. Botany wasn't her area of study, but she'd enjoyed a closer look at Earth's plant life. A glance at the clock on the stove told her it was past noon.

Scanning the kitchen, she saw Lucas digging through a cupboard built into a half wall that divided the kitchen from the living area. After a moment, he brought out two different tins, opened them, and poured the contents into separate cooking utensils, then set both pans on the stove. Again, the thought of his being so caring of her dietary needs gnawed a hole in her conscience. He could have left her to fend for herself or told her she had to eat what he prepared or starve, but he was going out of his way to find something palatable for her.

"What are we having for lunch?" she asked, trying to be cheerful when all she felt was guilt.

"Cream of broccoli soup for you and split pea with ham for me. And I found a box of crackers. Lucky for us, Martin keeps a well-stocked larder."

"Are you sure he won't be angry when he finds his supplies depleted? We've broken into his house, used his things, and eaten his food without permission."

Lucas opened the refrigerator, brought out a beer, and popped the top. He leaned back against the counter. "Martin? Hell, no. But you'll understand better when you meet him." He raised the bottle. "Care to try one of these?"

"I don't . . . no, thank you."

"Your people don't do alcohol, huh?" He took a swallow and sent her a sly smile. "Hmm, let's see. No meat and no alcohol, but your species does enjoy sex and playing mind games. Your planet sounds like a pretty confusing place, if you ask me."

"No one is asking you," Mira bit out, annoyed that he continued to bait her. "And who said I came from a planet other than this one?"

Lucas shook his head. "You just don't get it, do you?"

"Get what?"

"What's at stake here." He set the bottle on the counter and folded his arms. "Tell me, what will it take to convince you this is serious? Since a kidnapping attempt didn't do it, maybe you'll accept the danger when bullets start to fly. Or we fall under an all-out attack? How about someone's death? Because that's what might happen in the next day or so."

"Death? A little while ago you said that I—that an alien was a valuable commodity."

"The alien—yes. But me? Hell, I've been a thorn in the military's side for the past three years. I doubt they'd blink twice before killing me to get at you."

The cavalier words caused Mira to drop into the nearest chair. "They would kill you? But I thought you worked for the government?"

"I do, but conspiracy to commit treason or a half dozen other trumped-up charges could be leveled as their excuse to put me out of commission. They could claim *I* kidnapped *you*, so I could sell you to the highest bidder or gain the glory for myself."

The possibility of Lucas's being injured made her all the more determined to escape, especially if it was the only way to keep him safe. "I thought you said Martin would take care of the problem when he met with your leader."

"He will, but it might not happen before things escalate. I don't know how carefully your species has studied ours, but in this world a huge percentage of people are out for personal gain. If someone disreputable got ahold of one or more of you, you'd be the hottest ticket in town—hell—the whole world."

Another reason why Thane and the elders had shunned direct contact with the citizens of this planet.

Her people knew the dangers of individual greed and glory, while humans still seemed to be learning.

Lucas stirred each pan and poured the contents into large mugs. After adding a spoon to each, he set a cup in front of her. "Lunch is portable. Bring it with you while we take a look at what I wanted to show you earlier." As if confident she would follow, he sauntered away, carrying his food.

Mira sniffed the soup's steamy aroma, then tasted it. Wrinkling her nose, she decided she wasn't as hungry as she'd first thought. Her stomach had calmed while they'd been in the fresh air, but the combined smells of whatever was in his mug and her own made her queasy. She crossed the kitchen and walked in front of the sofa to stand beside Lucas as he gazed at a grouping of framed pictures. The images started on the far side of the living area and spilled over to a second wall.

"Let's start with this one," he said, gesturing to a photo in the upper-left corner with his spoon. The date under the photo read July 28, 1958.

"Who are those men?"

"The one at the desk with the pen in his hand is President Dwight D. Eisenhower, the others are probably prominent scientists of the time. He's signing the passage of the National Aeronautics and Space Act. According to historians, it was the beginning of our modern space program. The Russians had launched *Sputnik* about ten months earlier, and that kicked off the rivalry between our two countries in the race to conquer outer space."

The pictures were arranged chronologically, which made it easy for him to tell his tale. He explained the meaning of every photo, giving a brief detail of what had been accomplished with each event: Project *Mercury* and Alan Shepard, the first American to fly into space; Project *Gemini* and John Glenn, the first US astronaut to orbit the Earth; Edward White, the first human to go on a spacewalk; Project *Apollo*, the priority project that demonstrated the United States' superiority over Russia's efforts. And finally, *Apollo 8* and Neil Armstrong's historic walk on the moon.

"Who's that shaking hands with Armstrong?" asked Mira, focused on a snapshot dated the summer of 1975.

"Martin, meeting his idol right after he joined NASA. He even got the astronaut to sign the autograph to his 'good friend,' quite a feat for someone new to the organization."

The pictures continued. There were several of Martin Maddox shaking hands with whatever president was in office at the time. The engaging and interesting stories Lucas told about his mentor made her believe the ex-director was a powerful man who had aged gracefully in every aspect of his career except his retirement.

"What type of device is that?" She pointed to a grainy image on the bottom row.

A low whistle emanated from Lucas's throat. "I

shouldn't be telling you or anybody else what it is, but now that you've seen it . . ." He set his mug on the fireplace mantel. "Martin shouldn't even have it in his possession."

"It looks like some type of rocket."

"The X-37. It's NASA's top secret flight demonstrator, and as far as I know it's still under construction. They're hoping it will successfully take a manned crew farther into space than we've ever gone before. Since Martin still has a couple of dozen well-placed connections, it's anybody's guess how he got the image."

She faced him and waited to speak until he glanced her way. "I promise I won't tell anyone I've seen the photo, Lucas."

"No offense, but your word doesn't give me a warm fuzzy feeling. Especially since I know there's still an issue of trust between us."

"First a credit card thief, then an alien. Now you think I'm a spy?"

His lips twitched, a sure sign he was joking. "Hmm, I hadn't thought of that one, but now that you mention it . . ."

Mira sighed. "Did you mean what you said earlier, when you promised to tell me things about you . . . and your work?"

"If you agree to reciprocate, yes."

"I—I'm not sure I can do that."

"I can't remember the last time I met anyone as stubborn as you." He slid his hands into his pockets and sighed. "Okay, I'll go first. I assume you've figured out by now that my job has something to do with the United States space program?"

"Yes, but only indirectly." She almost blurted that she knew exactly what he did, but then she would have to explain her foray into his briefcase, which would have given him another reason to mistrust her. "It's obvious you're looking for an alien life-form, and you think it's me."

Lucas appraised her from head to toe and back again, inspecting her hair, her face, and finally her eyes. When he focused on her lips, she felt a rush of heat wash from her chest to her cheeks. Embarrassed, she concentrated on her bare feet.

"If you're an alien life-form, your existence is going to crush every single myth and hypothesis imagined by scientists, writers, and dreamers worldwide. When they hear about you there could even be a full-blown international panic attack. The powers that be will insist on running tests on your DNA to ensure you're not perpetrating a hoax."

She raised her head. "A hoax?"

"Have you taken a good look in the mirror? No one in their right mind is going to believe you're not a human being unless they see the proof with their own eyes." His expression turned hopeful as a smile played on his lips. "Unless you have seven toes on each foot or—"

She stiffened. "That's very amusing, but you've seen my feet."

"Hey, you can't blame me for trying."

"I'm glad you're having so much fun at my expense," she said with a half smile. "Why don't we finish with the pictures before we talk about your job?"

Lucas waved a hand. "There's not much of significance left. Most of it's private."

Despite the doubt in his voice, Mira stepped around him and stared at the area in question. The first photo showed several casually dressed people gathered around an outdoor table. "This one is nice. Friends getting together for—"

"A picnic," he finished. "It was a celebration for Martin's retirement."

"Who are the women?" Mira asked, hoping none of the attractive younger ones was Lucas's ex-wife.

He tapped a finger on the glass. "This is Peggy Britton. She's second-in-command in the department—has been for twenty years. And this is Janice, our administrative assistant. The other people are friends and family of Martin's." He moved to the next photo and said in a rush, "This is a group shot of everyone in the DIA. The rest is personal memorabilia."

His mouth set in a grim line, Lucas turned his back to the wall and took root in front of the remaining photos. "How about we hunt up some dessert or—"

Mira maneuvered into a position that had them shoulder to shoulder. His strange reaction forced her to study a picture of Martin Maddox holding a tiny bundle wrapped in blue, while Lucas and a dainty blond-haired woman beamed proudly.

Afraid she already knew the answer, she had to ask, "What about this one?"

He muttered a curse before responding. "That was taken at our son's christening. Martin was Kevin's godfather."

Moments passed while they stood in silence. Lucas figured he'd have to talk fast to get Mira back on track, or she'd begin a litany of probing questions. When he realized he'd balled his hands into fists, he loosened his fingers, eased out a breath, and used the time to collect his thoughts.

In exchange for her cooperation, he'd promised to be honest about his work—not his personal life. Though it had seemed like a good idea at the time, it was his stupid fault for bringing her to this corner of the room. He'd noticed earlier that his and Tina's wedding picture was missing, and prayed it was in the trash, but Martin had been thrilled when they'd asked him to be Kevin's godfather. He should have known the photo would be hanging in a place of honor.

"Your wife is very beautiful," Mira said, her tone soft and devoid of emotion.

"She's my ex-wife. Everything in that photograph is in the past. I'd rather discuss my job."

"You had a child together. Is he—is Kevin with his mother?"

"My son is—" Lucas swallowed a lump of regret. Would he ever be able to say the word without choking? "—dead."

Mira's subtle gasp was a knee-jerk reaction he'd

learned to take in stride. People always asked about each other's kids, even when they knew the parents were separated. There was no reason to make her uncomfortable when she was merely being polite.

Before he could again suggest she forget the subject, Mira touched his shoulder, and his spine went rigid in counterpoint to the intrusive action. He'd had his fill of pity—a useless display that wouldn't bring Kevin back.

"I'm sorry." She circled around to face him. "I didn't know."

"How could you?" And why would you care, he wanted to add. He stared into her eyes and noted they were shining with compassion. She blinked and a lone teardrop trailed down her cheek. "Don't waste your sympathy. It was two years ago. I've learned to live with it."

"How—how did it happen?"

"This was supposed to be a discussion about my profession, not my past. I'd rather not talk about it."

"I don't mean to pry, it's just such a shock. Children don't simply die." She swiped at her face. "Did he have an illness or a congenital defect or—"

Vowing to stay in control, Lucas kept his voice level. "Kevin died of SIDS."

"SIDS?" She tugged on her earlobe.

"Sudden Infant Death Syndrome. I guess that condition isn't prevalent where you come from."

Her unusual action momentarily distracted Lucas from his grief. It dawned on him that Mira often used the gesture when she asked a question. Were those diamond studs a type of translating device or speech enhancer? Did that mean her jewel-encrusted bracelet had power as well? He reined in his curiosity as she answered him.

"It's a recognized medical disorder that strikes children up to one year, occurring mostly in infants between two and four months of age. It occurs with no apparent cause while a seemingly healthy child is asleep."

Her monotone recitation of what he knew was a textbook description of the tragic phenomenon pretty much confirmed his suspicion. Incredible, to be tuned in to a miniature dictionary that clicked definitions whenever the subject needed information. No wonder she and the others had been able to slip into human mode so easily. He stored the knowledge and decided to give her a shortened version of his experience, with the hope it would end her curiosity.

"Over the past several years, pediatricians developed a list of preventative measures that have reduced the number of SIDS deaths, but it still claims innocent victims. We—Tina and I—did everything modern medicine recommended. We made sure Kevin slept on his back, didn't put anything in his crib that might cause an obstruction, used the proper mattress and blankets, but it didn't matter."

He recalled the avalanche of spiteful comments his wife had thrown at him long after the funeral, the finger-pointing he'd stoically endured while he told himself it was grief that made her bitter. He'd been the one to put his son to bed the night it happened, and he'd asked himself a thousand times since if there'd been anything he could have done to prevent the tragedy.

"I can't imagine what it would be like to lose a child," Mira said, echoing his pain. "You and your wife must have been devastated."

"We've moved on. Tina's remarried. I heard through the grapevine she's pregnant again."

Mira's eyes grew wide. Her lips formed an O of surprise before she said, "How nice for her."

The last thing Lucas wanted to hear were bleeding-heart comments for his ex. "I thought we had a deal. I share what I do in my job, and you tell me who you are and why you're here."

She tilted her head. "You're right. It's probably for the best if we don't get personally involved."

"Don't get personally involved!" She jumped at his near shout, and Lucas took a calming breath. "I'd say it's a little late for that. We've had sex in a half dozen assorted flavors, argued like cats and dogs, slept in each others arms—now we're running for our lives. If that's not personal, I don't know what is."

"I'm sorry. Learning you'd been married and had a child . . . I wasn't expecting it."

"Would you have done things differently that night at the elevator, if you'd known?"

Her face flushed pink. "I don't—I'm not sure."

"So your kind believes it's acceptable to have sex

with unsuspecting humans. What about those who are committed to another?"

"I thought we were going to discuss your work?"

Lucas stifled a smart-ass comment. He'd finally found the key to keeping her on topic. Simply quiz her about the morals and beliefs of her species, and wait for her to steer the subject back to what he wanted.

"I work for the Division of Interstellar Activity."

She tugged on her earlobe again, then frowned. "I've never heard of it."

A glimmer of pride sparked in his brain. If the branch wasn't in her mental dictionary, there might be other things her world wasn't aware of—things he could use to win her to his side. "The DIA was formed under Ronald Reagan in 1982." He paced to the sofa and took a seat, indicating she should join him. "His first choice to head the organization was Martin Maddox. At the time, Martin ran a covert operation within NASA whose sole business was to try and make sense of unnatural incidents reported by our astronauts when they returned to Earth from a mission. Translation: UFO sightings."

Mira sat on a chair facing the couch and tucked her legs beneath her. "Were there that many?"

"Enough for NASA to believe we were being watched. As years passed, the division's duties expanded until they were brought in on every reported sighting. Martin's group was supposed to be the brains, the military the brawn. But when the army brass started sticking their noses in his investigative process, Martin complained to Clinton, and the president gave him sole control."

"When did you become involved?"

"I was ten years old in '82, and hadn't a clue what I wanted to do with myself, but the idea of life on other planets always fascinated me. As I progressed from grade school to high school to college, I toyed with the idea of studying astronomy, but knew I didn't have the patience to sit and stare through a telescope all day. I even thought about joining the air force and applying for the space program, but after speaking with a recruiting officer—"

"Let me guess." Mira grinned. "You were too much of an independent thinker to become a member of the military."

Lucas almost blurted out one of his weaknesses—heights frightened him senseless—but he decided it wasn't relevant. Instead, he recalled getting the lowdown from Martin on how his high school teachers and guidance counselors had described him on his security check for the Secret Service. Stubborn, single-minded, arrogant, and a few other choice characteristics had topped the list, as well as his intelligence and leadership qualities.

"That's one way of looking at it." He relaxed in the chair when he realized she was genuinely interested in his past. "I knew I belonged in government service, I just had to find the right fit, so I talked to a few related bureaus and chose the Secret Service. After graduation, I climbed through the program until I was placed on a roster of agents assigned to protect the president and his family. My first high-profile job was working for Bill Clinton. Aside from his personal scandals, the man was a good ol' boy. He'd held enough conversations with people in Arkansas who claimed they'd met aliens to believe in the possibility of extraterrestrial life. He respected Martin, and pretty much let him do what he wanted."

"It was then you met your friend?"

"One morning I was given approval to sit in on a presidential briefing in which Martin detailed a sighting they were tracking in the northwest. After the meeting, I asked Martin to join me when I came off shift. The moment we sat down and began to talk, I knew I'd found my niche, my place in the government. Martin knew it, too, and asked them to place me on his team."

Mira yawned, not from boredom, but exhaustion. Embarrassed to be so sleepy, she shifted in the chair. "I'm sorry. I'm interested in what you're telling me, truly, but I can't seem to keep my eyes open."

Lucas raised a brow. "It's fine. We have plenty of time to discuss things. You need to stay on your toes in case our friends come to call, so it's probably wise we both catch a nap." He stood and held out his hand, helping her to stand. "The rest of the story will keep."

Mira's hand tingled from his touch, and she felt her face heat. Sympathy for his little boy and his broken marriage welled. She wanted to draw him to her breast and hold him close, tell him how much she loved him, but the idea of going to bed with him just then didn't feel right. The sooner she ended their personal involvement, the easier it would be on her heart.

"I can't—I won't—"

"I need sleep if I plan to stay alert tonight," he said. "There was no subconscious meaning to the invitation."

She sighed. "Then a nap sounds wonderful."

Fourteen

Peggy ducked into Lucas's office, closed the door, and slapped a steno pad on the desktop. "Where the heck have you been? And why weren't you answering your cell phone?"

Martin grinned, knowing full well he looked like a tomcat who'd polished off a bowl of cream. But it couldn't be helped. He'd just returned from tailing Harden and was itching to share his discovery. But seeing Peggy flustered always brought out the devil in him.

"I've been meaning to ask, when this is over and we've found Lucas, would you have dinner with me?"

Her eyes opened wide. "What?"

"Dinner. And not for business. Just the two of us."

"Are you inviting me on a date?"

"I guess so. Does that upset you?" Martin crossed mental fingers. "Because I—"

As if composing herself, Peggy tucked a strand of hair behind her ear, then set her hands on her hips and stared down at him. "No it doesn't upset me, and the answer is yes. Now exactly what did you mean by that cryptic comment you made to Janice earlier? Something about tailing a rat to the cheese?"

Martin kept his expression neutral, but his heart was doing a tap dance in his chest. As long as Peggy agreed to see him outside of work, he could wait to tell her more. He winked, hoping to prolong the moment. "And here I thought you knew me so well."

Her lips twitched. "Knew, as in past tense. And frankly, you've been acting a little odd lately."

"Peggy, my sweet, don't you realize that being again in your presence after all this time has me addled as a lovesick pup?" he teased. "You used to read my mind, answer my questions before I asked them. I hope we haven't lost that vibe."

"We haven't lost it, it's just been put on hold." She eased into a chair and studied his face. When she smiled, the years melted away. "You ferreted out something about Harden, didn't you?"

"That I did," he said, snapping to attention. "And it's a doozy. Janice told you he was in here this morning pumping her for information?"

"Yes, and she also said you heard every word."

"That's when I decided to follow him. I figured he had to be working for someone, since we both know he's not smart enough to take this anywhere on his own."

"And—"

"Major Everett Randall."

"Harden is working for the army?"

"Not the army. Randall."

Peggy's eyebrows shot to her hairline. "You mean he and Randall are in this together?"

"They're in something together, that's for sure. I just wish I knew exactly what." Martin beat a tattoo with the eraser end of his pencil. "I'm positive he's our leak."

"If that's the case, I'll solve the problem by firing his ass." Her blue eyes sparked flames.

"Don't be so hasty. It might be fun to play a little game of cat and mouse ourselves."

"If they figure out where Lucas is—"

"My guess is they already know, or have a strong suspicion. My man found two tracking bugs on Lucas's car. Randall has to know by now that the Hummer is missing. It's only a matter of time before he sends his goons to the cabin."

"We have to warn Lucas. He needs protection."

"I have a small arsenal stashed in the house, so he'll be armed. As soon as he's sure the president is back in the country, I'm betting he'll show with his guest in tow."

"His guest? You mean the woman you think he's protecting. The alien?"

"That's the one." He read her concerned expression and set the pencil down. "Unless you have a better theory?"

Peggy sighed. "Not better, it's just . . . the whole thing makes me dizzy. It's difficult enough to imagine Lucas meeting an alien—a *female* alien of all things— in his hotel lobby. To accept that they ran away together for no apparent reason—" She moved to the edge of her chair. "What if we have it wrong? What if the alien's taken him prisoner, and he's on his way to an unknown galaxy or worse?"

"Sounds like someone's been watching too much of the Sci-Fi Channel," he said, grinning. "Need I remind you of the business we're in? Nothing we do is real, Peg. It's one of the reasons we're so secretive about our work. I dare you to ride the elevator to street level and tell a single person strolling the sidewalk what we do in the basement of the Treasury Building—just one. Dollars to donuts they'll look at you as if you've escaped from a mental institution and run screaming."

"You're right." Leaning back, she smiled. "Sometimes, when my husband used to ask how my day went, I would tell him to watch a rerun of the *X-Files*, because it's more realistic."

"One day, I'm going to write a book," Martin said, repeating the threat he'd made upon his retirement.

"Uh-huh. Trouble is, no one would believe a word of it." She opened the steno pad. "Okay, help me make some logic out of the chaos, so I have it straight in my mind."

Ticking off fingers, Martin began with the night Lucas met the alien and worked his way through to their last conversation.

"That still creeps me out," said Peggy.

"Me too, but after what Lucas hinted at it's the only thing that makes sense. And since he's in my car, we can only assume Lucas and his friend are at my cabin, biding their time until—"

"The president returns?"

He shrugged. "I guess he's hoping I'll run interference and clear the way for him to bring in the alien."

"I made your appointment with the big boss, by the way. Two days from now, first thing in the morning."

"That might be too late, considering Randall and his minions will probably hotfoot it to the cabin tonight."

"You're sure about that?"

"The man is a pit bull. Stands to reason."

"And there's no way we can warn Lucas?"

"None I know of. We just have to keep our fingers crossed that he's a step ahead of them."

"Is there anyone you suspect is working with Harden?"

"My guess is one or two of the team captains. He mentioned men in the field during his phone call to Randall. If the major is on the ball, he'll have his own people in place, as well."

"But no one by name?"

"Nope."

A knock made them jump. The door opened, and Janice stuck her head inside. "Frank's on the phone for you, Peggy. The priority line."

"Thanks." Peggy rested her hand on the receiver

and rolled her eyes. "Do you suppose this is good news?"

Martin snorted. "I doubt it."

"Hello, Frank," she said into the phone. "What can I do for you?" She cocked her head, her attention totally focused on the man's words. "Uh-huh . . . uh-huh . . . I see."

Frank's babble carried out into the office, but Martin couldn't make heads or tails of the garbled words. When Peggy's cheeks grew red, his insides churned. Whatever the man was saying, the news had to be huge.

"Repeat that . . . uh-huh . . . how many . . . how big?" Peggy scribbled furiously on the steno pad. "And you say this happened last night? Why wasn't I called at home?"

Martin's pulse began to beat in double time.

"I see. Spell the name, please . . . and the names of the other civilians." She continued to write. "And the pictures?" She set down the pen and placed two fingers on the bridge of her nose. "No, don't arrest the people who interfered. But do inform them we have their names, and if there's a security breach, we'll come after them. I hope you and Chuck have the man in question in custody. Handcuffs—leg irons—the works—understand, Frank? Lose him, and you lose your job."

She slammed the phone in its cradle and hissed a string of curses so salty they'd embarrass a sailor.

"What the hell was that all about? Who is Frank supposed to have in custody?"

"I'm glad you're sitting down," Peggy said. Ironically, she stood and began to pace. "He and Chuck are taking the first plane out tomorrow morning and bringing in a photographer named Jack Farley."

"What happened to their suspect?"

"A man and his son, and a group of concerned citizens acted as vigilantes. Frank and Chuck saw the alien and the man and boy fly off in a spacecraft the size of a football stadium."

Mira lay awake in the semidarkness, nestled in Lucas's arms. It didn't surprise her that they'd slept through the afternoon. Ever since they'd arrived at the cabin, their days and nights had been upside down. Between her pregnancy, their morning hike to hide the Hummer, and the intense conversation they'd held earlier, it was no wonder she felt drugged. And Lucas, she suspected, was exhausted as well, and probably frustrated with her reticent behavior.

Now that she knew the truth, she understood why he hadn't wanted to speak of his personal life. His guilt and sadness were still raw, still alive in his heart. And not, she sensed, for the loss of his wife, but solely for the loss of his child.

She'd been told by the elders that humans didn't value children or care for them in the way they deserved. In the short time she'd been here, she'd read daily accounts of events that reinforced her planet's observations and studies. Babies here were often born to mothers who had little regard for their children's well-being; many parents left their offspring with humans so incompetent they were hardly able to care for themselves; a host of sexual predators prowled the streets and the Internet, preying on the weak, the small, the defenseless; poorer countries had more orphans, many of whom were dying of hunger and disease, than family units.

This world's disregard for life was one of the reasons Thane and the others felt no regret for sending the travelers here and ordering them to return with half-human fetuses. Earthlings didn't take care of the precious babies they were given; why not send the children to a society where they would be cherished?

But Mira knew not all humans were the same as those she'd read about. She'd seen loving families on the streets of Washington, parents who truly seemed to adore their progeny. She'd watched mothers sit on benches with little ones on their knees while they talked and sang and laughed. Even though she'd only had Thane, he had been caring in his own stern and officious way. They had been a formal but happy family.

She'd seen the misery in Lucas's eyes, felt the despair he harbored for the son he'd fathered who would never grow to be a man, and knew his pain.

As if envisioning the future, she imagined the baby she carried in her womb, saw his smiling eyes, his beautiful face and joyous personality. Her son would be a miniature of his father, a perpetual reminder of what she had gained.

And forever a memory of what she had lost.

Tears filled her heart and threatened to flow like the river that still raged in front of the cabin. When she left Earth, she would lose Lucas, and he would lose another child.

The cruelty of what she was forced to do overwhelmed her. His boy had died through an accident of fate, while her treachery was with purpose. Lucas's rigid posture and cynical expression had telegraphed the animosity he felt for his wife. When he realized she'd taken his son away, his hatred of her would be all-encompassing and so intense she could only imagine what he might try to do.

No distance would be too great, no situation too impossible to keep him from hunting down his child and bringing the boy back to Earth.

Mira's stomach growled, calling to mind how little she'd had to eat that day. No matter what happened with Lucas, it was imperative she stay healthy. Thinking to investigate the offerings in the kitchen, she rolled to the edge of the mattress and swung her legs over the side.

"What time is it?" Lucas muttered.

"Early evening." She peered at the clock, then glanced over her shoulder and met his drowsy gaze. "Almost seven."

"I feel like I've slept for hours." He swiped a hand across his face. "You want to cook?"

"I could, if you promise to eat whatever I make."

"I'm starving. Even nuts and berries will be all right, as long as they're filling."

"Nuts and berries it is," she said, standing. "What are you going to do?"

"Take a shower and change, provided I can find something else that sorta fits. You might want to hunt up a sweater and keep it handy. If we have to leave in a hurry, there won't be time to do more." He rose from the bed and walked to face her. "We can talk while we eat. I haven't forgotten about finishing our discussion."

"Neither have I."

Lucas cupped her jaw. "Honesty, Mira. That's what this is all about, remember?" Turning, he headed out the door.

Mira stepped to the closet and searched for something warm to wear, but all she found were cotton shirts and men's pants. She opened a dresser drawer, located a choice of heavier garments, and picked one in a soft, cool blue. Folding it over her arm, she went to the kitchen and set the sweater next to her tote bag.

After checking the cupboards and freezer, she decided on a meal of noodles, frozen spinach, and a jar of cheese sauce. Thirty minutes later, she assembled the softened noodles and thawed spinach, then stirred in the sauce and tasted the concoction. Not half-bad, she decided. A thump sounded from the back of the house, and she wondered what Lucas was doing to make the racket.

Moments later, a second thump caused her to spin

in place. Lucas stood in the doorway. His arms were full. A dark blue vest hung from each wrist, he held a gun in each hand, another larger weapon was propped against the pantry wall, and a carryall rested at his feet.

When he saw her standing with her hand over her heart, he frowned. "Sorry, I didn't mean to startle you."

"Where did you find those—those weapons?"

"On the top shelf of the closet in the second bedroom. I should have known Martin would have protection. He told me he'd run across a grizzly or two since he moved here, and I don't think he's squeamish about hunting. The Kevlar vests were a surprise bonus."

"Why did you bring them in the kitchen?" Mira spooned the noodle-and-cheese mixture onto two plates and carried them to the table. Weapons of any kind had been banished from her planet ninents ago. Just being in the same room with an instrument of destruction made her queasy.

"I suspect we're going to need them later," he said, his tone grim.

"You would use them on a fellow human being?" She sat in a chair and fisted her hands on the table. "You could truly kill another person?"

Lucas set the guns and protective gear on the counter and took a seat opposite her. Reaching out, he grasped her hands. "I could if my life were threatened. Or yours." Quirking a corner of his mouth, he eyed his plate. "What's for dinner?"

She wrested her hands away, picked up her fork, and moved her food from side to side, not sure she could swallow a bite. "Noodles and a sauce I found in the pantry."

Scooping a forkful into his mouth, he chewed. "Different. I've never had Velveeta on pasta before. What's the green stuff?"

"Spinach." Still uncomfortable, Mira slid her gaze to the counter. "Do you know how to use one of those?"

Lucas continued to eat. "If you're referring to the guns, I learned when I was in training for the Secret Service. I wasn't a crack shot, but I was proficient enough to pass the course."

"And the blue vests?"

"Body armor. It will help if one of us takes a hit to the torso. You're going to wear yours in case of stray bullets. I'm wearing one because I'll probably be a target."

"You still think you might be shot at on purpose?"

He raised a glass of water to his lips and drank. "I'm positive of it. With me out of the way, you're theirs free and clear." He wiped his mouth with a napkin. "Now, where did we leave off this afternoon?"

"You told me how you'd come to join the DIA." She picked up the plates and carried them to the sink, walking a wide berth around the weapons.

"Right. There's not much left after that. I worked with Martin and Peggy, we shared the same philosophy, Martin retired and named me his successor."

Mira refilled both their glasses with water, then sat across from him. "How long have you held the position?"

"Three years this summer."

"And what is it exactly that the DIA does?" If she told him she knew about his latest quest—to find the alien that had landed in Rock Creek Park and the other eight from across the country—he would realize she'd broken into his briefcase. Not a wise move when he was beginning to trust her.

"We investigate all reputable alien sightings reported in the United States, and we run a tracking station that's hooked to NASA, but they no longer monitor it—we do."

"Have you tracked many aliens?" *Besides me?*

"We get hundreds of reported sightings every year. I have a team that does nothing but check the stories for authenticity before we decide to investigate. We also work closely with a few of the more reputable independent agencies and groups funded by government grants, that sort of thing."

"I see. And has anyone ever found anything . . . concrete?"

"We've given credence to plenty of sightings, but we never had a handle on a landing until about ten nights ago, when we started tracking your pods."

Pods? Mira's heart stuttered in her chest. It was the closest correct human word she could think of to describe the vehicles they'd used to shuttle to the Earth. But how did Lucas know? "I'm sorry? What did you call them?"

"Pods. Martin and I imagine they resembled small, single-seater crafts. We know they were made from harmless, biodegradable material that melted or washed away in the storm, or a creek or lake or river, depending on where the pod landed." His smile was blatant. "Care to tell me how they were powered?"

Mira leaned back in her chair. "I don't have a clue."

"I thought we were going to be honest with each other?"

"I told you I wasn't sure I could ever explain who I was." She pushed from the table and opened the front door. "It's a clear night and the river is down to a manageable level. I can wade across it and be gone in a few minutes. Tomorrow, you can drive back to Washington and tell them whatever you like about my escape."

"Mira, be sensible." Lucas stepped beside her. "It's too late for—"

She cocked her head at a faint sound in the distance.

He grabbed her upper arm. "What are you listening to?"

"I'm not sure. A noise—"

Lucas walked onto the porch and gazed skyward. "Shit!" He trotted inside. "Douse the lights and gather your things."

"What is it?" Mira slapped at the switch plate, then pulled the sweater over her head and grabbed her tote bag.

He shoved a vest in her hands. "Put this on, now, before we go outside."

She did as ordered, talking while she struggled into the jacket. "What is it?"

"Helicopter." He slid into his vest and stuck a gun in each pocket, then slipped the carryall over a shoulder and picked up the largest weapon. Clasping her free hand, he led her to the porch steps. "We'll go on three. Stay low and head for the Hummer. Take the keys." He shoved them in her pocket. "If you hear shots, and I'm not beside you when you reach the car, get in and drive to DC. Go to the hotel and ask for Martin Maddox."

Mira grabbed his hand, and they staggered into the darkness. A dull noise hummed in the distance; but when she raised her gaze skyward the only thing visible was a sea of stars, not a helicopter or any kind of aerial craft.

"I don't see anything," she said in a strangled whisper, trying to keep up and search the sky at the same time. "Are you sure it's what you think?"

"From the sound, I'd guess it's a RAH-66," Lucas muttered. "I wasn't anticipating that sophisticated a machine."

She tugged on her ear with her free hand as they ran, but nothing appeared in her memory bank. She stumbled, and Lucas pulled her against him.

"Don't expect to find everything about us in that diamond dictionary of yours, sweetheart. There's a good chance the United States military's managed to keep some of our weaponry a secret." Clutching her to his side, he zigzagged toward the trees. "Stop worrying about what they're flying and get your butt in gear."

Mira swallowed her fear. The aircraft sounded lethal and extremely high-tech, which didn't bode well for their escape. She peered ahead, trying to gauge the location of the Hummer, but all was black. Before they reached the cover of the trees a wash of light blasted the area from behind. She turned and a gust of air swept in from above, blowing her to her hands and knees as it flattened the ground cover and vegetation. Blinded by the light, she shaded her eyes and squinted. The dirt in front of her scattered in a hail of bullets.

"Halt!" came a voice over the roar. "Stop and put your hands in the air."

"Get up!" Lucas pulled her to her feet and pushed her ahead of him. "Keep going. Don't stop and don't look back."

A second round of bullets split the night. "This is your last warning! Halt!"

Together, they lurched forward. More shots hit the ground. Lucas grunted and shoved her hard. "Straight ahead, about twenty yards."

His harsh tone told her something was wrong. Spinning in place, she stared at him. Backlit by the high beams, his face was a mask of determination. He dragged his left leg forward, and she gasped at the dark stain spreading over his thigh.

"You're hurt."

"It's nothing. Keep going."

Bullets again scattered the area. Lucas clasped her hand as he forged on at a hobble. "Damn but you are stubborn. Can't you do as you're told for once?"

"Not when you're injured. We have to stop the bleeding."

"It's not far." The words came in a rasp. "Veer right."

They'd stowed the Hummer in a clearing off the path. The light from the helicopter stopped at the tree line, forcing them to feel their way over the downed branches, rocks, and ruts. Crashing through the brush, they fell against the vehicle's bumper. Mira's breath hitched when she realized the humming noise had petered off to a barely discernible buzz.

"They'll be on the ground as soon as they find a place to land safely," Lucas said with a growl. "Hurry. Get in the driver's seat and start the engine."

She clambered in, pulled out the keys, and met his eyes as he settled in the passenger side. "You expect me to drive?"

"It's a stick, and my left leg isn't worth shit right now. It's up to you to get us out of here."

"I don't—I can't—I've never—"

"—driven a stick?" Gun in hand, he leaned out the window and fired, then rounded on her. "Guess it's time you learned." He reached over and flipped on the lights. "Put your left foot on the clutch pedal—the one on the left—and push down, then start the engine and do exactly what I say—no arguments."

She turned the key, and the vehicle came to life.

He spoke rapid fire. "Shift the gearshift to the left until you hit a notch. Step on the gas with your right foot and ease up on the clutch."

The Hummer bucked, the engine chugged.

"Hit the clutch!"

Mira slammed her left foot so hard she thought it would go through the floor.

"Good girl. Depress the clutch whenever that happens, and you won't kill the engine. Now try again, same as before—ease up on the clutch and give it some gas." He edged out the window with the gun raised and answered a volley of bullets with a round of his own.

The car jerked forward and she pressed with her left foot.

"That's the way. Lighten up on the clutch, feed it a little gas, and steer us out of here. Keep it in first if you have to, but get moving."

Bullets hit the rear of the Hummer. Mira screamed.

Lucas turned and sent off a few shots. "Go! Now!"

Heaving a breath, she concentrated. The vehicle jackrabbited into the forest, dropping its covering of branches. The narrow path, barely more than two ruts, was strewn with debris. She jerked the wheel hard to avoid contact with what appeared to be a downed tree, then steered back onto the shallow road depressions.

Lucas pulled from the window. "Looks like they've gone back to the chopper. Lucky for us it's valuable or they'd follow on foot." He covered her hand on the gearshift. "You did fine. Want to try putting it in second?"

Mira stepped on the clutch and let him guide her as she moved the stick straight down.

"Let up on the clutch."

The car bucked and she pitched forward. Pressing her foot to the floor, she fed the car fuel then eased out the clutch. The Hummer jerked and settled into drive rhythm. Still shaky, she decided she'd pilot a landing pod any day before she drove another Earth vehicle.

"Hey, you're not bad at this. Keep on the path until we get a clue."

"Do you know where we are?"

"In the mountains."

She groaned as they bounced over the hardscrabble terrain. "I know that. Where in the mountains?"

"I'm not sure. Martin took me this way once to buy supplies at a country store. I think it's about two miles. I remember there was an intersection that led to a series of paved roads. I'm sure we can find our way from there."

"You need a doctor."

He glanced at his thigh, laid a hand on the bloody fabric, and grunted. "Probably. But I think the bullet went through. It'll be fine with a few stitches." He opened the glove compartment and pulled out a case.

"What's that?"

"First-aid kit. Martin was a Boy Scout."

Mira had a hard time concentrating on the path. "Why don't we stop and take a look?"

"Can't stop now. The guys in the chopper will be searching."

"They can't bring that thing through the trees. It might be better if we turn off the lights, pull over, and wait until morning. That way, we can tend to your wound, and they won't see us from above."

As if considering her idea, Lucas looked out the window, inspecting the thick overhead canopy in silence. "Maybe you're right. But one of us has to stay awake."

"You're hurt. You need to rest." She slowed and went around a good-sized fallen log, then righted the vehicle and gave it more gas.

"I doubt I'll be able to sleep. This thing is starting to hurt like a son of a bitch. Stop when you feel comfortable and douse the lights."

Mira went a few more yards, then steered to a stop in a cutout in the trees. Swiveling in her seat, she waited while he fumbled in the glove compartment and pulled out a flashlight.

"Set this on narrow scope and aim it at my thigh. I'm going to do a patch job."

Raising his hips, he slid his pants to his knees. She gasped when she saw the angry red tear seeping blood on the edge of his thigh.

"See, a flesh wound. Nothing to worry about." He popped open a roll of gauze and wrapped a strip around his leg. Then he ripped into a packet, took out a wet pad, and dabbed at the gash. "Shit, that stings."

Mira gave a sigh of relief. The wound was raw, but didn't appear life-threatening.

He tore open a series of bandages and arranged

them over the injury, then wrapped them with more gauze. "That ought to do it," Lucas said, tugging up his pants. "Douse the light."

Mira did as she was told. "What next?"

He stowed the flashlight and first-aid kit in the glove compartment. Turning to her, his teeth flashed white in the darkness. "You sleep. I'll stand guard."

Fifteen

*M*artin and Peggy waited for the U.S. marshals to escort Frank, Chuck, and the troublemaking photographer to the office from Reagan National. Peggy had canceled the 7:00 A.M. meeting, choosing instead to interrogate the men before they brought the local team members up to speed. The only other person they'd invited to the questioning was Jonas Harden.

A knock sounded, and she nodded at Martin. "You ready?"

"As I'll ever be. Anything I can do to make this easier?"

"I doubt it." There was a knock at the door, and she rubbed the bridge of her nose. "Yes?"

Janice rounded the corner. "They're here."

"Give the marshals a cup of coffee and have them

wait in Conference Room B, then ask the Jonas, Frank, Chuck, and their guest to step inside."

Janice ducked out, and the door opened wide. Chuck walked in first, his tie askew and his face stony, followed by Jonas Harden, whose eyes darted from Peggy to Martin prior to taking a seat at the far end of the table. Then came the man of the morning, Jack Farley, an aging hippie with a scruffy ponytail, droopy mustache, and cocky expression. Frank brought up the rear, his face grim, his gaze narrowed.

"Gentlemen," began Peggy, "have a seat. Can Janice get you something to drink?"

"You can get me a lawyer," snapped Farley. "I'm not saying a word until I speak to an attorney."

Peggy gave him a friendly smile as she held out her hand. "This is merely a meeting, Mr. Farley. I'm Peggy Britton, assistant director of the division, and this is Martin Maddox, our first director, now retired."

Despite the handcuffs, Farley raised his arms and accepted her gesture. "The division? Do you people still call yourselves Operation Roswell?"

"Operation Roswell?" mouthed Peggy.

"I thought not. How about the Division of Interstellar Activity?"

Martin took a seat, as did Frank and Chuck. "I don't think we're here to quibble over a few letters."

"Martin is right," said Peggy, pulling up a chair. "And for the record, you aren't under arrest."

"Then how come I was brought here by an armed guard—in chains?" He raised his shackled wrists. "I know my rights. You can't hold me unless I'm charged with a crime."

Peggy nodded to Frank. "Remove the cuffs. We don't want Mr. Farley to be uncomfortable."

As soon as Frank unlocked the handcuffs, Farley lunged for the door. Grabbing the knob, he spun in place when he found it locked. "I want to make a call. I'm entitled. It's the law."

"That would be the case if you were under arrest. You're merely being detained in order to share information about what happened on the night in question. By the way, if you have no objection, we'd like to tape this meeting—for the record."

"I'll just bet you want to tape things *for the record.*" His lips curled in a sneer. "I'm sure your bumbling agents would love to have the story of how they fucked up the biggest find of the last thousand years recorded for posterity."

Chuck shot to his feet and charged for the door, grabbing Farley by his collar. "Shut up, you idiot."

Martin stood. "Hey now, none of that. Sit down, Chuck. We'll get to the bottom of things soon enough."

Farley pulled away and smoothed his shirt. "Stupid sons of bitches," he muttered. "I want those two arrested for false imprisonment and interfering with a private citizen's right to earn a living, plus destruction of personal property—you got that?"

"Duly noted," Martin said, trying to keep a straight face. "Now, let's behave like civilized beings and start at the beginning."

Peggy clicked on the recorder and gave the date and time, then listed the names of everyone present. Gazing at each man in turn, she said, "Frank, how about if you go first."

Frank Kaufman, an older man with a balding head and florid face, swallowed visibly. Martin had hired the senior agent twenty years ago and knew him to be competent but disgruntled. Lucas had told Martin that since he'd been appointed director, Kaufman's sullen attitude was hard to ignore.

"You've read our daily reports, so you know we suspected the woman—this Zara person—almost from the get-go, right?"

"The waitress. She came to town the day before you arrived and got a job in the local eatery," Peggy read from her notes.

"I knew there was something odd about her from the moment I saw her," said Chuck.

"That's enough, you'll get your turn," said Martin. "Go on, Frank."

Frank told of the woman seeing a young boy through an asthma attack. The child's father, a man named Daniel Murphy, and the woman started an affair only days after meeting.

"So you think the man in question—this Daniel Murphy—was the alien's target? She didn't ask about your job or our government or anything suspicious?"

"Nothing. In fact, she didn't have eyes for anyone after she met Murphy and his son."

"Then what happened?"

"She got sick at a shopping mall. Claimed it was an allergy to perfume, but her reaction seemed off the mark. The next day her eyes changed color and she fed everybody a cock-and-bull story about wearing tinted contacts. I knew it was a lie because I'd already searched her cabin. There was no saline or case, no extra contacts—nothing."

"I see." Martin turned to Farley. "And when did you arrive in town?"

"The day after your agents."

Peggy put down her pen. "What brought you to Texas?"

"I had a tip from a reliable source that the government was tracking UFOs. At the time, I was in Dallas on assignment, so I drove north to check it out."

Jonas Harden took that moment to rise from his chair. "I'm going for water."

Peggy held up her hand. "Stay put. Martin, would you go out and ask Janice to bring in a pitcher with cups and ice." Peggy continued. "Who, exactly, told you that we were tracking a sighting, Mr. Farley?"

"A journalist never reveals his sources. You know that."

"And you should know that whatever goes on here is top secret. Your refusal to name the informant could result in jail time."

"So send me to prison. Thanks to your so-called agents I don't have the photographs—I don't have jack shit. In my business, that means my career is over."

Martin came back in with a tray. Harden accepted a glass of water and sat down as far from Farley as was possible.

Frank continued with the story until the day of the final confrontation. "We caught her as she was leaving town and brought her to the office. Farley insisted he be there when we took the woman in. It's because of him she managed to get to her bracelet. The stones are hooked to some kind of device that can freeze a body like a rock."

"Freeze? You mean you were immobilized?" asked Peggy.

"Yeah, immobilized. The woman left, and we were stuck like statues. Couldn't move for about two hours. As soon as we could, we took off after her."

"To Oklahoma?"

"Right. She didn't try to hide her tracks. Probably thought she'd be gone before we found her. Trouble was, Murphy and his son reached her first. We surrounded them, and Chuck held the boy for leverage until it looked as if the alien was ready to give up."

"You took a civilian—a child—as hostage?" Peggy frowned. "Since when is that in the rule book, Frank?"

The older agent balled his fingers. "It didn't mean anything. We wouldn't have harmed the kid. It was our only hope of getting her to cooperate."

Martin removed his glasses. "Okay, then what?"

"A group of vigilantes, town idiots really, followed us and decided they were going to rescue the alien.

They overtook us with guns blazing. It was about then that the ship showed up."

Chuck half rose from his seat. "They held us at gunpoint, and let the woman run. Before we knew it, the kid took off after her, and the man followed. I tell you it was like something out of a damned *Star Trek* movie." He lowered to a sit. "The spacecraft was big as a football stadium. It hovered while the alien, Murphy, and his son broke into little pieces and got sucked up in a beam of light. Then the ship disappeared in absolute silence."

Martin glanced at Peggy. They'd discussed the manner of transport and type of vehicle another world might use a thousand times when they'd imagined the first contact. "And what were you doing while all this was going on, Mr. Farley?"

"Taking pictures. I had my camera set on night light, high-speed film, the works. Those photos would have been worth millions—"

"Would have been?" asked Martin.

"One of those town idiots punched me, opened the camera, and ruined everything. I'm suing his ass, too."

Peggy sat back and heaved a sigh. "So you have no physical evidence of the encounter?"

"Nothing but what we saw with our own two eyes," said Frank.

"Do you have anything to add?" Martin asked Chuck.

The younger man pushed back from the table. "Just

that it was damned spooky, the way the woman zeroed in on Murphy. In the end, she tried to leave him and the boy, but they wouldn't let her. They wanted to go with her—they had to go with her."

"There was no coercion on the alien's part?"

"Hell, no. She begged them to stay put and let her leave on her own."

Martin set an elbow on the table and cupped his chin. "Do you believe she was a woman?"

"What do you mean?"

"Was the form hers, or did she take on the form, as if she were wearing a disguise or shapeshifting?"

"She was as much a woman as any I've seen on this planet," interjected Farley. "If a man saw her on the street, he might size her up because she was attractive and had a great body, but you'd never suspect she was an alien."

Peggy glanced at Martin as she turned off the recorder. He shrugged.

"That's all for now, gentlemen." She stood and pressed a button on the phone. "Janice, please ask the men who escorted Mr. Farley here to return." She smiled. "We have a lovely apartment with all the amenities of a four-star hotel at your disposal, compliments of the government."

Farley's cheeks turned red, his expression mean. "You said I wasn't under arrest."

"You're not. But we are going to detain you while we sort this out." The marshals filed in. "You have your destination and orders?" she asked the man in charge.

"Yes, ma'am."

Martin shook his head as Farley fought the marshals like a trapped mountain lion. By the time they dragged him away, he and his newspaper were suing everyone, including the president and his family.

He turned to Harden. "Since you're senior operator, we thought you'd want to be in on this, Jonas. We're going to tackle Frank and Chuck's story again, piece by piece. Peggy and I have a few questions we couldn't ask while Farley was here. Feel free to chime in if you think of anything."

Lucas gave a sidelong glance at Mira, then winced at the throbbing in his leg. Good thing she was asleep, or she'd insist he take something for the pain. The first-aid kit held a treasure trove of drugs—everything from aspirin to muscle relaxants to codeine, but he couldn't risk easing the ache. Their lives depended on him staying alert.

Recalling the gunfire they'd survived, he felt positive he'd been hit by a stray bullet. Once he and Mira were in the middle of those high beams, there was no way they could be missed unless it was on purpose. The knowledge that he had yet to be selected for termination was of slight comfort when combined with all that he knew might happen to him.

Leaning back, he tried to come up with their next

move. He suspected the Hummer was running on fumes, and they needed a way out of the mountains that was undetectable. If his memory was correct, the RAH-66 was built to carry three men. He imagined their would-be captors had left a man at the cabin, which put two on the receiving end at the convenience store. Since there were no rest or truck stops this far off the main highway, the goons probably thought they had their prey trapped between a rock and a hard place.

Sadly, that wasn't far from the truth. He'd taken a few survival courses, knew how to start a fire, build a shelter, and locate north, but that was about it. If he and Mira headed out on foot, they'd have to find a place to ford the river, then stay to the woods until they had no choice but take the highway and hitch a ride. They had no choice but to return to DC and meet with the president, but given the state of his leg, he doubted they'd get there in one piece.

And once they got to town, who besides Martin and Peggy could he trust?

What if Randall or whoever was running this show got to the president and convinced him they had to handle the aliens as they would an enemy invader? Mira had yet to admit the truth about herself, so why would she tell the supposed leader of this planet?

Why didn't she trust him?

Lucas sighed and stared at his watch, noting they had about two more hours until sunrise. The minutes were crawling by, and his mind was in meltdown.

Why couldn't he concentrate or get a handle on how to fix this situation? What the hell was wrong with him?

A mist appeared in his mind, and through it he saw a serene glade with beautiful flowers and a waterfall that emptied into a tranquil pool. Dressed in a figure-hugging sarong, Mira stepped from the tropical green-ery and beckoned with a curled finger. Lucas envisioned himself inching toward her, amazed at how real the experience felt. When he reached her, she held out her hand, and together they slid to the grass-covered ground. Without a word, he stretched out and placed his head in her lap. His eyes closed as she soothed his temples with her fingertips.

A gentle rest will better prepare you for your task.

Lucas tensed, but he couldn't stop the lethargy, the total relaxation of his muscles. He swiped his hands over his face, but it didn't matter. Damn, but he was losing all control.

A few minutes' sleep is all you need. The time will be well spent. It will ready you for the journey ahead.

He muttered a curse as he glared up at her, and the vision smiled. *Sleep. Close your eyes and sleep.*

Moments passed before Mira dared glance in Lu-cas's direction. He sat with his head upright, but his eyes were closed, his hands relaxed in his lap. He would know the second he awoke that she'd done this. Bit by bit, she was revealing herself to him, but it couldn't be helped. All that she'd done since she'd left the hotel had been for his good. If she had thought she could get away without detection, she would have contacted the mother ship and left. But that wasn't possible.

The ship wouldn't make a pickup in daylight, and, somewhere, trained enemies waited and watched.

It was logical they were at the convenience store Lucas had told her was at the end of the path. She imagined the men had scoured the area and felt secure in waiting there. She'd read the fuel gauge and was aware the Hummer needed gas, and Lucas had to reach Martin. They could do neither without getting to the store.

Mira gazed at her bag. Thane would be angry when he found out she'd been in danger and hadn't notified him. With Lucas in a deep sleep, she could use the transmitter to contact him, but it was too close to daylight to send the mother ship.

When she arrived home, she would insist the next mission be planned more carefully. The travelers had to have a way to communicate with each other. The women needed proper Earth identification, current clothing, and a reasonable amount of currency, as all would have made the job easier. Other than attaining her goal, she'd done little but worry about her sister travelers. Had they come up against the same problems? Had any of them been captured?

How many had been as foolish as she and fallen in love with their targets?

She settled into the seat and peered through the trees. It would be daybreak soon. Common sense told her they should leave the car, because the men would be watching for it. They could forge a path on foot, find a place to cross the river, and obtain a ride to the nation's capital.

Resting a hand on her belly, Mira let slip a smile. The gesture seemed to come so naturally that she now thought it had always been a part of her. The knowledge that her son would be a leader among their people, an honorable and caring man like his father, warmed her.

If only she could change the rules. She would confess who she was and why she was here. She would tell the president, too, in the hopes he could find a way to come to terms with her world's government.

But she wasn't in charge. She was a citizen on a mission. And betraying her mission was tantamount to betraying her people. No matter how much she loved Lucas or commiserated with him on the loss of his son, her world and her child came first.

Lucas shifted in his seat. His mouth felt dry as a ball of cotton. He peered into the forest. Gray light filtered down from the overhead canopy in narrow, dappled streaks, illuminating a watery mist that seemed to hang in the air.

His watch read 5:36.

Angry that he'd fallen asleep, he bolted upright and took in the empty driver's seat, the space where Mira kept her bag, the keys dangling from the ignition. Cursing, he inched open the passenger door. When his feet touched ground, his thigh felt as if it were on fire, and he fell to his hands and knees.

His last coherent memory, a waterfall, a tranquil pool, his head in Mira's lap while she soothed away his tension, rose to taunt him. Damn if the woman hadn't messed with his mind again.

After struggling to a stand, Lucas probed his wound. If he didn't know better, he'd think the bullet was lodged inside. He lurched against the Hummer. Great. He was crippled, and he'd allowed his prisoner to escape. How long had he slept?

Hissing out a breath, he tested his injured leg. After a few creaking flexes, he was able to take a couple of steady but painful steps. Working to stay quiet, he pressed the Hummer door closed and eased open the rear passenger-side door to collect his backpack, spare gun, and ammo. Then he tottered to the driver's side and put the keys in his pocket. Unless something disastrous occurred, Martin's car would be safe until his return.

Once Mira reached her ship he'd never catch her. And he still had to deal with the goons in the chopper—not to mention the president, the military, the press, and anyone else involved in this debacle.

Best-case scenario, she had arranged a pickup and was out of harm's way. Her departure would blow his job to hell and back, but the most important thing was her well-being. He was responsible for her, so he had to follow her trail until he knew she was safe. In an ideal world, he would deny to Randall and the press that this entire episode had ever occurred—at least where he was concerned.

Of course, he'd have to admit everything in his report to the president—just before he resigned his post. On a more personal level, he wasn't sure he would ever accept that Mira was out of his life for good.

He stepped off the path and glanced around, pleased to note how well the soggy earth muffled his footsteps. He assumed Mira wasn't stupid enough to return to Martin's cabin, and she had to know what was waiting for her at the opposite end of this trail. The only place for her to go was the woods. But in which direction?

Civilization lay to the left, but to reach it she had to cross the stream. Higher ground rose on the right. The elevation would make it easier to send a signal, keep watch on the area, and take her closer to a possible rescue craft.

He took three hesitant steps into the vegetation and propped himself against a tree to scan the ground. Lucas was no trained scout, but he was fairly certain the sneaker imprint he spied in the mire belonged to Mira. Straightening, he heard a sound, ducked behind a large pine, and held his gun at the ready. Moments later, he tensed from head to toe when a hand touched his shoulder.

"Lucas?"

He relaxed his grip on the trigger and frowned. Some ground commando he was turning out to be, letting a visitor from another world get the drop on him. Slipping the gun in the waistband of his slacks, he swallowed a ragged breath, set his lips in a line, and slowly turned.

"How is your leg?"

"Bearable."

Mira smiled, and he resisted the urge to pull her to his chest. At least she'd trusted him enough to return.

"Where the hell have you been?"

"I think the correct military term is *reconnoitering*."

"You went on a search alone, in unfamiliar terrain?" He raised a brow. "You are certifiable."

She took a step nearer and dropped her voice. "I'm as sane as you, probably more so. I got to the store and spotted two men undercover on the far side of the building. They were dressed in utilitarian brown-and-green uniforms, and had weapons tucked under their jackets."

He grabbed her upper arm and drew her deeper into the forest. "Did you see a helicopter?"

"Later."

"Were they talking?"

"One of them mentioned waiting for the proprietor. Mostly, they kept their eyes on the forest."

His lips itched to kiss her. Instead, he swiped a stray strand of damp hair from her cheek. "Where were you? Floating overhead on a cloud?"

"Of course not. I sneaked around the rear of the store. The ground and everything on it is so wet nothing crackled. It was easy to stay quiet." She gave a little-girl smile. "They finally took off in the helicopter. I doubt we'll hear from them until we're back in DC."

"Mira—"

"There's a pay phone mounted on the outside of the store. I think we should phone Martin."

"What did you do?"

"Nothing."

"Then how do you know those men won't be coming back?"

"It's just a feeling I have." She hoisted the tote bag higher on her shoulder and edged around the Hummer. "Come on."

Lucas recalled his vision, the waterfall, his restful sleep. "You used that mind-meld thing on them, didn't you?"

She opened and closed her mouth. "I—I had to. You needed time to heal."

He limped to her side. "I remember what you did in my hotel room. And this morning, when I was trying to stay awake, you gave me a dream that encouraged me to sleep."

"I did what I thought was best." She tried the door, found it locked, and headed up the road. "I'm going to the store. It should be open soon."

"And then what?" He hobbled behind her and took her hand. "Mira. What about the man at Martin's cabin?"

"What about him?"

"He's only about a couple of miles back. When he realizes his friends aren't returning, he'll make a trip to the store. Or he'll call his pals, since he's sure to have a radio. That will set everything in motion all over again." Lucas held on to her shoulders. "It won't stop."

She heaved a sigh. "It would if you'd let me go."

"I can't do that, and you know it."

"I don't understand. I haven't hurt anyone or infiltrated your national security. I just needed—" She shrugged from his grip. "I've said enough. If you don't want to call your friend, I'm leaving."

"We made a bargain. I kept up my end when I told you about my work." Determined to get the truth, he stepped into her and clasped her elbows. "Is that the way your kind handles honesty? You pretend to keep your word until you get what you want."

Sighing, Mira focused on his shirtfront. If she could have left the night before, she'd have sent out the signal for an emergency pickup and been well on the way to meeting the ship. Instead, she was still in Lucas's debt. She owed him so much, and he'd guessed correctly at most of what she was up to. Maybe honesty was the only way to repay him.

"All right. I'm from another planet. Is that what you want to hear?"

"It's a start."

"There's nothing else to tell."

"You're kidding, right?"

She closed her eyes and shook her head.

"Are you here to run experiments on us or check out our space program? It can't be for our technology, because it's obvious you have us beat on that score." Lucas gazed at the overhead canopy, then shifted his stance. "Maybe you should start with where you come from, or why you're here. What's going on in the other eight states? And why did you pick me as a contact?"

"We're a curious species," she began, using the answer she'd been told to give by the elders. "We investigate foreign planets to take stock of their development. Earth is just one of many we're looking into."

"For what?"

"A vacation resort!"

He bit his lip, but couldn't hide his grin. "I cannot believe I'm sparring with an alien who thinks she's doing stand-up at a comedy club."

"I'm not trying to be funny. I've said too much already. You know I never promised to tell you everything."

"Yet you let me talk my fool head off."

"I would never betray you by repeating a word you said."

"You believe I told you the truth?"

"Yes."

"Then why can't you do the same? Why can't you tell me the entire story?"

"What if I promise to accompany you to the capital so we can sort this out?"

"Only if you promise not to use that mind-meld thing."

"On just you or everyone?"

He narrowed his eyes. "Don't use it on anyone."

"Fine."

She stormed ahead of him on the path. A moment passed before she heard Lucas stumble along behind.

Sixteen

Lucas slammed a hand against the peeling bark of the log cabin store and disconnected the call without leaving a message. Where in the hell was everyone? He thought he'd at least reach Janice. Though it wasn't quite nine o'clock, the office should have been humming. Unless things had gotten so chaotic since he'd left no one was in charge of the show.

Wouldn't happen, he told himself. Even if Martin hadn't picked up on what Lucas hoped were his logical clues, Peggy would have beaten the information to death until his disappearance made sense.

Then it dawned on him—it was Saturday. Normal people took a day or two off on the weekend. Even his local team leaders would need a day to recharge. Especially if things were as dead in the water as he suspected.

He eyed the battered truck the store owner had pulled up in just about the time he and Mira stepped onto the porch. The old codger hadn't seemed surprised to see them, nor had he batted an eye when Mira made polite small talk and followed him inside. The idea that she could charm an ancient mountain man as easily as she had him made Lucas smile. What would the guy say if he knew he was talking to an alien?

Mira's throaty laughter drifted outside, and he sidled to the entryway. The store was dark, with about as much sales appeal as a tin can full of rusty nuts and bolts. He hobbled to the screen door and pushed it open, ignoring the haunted-house creak as he inhaled the aroma of tobacco, leather, and vinegar. To the owner's credit, the floors were clean, and the dry goods were neatly arranged on several banks of shelves.

He spotted a huge pickle barrel to the left of the door, which explained the briny smell. A cold case ran along the wall behind the main counter, while a series of slanted wooden boxes held tomatoes, potatoes, onions, and apples under the front window. Stacked in a row over the vegetable bins were half gallon jugs of what he guessed was apple cider.

Mira stood at the counter in front of an assortment of candy bars. He walked beside her, and she sighed.

"Hungry?"

"Starving. How about you?"

Lucas raised his gaze to the proprietor, who seemed

intent on wiping down the fogged doors of the cold case. "Excuse me, what have you got to eat that's fresh?"

The man kept his hands in motion. "For eatin' now or later?"

"Now would be good."

The storekeeper turned, his face brown as a pinecone with about as many pits and ridges. "Everything here came in before the bridges went out. Sale date's still good on most things."

"Got any fresh coffee or a microwave we could cook a couple of eggs in?"

"Coffee's already on, fifty cents a cup. I can do up hard boiled eggs in the microwave." He aimed a thumb toward a doorway in the rear of the store. "If you want lunchmeat, you'll have to buy it by the package."

Mira wrinkled her nose. "Not for me, thanks."

"The eggs will be fine. Four, if it's not too much trouble." Lucas walked to the vegetable bins, chose two apples and brought them to the counter. "I'll take a cup of coffee." He glanced at Mira. "What about you?"

"Orange juice?"

"And an OJ."

The man removed a container of juice from the case along with an egg carton. After setting down the juice, he ambled through the far doorway. Lucas reached for a candy bar. "Do they have chocolate where you come from?"

She tugged on an earlobe and shook her head. "No, but it sounds interesting."

Lucas picked out an Almond Joy, a package of Reese's Peanut Butter Cups, a Milky Way, and a single serving bag of M&Ms. "Then there's reason for dessert."

"Did you reach Martin?"

"No one answered, but I forgot it was Saturday."

"Did you try his hotel?"

"I will as soon as we finish here. You getting worried?"

"A little. It's a long way to Washington on foot."

The shopkeeper trundled out holding a Styrofoam cup. Itemizing the rest of Lucas's purchases, he rang up the sale.

Lucas paid the requested amount, then decided he had nothing to lose by asking. "Do you know Martin Maddox?"

"I might," said the old man.

Lucas caught Mira twitching her lips and rolled his eyes. "He lives about three miles from here, down the trail that cuts through the woods. We arrived at his cabin the night of the storm. This morning we needed supplies so we took the path. Left his car a mile back. It might be out of gas."

"That's why you're here on foot, I imagine." A *ding* echoed from the back room. "Eggs are done."

Mira didn't speak until he disappeared. "Do you think he's going to help us?" She opened her orange juice and stuck a straw in the carton.

"We'll have to wait and see." Lucas handed her a

section of Almond Joy. "Here. Try this and tell me what you think."

Mira bit into the candy and chewed. Her tongue tingled with the combination of flavors. Bits of sweet mixed with a darker, deeper intensity of taste. She swallowed, saddened at the loss of such a wonderful sensation.

"Good?"

"What was that?" she asked, hoping to mask her pleasure. But she vowed to find a way to sneak a candy bar aboard her spacecraft. It would give the scientists who worked the replicators a challenge.

"Coconut and dark chocolate. Here, this one is my favorite." He opened an orange wrapper and took out a round flat lump molded in a paper cup. "Chocolate and peanut butter."

Inhaling the familiar scent of peanuts, she recognized the aroma of chocolate. She tried to take a dainty nibble, but the tempting scent encouraged her to bite the patty in half before sliding the rest into her mouth. She raised her gaze and found Lucas grinning.

He chose another from the display and set it on the counter just as the owner returned with the eggs, two each in white paper bowls. Lucas handed the man more money and tossed the extra candy into the bag.

"Mind if we eat on the front porch?" he asked, passing Mira her eggs.

"Makes no never mind to me."

They carried everything to a pair of rockers and set

their meal on the barrel that stood between them. Mira ate slowly, while Lucas swallowed his eggs at a break-neck pace.

"I'm going to make a few more calls. Give me a minute."

He stood at the pay phone and began to feed change into the coin box. Then he turned to her with a scowl and thrust out a bill. "Go inside and see if the guy can give you change—all quarters. This has to be the last pay phone in America that doesn't take anything but coins."

Mira walked to the register. "Excuse me. My friend needs money for the phone. Can you help?"

The proprietor took the bill, counted out change, and handed her a palm full. She smiled. "Thanks. If you have a minute, I'll be right back."

Without getting his answer, she sped to the door, handed Lucas the coins, and returned inside. The shopkeeper had his back to her and was again wiping down the cold case, but she had a feeling he'd been waiting. She'd learned to deal with hundreds of older gentlemen on her planet and thought most were kind, though set in their ways. Surely the senior citizens of Earth were the same?

"This is a nice store. Have you owned it long?"

The proprietor turned and used the rag to mop the counter. "My momma and daddy had it first, then me and my wife."

"I guess you do a pretty good business."

He straightened a row of plastic-wrapped items labeled BEEF JERKY. "Good enough to put two sons through college. Course they're too busy with their own lives to take it over anytime soon. Might have to close the doors one of these days."

"Maybe you could sell to someone who wants to live here. The mountains are beautiful."

"We like it." His lips morphed into a smile. "Don't get too many city folks this way."

"I'm Mira." She held out her hand. "It's a pleasure to meet you."

"Osgood Fairly," he said, pumping politely.

"I noticed you have a truck."

Osgood gazed into her eyes as if trying to read her mind. "Yep."

"Have you ever thought of selling it?" It was a given that the men who were after her would recognize Martin's Hummer, which made a nondescript older vehicle a perfect choice for their return to DC.

His face turned into a road map of unhappy wrinkles. "Not in a heartbeat. Sadie and me been together almost thirty years. I couldn't sell her. It'd be like sellin' my wife."

Mira nodded. "Maybe Sadie would like a change of scenery."

"A change of—?" He narrowed one eye. "Say, you tryin' to pull a fast one?"

"Me? Oh no. I just thought maybe we could make a trade. Martin's Hummer probably has enough gas to get it here, and you have a gas pump so you could fill it up. We'd let you have the Hummer if you'd let us take Sadie. Martin would return her when he picked up his car."

Osgood leaned against the counter. "And just where would you want to be takin' my Sadie?"

"Not too far. Washington, DC."

"The capital? That's more'n two hundred miles away."

Mira sighed. "You're right. Sadie's old. The trip is probably too long for her. Never mind." She waited a beat, then said, "Before you know it, she'll need to be retired."

The shopkeeper fisted both hands on his hips. "Retired! My Sadie runs as good as the day I got her. You young people don't know reliable unless it reaches out and slaps you in the head." He glared at the door. "I know Martin, and I know that fancy car he drives. Gets 'bout ten miles to the gallon. You'd have to pay me to tank it up, and I'd expect Sadie here in one piece in a week."

"We'd have her back in perfect shape. I promise. It'll just take us a while to get to the Hummer and drive it here." Mira walked backward out the door. "I'll talk to my friend and be right back."

"Martin is not going to believe it when I tell him this is what we got in trade for his baby."

Mira held back a laugh. It had taken two hours to walk to the Hummer and deliver it to Osgood. Then they'd had to listen to a half hour dissertation on the care and feeding of Sadie before the old gentleman let them leave the store. After that, they'd driven an hour out of their way to find a place to cross the swollen river, and had their second meal of the day.

Sadie performed like a champ throughout the trip, though it had been difficult getting her speed over forty miles per hour. Now, at close to ten, the lights of the capital stretched before them, glittering like diamonds in the clear and starry night. Lucas had grumbled and groaned through most of the ride, convinced Martin was going to have heart failure or sic the law on him when he found out what Lucas had traded so he could deliver an alien.

Alien. Mira was getting used to the harsh description though she didn't agree with it. She would much prefer being referred to as an off-world visitor or an extraterrestrial, even a nonhuman, before being awarded the negative denotation the word had on this planet. Then again, did it matter? When Lucas found her gone, *alien* would be one of the kinder names he would call her.

In between his complaining, he had asked questions that encouraged her to talk about her world. She'd answered hesitantly, explaining that she thought it best to tell her story to everyone involved at the same time, rather than repeat herself. He wasn't happy with her reticent attitude, but seemed to understand her reasoning.

"Can you at least tell me the name of your planet?"

"It's nothing you would recognize."

"Humor me."

Mira gazed through the windshield at the star-filled sky. "How well do you know the constellations?"

Lucas shifted gears as he took an off-ramp. "It's my job to be as educated as most of our astronomers. Of course, we don't have the same names for the star clusters as you do, which could make things confusing."

"You're correct," she agreed. She needed one locator stone to send the signal for an emergency pickup, which meant she could use one to call up a hologram of the heavens. Dare she show Lucas a road map to her world?

"You still don't feel comfortable telling me the truth, do you? Even though I've done everything I've promised." He drove into town without glancing her way. "I can't do more unless I know the whole story."

Mira caught the wounded tone in his voice and held her hand to her stomach, but that only reminded her of how much she was taking from him. She imagined how impressive a star map would look to someone unfamiliar with the sight. Perhaps a glimpse of one would soothe his wounded ego. "I could show you. If you recognize it, you can tell me what you call our world."

"Show me?" He raised a brow. "The planetarium isn't open this late."

"We don't need a planetarium, just a dark, quiet area."

Lucas steered the truck through a traffic circle and exited onto a side street. He had to drive for several blocks before he found a passable parking spot, and even then the back end of the truck edged into a driveway. "Keep your fingers crossed the Metro Police don't pass by, or we'll be asked to move."

Mira checked out her side window and noted all was still. She removed a green stone and inserted it into the clasp, then sent a bead of mental energy into the stone as she pressed the outer ring of the clasp. In scant seconds Sadie's windshield filled with a mesmerizing vision.

Lucas stared at the window, his jaw slack with amazement. Closing his mouth, he swallowed as he took in the swirling planets, shooting stars, and distant galaxies dancing in front of him. Every spectrum of the color wheel filled the truck's interior, from the darkest red to the brightest yellow, to the coolest blue and the deepest purple.

Finally, he rasped out a reverent, "My God."

"Can you make sense of it, or do you need a guided tour?" she asked, smiling inside. If only there was some way to give him this map when she left.

"Uh . . . let me get my bearings." He lifted his hand. "Can I touch it?"

"If you feel it's necessary, but the energy needed to keep up the transmission might tingle."

He prodded the planet Earth with his index finger, then jerked back his hand. "Tingle? It's more like a buzz. You said energy. Does it come from the bracelet or the stone?"

"The data comes from the stone. The energy comes from my mind. The bracelet is the conduit that links the two."

He touched the map again and kept his finger in place. "I guess you get used to it."

"You're pointing to Earth. From there you can follow the planets out of your galaxy. Continue upward and to the right about forty-five degrees."

"What about the activity?" He gestured to the miniature bodies covering the map. "The swirling gases and shooting stars—are they happening in real time or is that something you're doing with your mind?"

"It's happening as we speak. Once the stone is set in place it locks into the universe, and my mental energy brings to light whatever it reads."

"I don't know what to ask first." He rubbed his eyes. "It's a lot to absorb in one look."

"You want to know where I come from, so why don't we start there? Can you go to what you call the Milky Way?"

Lucas felt as if he were in high school all over again. But this teacher knew things his science instructors could only guess at. He pointed to a large pearly cloud.

"Follow past it to the north. I believe you call the mass Ring Nebula M57."

Lucas found the gaseous body and repeated what he knew of the dying star. "You can't live there. We understood this body to be an exploded star bigger than our own sun."

"We're positioned behind it, but not so close as to be harmed. The star has given us good protection from some of the more capable and warlike species in the universe." She gestured upward. "Look beyond it to the small planet with twin suns and smaller moons."

"I don't think our telescopes reach that far."

"You're correct, but ours can see to the Earth and beyond."

"How old is your world?"

"Ancient compared to yours, although there are other civilizations that are older."

"Have they come to Earth?"

"A very long time ago, but not recently. You were such a young world, they didn't want to disturb your growth. I imagine some of them have forgotten you exist."

Lucas found the information frightening. "Would they harm us if they knew how far we'd advanced?"

"Far?" Mira tried not to grin. "Oh, Lucas. You have no idea how much greater a journey you have before they'd be interested in you again. To them, Earth is a fledgling with nothing to offer. You won't be invaded, but they might send ships to keep tabs, just as we did."

"Are we that stupid?" he asked, insulted by her comment.

"Not stupid. Merely uneducated. They prefer, as do we, that when you ask the questions you find the answers for yourself."

Lucas sat back and sucked in air. At least he could inform the president that it was doubtful they'd be attacked by a ravaging horde of aliens. He slid a sidelong gaze at Mira, who was studying the map.

"I've asked this before, and you haven't answered. Why did you come here?"

She straightened in her seat. All business, she opened the clasp and the map disappeared from view. "I told you I'd explain it all to your government in our meeting."

"You didn't give me a name for your planet."

"It doesn't have one in your language. Would you care to hear it in mine?"

He nodded, afraid to speak and destroy the one small concession she was willing to give him. Mira met his eyes and a string of soft notes, not exactly a bird's call but closer to it than anything else he could describe, filled the interior.

"That was beautiful," he admitted. Things that he'd only imagined existed in the universe were becoming very real. "Was I right about the diamond studs? They're translator chips?"

She tapped her left ear. "This one intercepts and translates your language, and sends mine to you in an understandable manner. This one"—she touched her right ear—"works as a miniature dictionary. Very clever of you to have figured it out at the cabin." She clutched at her tote bag, hugging it to her middle. "Isn't it time we got to the hotel?"

Lucas could tell by her no-nonsense manner that she was finished sharing information. He started the truck engine and eased into the street. "You're right. It is late. I guess we'd better head for the Hay-Adams."

* * *

Mira breathed a sigh of relief when they pulled into the hotel garage. "Does Martin know we're here?"

"He's aware we're getting in late. If he needs us, he knows how to find us."

"What about the men who are after us?"

"If we're lucky, they're still looking for the Hummer. Better yet, they think we're on foot."

"How much did you tell Martin about me?"

"Enough to prepare him. When you two meet I want you to imagine seeing yourself though his eyes. You're the prize he's been waiting for his entire life."

Not comforted by the words, Mira frowned. She wasn't a prize. She was a woman on a mission. And at that moment she felt as if she'd failed. Yes, she'd accomplished her goal and conceived a child . . . but at what cost? Thanks to her, Earth was aware of her planet's existence, and Lucas knew so much more. If she didn't escape, everyone would also know of her world's problem.

Technology in the United States was advancing in great strides. Soon humans would be capable of space travel outside the reaches of their own galaxy. People of Earth still lived with a "conquer or die" mind-set. If the military found out the coordinates of her planet, her peaceful brothers and sisters might fall victim to their demands. And it would be her fault.

They parked, gathered their gear, and headed for the elevator. Mira walked beside Lucas, warily taking in the dark and gloomy garage. On her last visit there, she'd been in grave danger. Lucas had a gun and would keep her safe, but icy fingers of fear still skittered up her spine.

"Do we have to stop at the desk?" she asked, when they were in the elevator.

"Nope. I still have my key, and Martin had my suite checked for bugs and held while I was gone. He even had them move what little was left in your room to mine. Everything should be ready and waiting."

The elevator opened and he steered her to the door. Once inside, they set their parcels on the sofa. Feeling edgy and a bit awkward, Mira strode to the window and took in the view. The government buildings were bathed in cool white light, direct counterpoint to the hot dark fear building in her core.

"See anything interesting outside?"

She turned and Lucas limped toward her. Mira held back a sob as she took in his torn and bloody pant leg and pale haggard face. "Are you in pain?"

"Nothing a few ibuprofen won't handle, but I should make a trip to the ER tomorrow to get a tetanus shot and stitches."

She bit on her lower lip to keep from crying.

"Why so glum?" he asked, sending her a smile of encouragement. "We're safe here."

Safe? Maybe. But their relationship was doomed. Lucas needed rest to bring him back to full strength, or he wouldn't be able to give a plausible explanation when she turned up missing in the morning. He took her in his arms, and she rested her head on his shoulder, but her panic continued to build.

"You okay?"

"I'm fine. Just nervous. Those men could come back, and—"

"I told you there's nothing to worry about. Randall knows we're on to him. He wouldn't dare invade a public hotel—too easy to get caught and too much bad publicity if he doesn't find us. The president arrived home today, and tomorrow Martin will brief him on everything. We have tonight to catch up on our sleep and tomorrow to talk with Peggy and plan strategy. By the time we meet in the Oval Office it'll be a done deal."

"If you say so."

He drew back and stared into her eyes. "I haven't lied to you yet, have I? Trust me." He kissed her forehead. "I'm going to take a shower and see what I can do about this wound. You get comfortable and raid the honor bar. If Martin doesn't call, we'll go to bed."

She raised her gaze, and Lucas bent forward, brushing his lips lightly against hers once, then more slowly a second time. His tongue teased the seam of her mouth, and the erotic sensation cut through her like a laser, reminding Mira of what she'd be missing when she left. She raised her arms to his neck and pulled him close. Opening to his desire, she poured her essence into the kiss.

After tonight, she would never see Lucas again. If she had nothing more than the next few moments, she was going to make them memorable.

Lucas accepted her offer and searched her warm wet heat. His hands moved from her back to her front, slipping under her sweater and thin shirt. Palming her breasts, he caught her nipples between his fingers and squeezed.

Mira arched into him and ground her pelvis against his. Breathing as one, they clung together until he rasped out a shaky laugh.

"Hold that thought. I'll be out in a few minutes." He waggled his eyebrows. "Unless you want to join me."

"I don't think that's a good idea."

"I understand," he answered, his voice resigned. He stepped away and held her hands. "Just remember, now that you've agreed to surrender, things will be fine."

Surrender. She blinked, cringing at the hole the word ate in her heart. This was the first time he had used the distasteful description, and she couldn't help but compare it to the oral salvo of a conquering nation.

Stepping around him, she picked up the remote. "I'm going to sit and listen to the news. I want to see if there's anything pertinent we need to worry about. I'll shower when you're through."

He stroked her cheek with the back of his hand. Pushing a lock of hair behind her ear, he cupped her jaw. "I promise everything will be fine."

Mira watched the man she loved hobble away. Swiping at a tear, she was thankful she had kept silent. There would be no angry sentiments to remember when she recalled their parting. Lucas would be furious that she'd betrayed him, but eventually he would understand. They would never see each other again, but she would have his child to remember him by.

The bathroom door closed and the shower started. She grabbed her bag and tiptoed out the front door. Assuming the television would muffle any odd sounds, she opened the door to the stairwell and headed down.

Dim light guided her through warm humid air that smelled of chemicals. Intent on avoiding the parking garage, she hoisted the bag higher on her shoulder and eased into the lobby. The bellman's stand was vacant, the gift shop closed, and she didn't recognize the lone clerk on duty at the main desk. She walked toward the front door, then thought of the one thing she had decided to bring back with her.

She opened her bag, found coins and bills at the bottom, and approached the desk. "Excuse me, is there a place I can buy some chocolate?"

The young woman grinned. "The best selection is in the gift shop, but that's closed until eight o'clock. There's a snack machine around the corner from the elevators. I think there might be a couple of candy bars inside."

"Thank you."

Mira followed directions and found an assortment of machines tucked in an alcove. Assessing her choices, she considered how long it might take for an emergency rescue. She selected a bottle of water, two packages of cheese and crackers, and two of the peanut butter and chocolate cups. After tucking the prizes into her bag, she turned to leave the area.

When an elevator dinged its arrival, she ducked behind the wall. Peering around the corner, she blinked back her surprise. Two men, dressed in the same-style fatigues as those she'd seen their would-be captors wearing that morning, were walking quickly from the elevator. Between them, dressed in identical khaki and brown, stumbled a third man with his arms thrown over their shoulders in an air of camaraderie. But instead of walking under his own power, it looked as if he was being dragged.

"This isn't the parking garage," one of them hissed.

"We're behind the hotel, remember. This will be closer," the other man answered.

"Let's just hope we can find the rear exit from here," growled the first.

Mira shuddered at the sound of their voices. Inching across the lobby, she ducked behind a potted palm and watched as they stopped to hoist up their middle companion. They laughed heartily as they continued over the marble floor toward the stairwell. When they opened the door, the man stumbling between them jerked as if struggling to break free.

He swung at one man and tried to get away, but the other escort punched him in the back. As if made of paper, the middle man crumpled to his knees, only to be dragged along and pulled through the door.

In the fray, he whipped his head around and Mira bit back a cry. His face was battered, his nose bloody, but there was no doubt of his identity.

Lucas was being kidnapped.

Seventeen

*M*ira scanned the deserted lobby and decided searching for assistance was futile. Even if the young woman who'd directed her to the candy dispensers was there, what could she do to help?

Hands on her temples, she paced the marble tiles. Men resembling those who'd come after them at the cabin were kidnapping Lucas. When she'd been accosted, he'd rescued her. She owed him assistance, but if she failed they would both be trapped. If they took her bracelet, she would be at their mercy. Once caught, there was only so much she could do with her mental gift.

Maybe it would be best if she continued with her escape. Eventually his captors would have to believe Lucas when he told them he didn't know where she'd gone. After that, they would release him, and he could continue with his life.

I'm expendable. They won't think twice about killing me.

The ugly words echoed in her mind, forcing Mira to admit Lucas was right. He'd been shot; he knew about the helicopter and the military. Now he could identify these men. When the culprits and their leader found out he'd let her go free, they might be angry enough to kill him for ruining their plans.

She wracked her brain as she paced, barely noticing when the hotel door opened and a man ambled into the lobby. Apparently he, too, had a lot to think about, because he stepped into her as she passed and almost knocked her over. When he grabbed her arms to steady her, she gazed into a pair of warm brown eyes identical to those she'd seen in dozens of photos over the past two days.

Smiling, the man said, "Sorry, miss. You okay?"

"You're Martin Maddox." Mira gripped his forearms with steely fingers. "I need your help. They've got Lucas."

"Lucas Diamond?"

"Yes, Lucas Diamond. I'm a . . . friend."

Raising a brow, he studied her. "You're Mira."

"Please, you have to do something." She jogged toward the stairwell. "I heard them say their car is behind the hotel."

Martin followed her, talking as he walked. "Who has him? Did you recognize them?"

"I've never seen them before, but they reminded me of the two men who attacked us last night. Lucas says they're military—they'll kill him if they don't get what they want."

"Where were you when this happened?" They skimmed a short flight of stairs and opened a door marked DELIVERY ENTRANCE.

"I left the suite when Lucas took a shower. I wasn't there when they came in."

Together, they peered into the darkness. In the distance came the sound of an engine, then the flash of taillights. "We need transportation. Where did you park the Hummer?"

"In the parking garage." Mira dashed back inside with Martin on her heels. Charging down the stairs, she slammed open the parking level door and led him across the garage to the rusted truck. "This is what we used to return to town."

He glared at the vehicle. "Osgood gave you Sadie!"

"Yes, but she's locked, and I don't have a key."

He squatted and searched under the back left wheel, grinning as he stood. "God bless Osgood Fairly." Rushing to the driver's side, he shouted, "Get in and buckle up. This could get dicey."

Mindlessly, Mira scrambled into the truck. Before she could reconsider, Martin jammed the vehicle into reverse and drove to the exit.

"Government business," he announced to the attendant. Crashing through the gate, he forged into the street, then shot to the corner. Far ahead, a shimmer of red lights veered to the left. He gunned the engine as he shifted gears. "Any idea where they're going?"

"No."

He pulled a cell phone from his pocket.

"Who are you calling?"

"A friend."

"Is he in the military?"

"He was once. Now he's an independent."

"Can he be trusted?"

"He's never let me down." The distant lights flickered as the car disappeared to the right. "Headly? It's Maddox. I need some information, and I need it now."

Mira hung on to the seat-belt strap as the truck took the next turn. Lucas trusted Martin, but she didn't know him or any of his colleagues. How far would he go to make certain she was brought to the president?

"Major Everett Randall. He has a house in McLean, but I need to know if he owns a farm or acreage within driving distance of Washington. The tract would be isolated with plenty of land." The truck engine chugged, and he thrust the phone at Mira. "I need both hands to manage this thing, or I'm going to lose them. Introduce yourself and tell Headly to get back to me at my cell number ASAP."

Mira held the phone to her ear and did as he instructed. "Now press the red button."

She did and attempted to hand him the device.

"You keep it. When he calls back—answer." He shook his head. "Osgood would shit a brick if he knew what Sadie was doing right now."

Worried she might lose the phone on a sharp turn, Mira dropped it into her bag. "Do you see them?"

"Just barely," he muttered. "Bastards are driving the limit, but once they get on the Beltway all bets are off. We'll never keep up in this bucket of bolts."

"Where do you think they're going?"

"Lucas told me they came after you in a RAH-66. Since I doubt the major can order that type of chopper from one of the local bases without arousing suspicion, my guess is he found a way to help himself. His chopper is probably stored somewhere only Randall and his minions are aware of. Trouble is, I was too busy to call Headly today and have him get me the info." He leaned forward in his seat. "Hang tight. They're getting on the Beltway. The best we can do is head in the same direction, maybe keep them in sight."

They veered into traffic and settled in the slow lane. Though it was late, cars dotted the highway, and Mira had no idea which one they were following. "Can you still see them?"

"I think so. They're in the middle lane doing about five miles over the limit. Not fast enough to interest a radar unit, but if they keep going at that clip, we'll lose them in the next few minutes."

Mira swallowed hard. Lucas was disappearing before her very eyes, and there was nothing she could do to stop it.

"You okay?" asked Martin, after a few minutes of silence.

"I'm worried about Lucas. He said they would kill him."

"Did he now?" He patted her knee. "We have a saying on this planet that always makes me smile. Care to hear it?"

"All right."

"It ain't over until the fat lady sings."

Mira had no idea what the adage meant, even after she tugged on her translator chip, but the odd words did bring her a modicum of comfort.

"Care to explain why you weren't in the suite when the men broke in?" He gave her a sidelong stare. "I can't imagine Lucas taking a shower and allowing you to explore on your own."

"I was . . . in the lobby."

"You were running away?"

"No. I was looking for chocolate."

"Chocolate?" His tone rang with disbelief. "And once you found it, you were going to make your escape."

She rubbed her burning eyes. "I have to leave. Lucas has enough information about me to satisfy your government. In time, he'll forget this entire incident. You all will."

Martin chuckled. "When this mess is over, you and I are going to have a talk about the tenacity of the human spirit. And if you believe that about Lucas, you don't know him."

"What do you mean?"

"He cares about you, and not just because of who you are. If you disappear, he'll never stop searching."

Her heart stuttered in her chest. "He told you he cared about me?"

"Not in so many words."

"In that case, I'm sure he was thrilled when he realized he'd captured an alien," she said, daring to use the distasteful word.

"He never called you an alien when he talked to me. But he did say you were one hell of a woman."

"Oh." The information left her short of speechless.

"Said you were smart, brave, and stubborn. I think it was the stubborn part he was most intrigued with."

Mira smiled. "He's more stubborn than I am. And opinionated. He won't take no for an answer."

"Is that right?"

"I guess you're already aware of that."

"It's the reason I groomed him for my job. Taking no for an answer won't cut it in this business."

The phone rang, and Mira jumped.

"Open it and say hello. Then repeat Headly's information word for word."

"Hello . . . yes, this is Mira."

The man began a list of instructions complete with road names and directions. Mira echoed Headly's words as Martin weaved the truck around a vehicle ten times the size of Sadie.

"That's it. I've lost them. Tell him to give you that last turnoff again."

She recited the directions a second time. Martin held out his hand and she gave him the phone.

"Thanks, Pete. I owe you . . . no, I think I can handle it on my own." He passed the instrument to her. "Keep this close in case we get caught. I doubt they'll think you have one."

Mira tucked the phone in her bag. "Where are we going?"

"About two hours southwest of DC. I know the area fairly well. Should have figured Randall would head that way."

"What are we going to do?"

"Isn't it obvious?" He flashed her a grin. "We're going to rescue Lucas."

"We're here."

Mira woke with a start, and glanced in the direction Martin was facing. The outline of a three-board white fence ran the length of the road. They were parked on a narrow dirt lane across from the property, and though it was dark, she also made out the shape of huge iron gates with a large capital R gracing the top scrollwork.

"Where are we?"

"Horse and farm country. It's isolated, and the fence looks as if it runs the entire perimeter. My guess is it's a sham. Once we get closer, we'll find out."

"What are you planning to do?"

"Go inside and find Lucas. You game?"

Mira swallowed her fear. Lucas had done so much for her, saving him was the least she could do. But she had their baby to think of. And her planet. "I won't fire a gun," she warned. "I—my world doesn't believe in them."

"Since we don't have one, that's not a problem." His expression turned questioning. "Correct me if I'm wrong, but I heard you were equipped with other weapons."

"Other weapons?"

"The two men who covered Texas for us met your friend Zara. Claimed she had a bracelet like yours that was capable of a few interesting tricks."

Mira gasped. "Zara's been captured?"

"Was. She escaped in a spacecraft. I bet it's the same one you were hoping to find tonight."

She ignored his blatant guesswork. Though Zara was safe, she must have been forced to use her bracelet or explain its special qualities, another thing the elders had forbidden. Mira had thought about using the gems to rescue Lucas, but that was when she'd been on her own. Now that she was with a stranger . . .

"Explain how that thing works." He focused on the bracelet. "Once I know what it can do, we'll figure how to get ourselves inside."

An image of Lucas being dragged from the hotel elevator filled her mind. There was no time to think of herself, only the man she loved. "It's not a weapon, exactly, but it does have the ability to hold someone in place in a sort of suspended animation."

"How many people can it be used on?"

"Each stone can take care of three or four living creatures—people, animals, anything with a heartbeat."

"And you have how many stones?"

"Three."

"Okay, so depending on the numbers we might be able to suspend up to a dozen of them. That should be doable. How long will it hold them in place?"

"Several hours."

"What about your . . . mental skills?"

"My mental skills?"

"They told me Zara was a healer. Can you do the same, or are you proficient in another type of extrasensory perception?"

Mira bit her lower lip. Even Lucas wasn't aware of everything she could do with her mind. After she told Martin what she was capable of, he would know all her secrets.

"I'm still in the development stage of the skill, but I'm able to see into minds, and sometimes . . . I can influence people with my thoughts."

"Get out of here."

Her lips twitched at his childlike comment. Instead of saying more, she imagined an itch. Then she placed the itch on Martin's knee. He scratched. She moved the itch to his stomach and he followed with his hand. When she shifted the itch to his head, he rumpled his hair.

He stared at his fingers, then gazed at her. "Well, I'll be—that was impressive." He narrowed his eyes. "Anything else I should know?"

"You're thinking about a woman named Peggy. You can't wait for the two of us to meet, so I can do to her what I just did to you."

"Son of a gun." He continued to stare with an expression of awe. "Amazing."

"I'm afraid that's it," Mira said sadly. "The elders assumed we wouldn't get caught and, if we did, could take care of it with our mental powers. They didn't think we'd need more."

"And your world doesn't believe in weapons, either for individual use or mass destruction?"

"We used them ninents ago and almost annihilated our planet and our people. All substances deemed harmful to our species were banned: weapons, chemicals, drugs—anything that proved to be a danger to our well-being was destroyed. None of it exists on our world any longer."

"Really? Maybe you can tell me about it later. Right now, I'm going to inspect Sadie's toolbox and see if she's carrying something that will give us a leg up." Martin opened his door. "Try to stay quiet and keep your eyes on the farm. If you see anything interesting, let me know."

Mira got out and propped her backside against the front fender while he swung into the truck bed. Far in the distance, she saw lights coming from a large building. The trees rustled on a breeze, and she smelled rain. Thunder rumbled as creaking noises and metallic rattles told her Martin was still digging.

Moments passed before he jumped from the truck

and stood by her side. "Osgood doesn't have a hell of a lot, but the wire cutters should come in handy, as will the flashlight."

"What next?"

"Did you see anything that might tell us where they have Lucas?"

She pointed to a large shape, maybe a barn or house. "I saw lights go on and off in that building. Otherwise, it's been quiet."

They locked gazes, and Martin's mouth stretched into a grim line. "Before we begin, I have to tell you that I know we didn't start out the way I'd hoped. It's important you realize Lucas is my friend. I'll do whatever it takes to keep him safe, including sacrificing an alien if you try to sell him out."

She pressed her hand to her stomach. "I would never do that. I want him safe, too."

"You care about him?"

"Yes. I—" She shifted her focus to the road. "Yes."

"Then I'll do my best to make certain you're protected. There's just one thing. If I tell you to run, no arguments. The keys are in the truck. Get back here and hit the green button on the cell phone. It'll automatically redial Headly. Tell him I need help, then drive this heap wherever you have to and hightail it to your mother ship and your planet."

"But Lucas—"

"Would never forgive me if I let anything happen to you. Go home and find a way to return later. He'll understand."

* * *

Since her nap, Mira had lost track of time, but she assumed it was close to sunrise. She tiptoed after Martin, emulating his crouched body and cautious movements. They arrived at the fence and followed it to the left, around the perimeter for several hundred yards to where it turned down another side of the grounds. Once the building she thought was occupied was directly across from them, Martin inclined his head and eased himself through the slats in the fence. Holding out his hand, he indicated she should do the same.

Mira slipped between the boards and stood. Martin was a few feet in front of her, appraising a ten-foot-high, open linked metal barricade with a flourish of barbed wire on the top that had been invisible in the darkness.

Putting a finger to his lips, he whispered, "It might be live. Don't touch it until I check." He squatted and lightly tossed the wire cutters toward the base, where they hit the fence and bounced to the ground. When nothing else happened, he signaled her to inch forward.

Working from the bottom up, he snipped at the fence until he cut out a doorway barely large enough for them to crawl through. Peeling back the metal, he indicated she should go inside, then he did the same and left the opening askew.

Bending at the waist, she stayed with him as he zigzagged across an open field. As they neared the building, she tugged on her ear and deduced it wasn't a barn but more of a storage hangar. Probably home to the helicopter that had come after them and possibly other types of weaponry.

Martin stopped at a dilapidated pile of machinery and waved her to get down. She crouched and moved near. He pointed, and she spied two men holding weapons propped against the outside of the building. Instead of keeping an eye on the area, they faced each other and talked in hushed voices.

When he grabbed her arm, touched a finger to his temple, and closed his eyes, it took a second before Mira understood what Martin wanted her to do. Concentrating, she imagined the same relaxing glade she'd shown Lucas. Then she planted the suggestion of a restful sleep. Beside her, Martin stiffened as he waited. Moments passed before the two men slid along the building and landed in a sitting position. Their guns dropped to the ground, and they slumped sideways.

"Not bad," he muttered, stepping from behind the machinery. He took her hand and led her to one side of the structure. Raising a finger to his lips, he made a motion that told her he was going to investigate. Then he took off in a crouch.

She cupped her elbows for warmth. A light rain began to fall, and she shivered. Taking a few paces backward, she noted that this side of the hangar had no windows. Unless the far end had a few, it would be impossible for Martin to see inside.

She edged to the corner and peeked at the two men, giving them another command to rest more deeply. Then she pressed her ear against the metal wall of the building and probed with her mind, hoping to find Lucas. In seconds, she learned there were four men inside, and three were awake and alert. She had surprised herself by putting two men to sleep at one time. She doubted she could take care of three at once. And was the dormant man Lucas?

The wind kicked up, rattling the hangar roof. Thunder rang in the distance, and lightning stroked the sky. She sensed a presence behind her and saw Martin slip from the back of the building and head in her direction. When he raised three fingers, she nodded. Then she mouthed "Lucas?"

He jerked a thumb toward the hangar. Mira wiped the water from her face. She read Martin's worry in the next bolt of lightning and knew Lucas was in less-than-perfect shape. He pointed to her bracelet, then gave her the high sign. She nodded and followed him, cutting a wide path around the dozing guards.

Martin picked up their weapons, clutched one to his waist, and threw the other out into the night. Together they peered into the narrow opening of the hangar's sliding doors. An enormous black helicopter sat in the center of the floor, reminding her of a huge bird of prey.

He inclined his head, and she looked past the machine to three men in the rear of the building—two playing cards at a table and one propped against a wall. Next to the standing man was a cot, and on the stretched canvas lay Lucas.

Covering her mouth, Mira stifled a gasp. Even though she was a good distance away, she saw clearly his bruised face and swollen lips. Blood trailed down his jaw and onto his T-shirt. She wasn't sure whether he slept or was unconscious, but feared the latter. At least he was still alive.

Martin made a motion, indicating she should retreat from the doorway. Then he held up his wrist, inviting her to use the bracelet. Mira quickly chose one of the clear gems and slid it into the clasp. Pressing down, she closed her eyes and imagined the men's immobilization. Seconds passed before she heard a chuckle.

"That did it," Martin whispered. He took her hand. "Come on, we have to work fast."

Mira trotted at his side. Martin busied himself collecting weapons while she knelt next to Lucas. When she placed her lips to his forehead he moaned. Not wanting to frighten him, she sent him a small thought wave of hope.

He blinked and opened his uninjured eye. Focusing on her face, he smiled. She cupped his jaw and gently kissed his lips. He flinched, but he didn't hesitate to deepen the contact. Then he struggled to a sitting position and held out his tied hands. Mira undid the rope, and he ran his fingers through his hair in what appeared to be a wake-up gesture. She helped him to stand, and he hobbled toward Martin.

The older man thrust a gun into Lucas's hand, then shook his head. "You look like hell."

"Nice to see you, too."

"Any other goons we need to worry about?"

"I remember five. These three plus two outside."

Martin thrust his chin toward Mira. "Your friend took care of them."

Lucas sent Mira a frown and limped to the man who was standing. He poked the guy in his chest, then waved a finger in his face. "What the heck did she do?"

"How about if she explains it while we get back to DC. I don't want Randall to find us just yet."

Mira drew herself up, determined to be treated as an equal. "Can you walk? What about your leg?"

"It's been better," Lucas said. He stumbled toward her, and the leg folded under him.

Martin bit out a curse and hoisted Lucas up by one arm while Mira took the other. Together, they kept him steady as they shuffled into the sunrise.

Eighteen

*P*eggy sat in the lobby of the Hay-Adams and hung the house phone in its cradle. It was after nine, and she'd started calling Martin's room ten minutes ago. Strange of him not to answer since he was supposed to be awaiting her arrival.

She walked to the front desk and stood to the side while a family of five checked out, then approached the clerk. "Excuse me. I'm trying to reach a guest, and I'm not having any luck with the lobby phone. Could you ring his room for me?"

"Yes, ma'am. Guest's name?"

"Martin Maddox. And please check to see if he left a message for Peggy Britton."

The desk attendant consulted the computer and dialed a number. She heard the room's voice mail pick up in the quiet of the lobby.

"Sorry, there's no response." He fumbled around the desktop. "And no message. Maybe your friend is in the shower or in the restaurant having breakfast."

Peggy imagined Martin rising at dawn and eating in the privacy of his room, then pacing until it was time to meet with Lucas and his companion.

"Can you try Lucas Diamond's suite?"

The man followed the identical procedure and received the same result. "No one's picking up there either." He set the phone down. "Would you care to leave a message?"

"No, thanks."

He smiled. "Let me know if there's anything more I can do to help."

Puzzled, she walked to a group of chairs and took a seat. Martin had been clear in his plans for the day. He had a 10:00 A.M. appointment with the president, while she was supposed to spend the day briefing Lucas on Jonas Harden, the investigative team from Texas, and the intrusive photojournalist. She was also expected to get acquainted with Lucas's alien and put the pieces of the woman's visit together.

She and Lucas then needed to regroup with Martin and the president to discuss how they should handle things before they faced the public and the press. In between, she had seven field team captains to reach. Depending on what she learned from the alien about their communication network, she would either recall the teams or send them to rendezvous with their targets.

The big boss had just returned from a peace summit. The alien visitation was only a small portion of the data he had to digest in order to perform the duties of his office. If the president had changed the meeting time, Martin would have left her a message. With one last check of her watch, she decided she would worry about what had happened to Martin and Lucas while she hotfooted it to the White House to smooth things over with the commander in chief.

She used the house phone again with no luck. Determined to carry forward as if everything were under control, she stepped from the Hay-Adams into the warm May sunshine. On the way to the Oval Office, she noticed a crowd gathering on the Mall and guessed it was the usual Sunday-morning protest contingent. Over the last few years, a variety of organizations had obtained permits to carry out orderly demonstrations. Because of the day's nice weather, there might actually be several different factions hoping to garner the attention of the press, the president, and any number of political activists.

While waiting for the light to change, she blinked at the glare reflecting from the participants. Taking in the group of mostly senior citizens, she saw that they all wore headgear composed of something shiny—aluminum foil?—which glinted brightly in the sun. And they carried signs that made her stomach churn.

EASTERN SHORE ALIEN WATCH.
PROTECT US FROM INVASION.
ESAW.
WE'RE WATCHING OUT FOR YOU.
JOIN ESAW.
SEARCH FOR ALIENS.

A few days had passed since they'd heard from Edith Hammer and her aides. Edith had driven from DC to Wallops Island and picked up a mobile cruiser disguised as a bird-watching trailer to use as their home base at the tip of the eastern shore. Had these older folks somehow found out why Edith's team was in town? Was Edith in cahoots with Jonas Harden and Randall and hoping to break the story in this showy manner?

Police cars parked on the street facing the Mall. Several officers spoke with a man who seemed to be in charge of the demonstrators. A truck pulled up behind the patrol cars, and the driver started unloading a series of boxes and stacking them into a makeshift podium.

A crowd of bystanders gathered. She also recognized a few bottom-feeders from the various tabloids milling around the fringes and talking to whichever senior citizen would answer. One of the reporters caught the attention of the man she thought was their leader. He began to pontificate while the reporter scribbled furiously.

Inching toward the throng, Peggy overheard a few of the questions the tabloid media threw at the gentleman.

"When did the aliens land in town?"

"Preston's Ferry? Where the hell is that?"

"How many government agents were involved?"

Peggy made a mental note to call the DIA informant at Wallops, and send him on a fishing expedition to Preston's Ferry. There was no immediate way to find out how these old-timers knew of Edith Hammer's existence, but it was obvious the agent's cover was blown.

Close to being late for Martin's meeting, she headed across the street toward the White House. Since Martin's name was on the appointment list and hers was not, she had to wait before getting approval to enter. Much as she'd tried to be prompt, she arrived at the Oval Office fifteen minutes behind schedule.

She made a beeline for the commander in chief and shook his hand. "Mr. President, sorry to have kept you waiting."

"Peggy." He indicated she should take a seat, then smiled. "I got a call from Martin about an hour ago. He told me he was certain you'd be here to keep his appointment, and he asked that I tell you to turn on your cell phone."

"Oh hell, uh, heck," she stammered, feeling like a fool. She had a bad habit of turning the thing off when she hit home and forgetting to start it up when she left for work. This would teach her. She reached in her bag and activated the device, noting two messages in the hopper—probably from Martin. "I was supposed to meet him at the hotel this morning to go over things before he saw you. Did he say what went wrong?"

"Not in so many words. But he called from a hospital."

"A hospital? What . . . who . . . ?"

"Lucas. Something about a bullet wound, and a run-in with the army." The president furrowed his brow. "He said Lucas was fine, and he'd explain after they had a chance to regroup and speak with you. You're to meet them at Lucas's town house, but first you're supposed to fill me in on everything that's gone on since I left. Is it true you've captured an alien?"

"Not me. But the team in Texas had one in custody until a tabloid photographer ruined things. He's been brought here and detained for questioning, as well as the two agents. Then there's Lucas."

"Lucas captured an alien?"

"Martin and I believe he apprehended the one who landed in Rock Creek Park. Unless there was a problem, I imagine the woman will be attending our meeting later today."

"The woman?" The president leaned back in his chair and removed his glasses. "These extraterrestrials are human?"

"Humanoid," said Peggy. "I hope to know more when I see everyone at Lucas's."

The world leader steepled his fingers. "I guess I'd better prepare myself. Do you think we'll need extra security for our meeting?"

"If she's still in Lucas and Martin's care, I doubt it."

"What do you mean—if?"

"Things got complicated a few days ago, and Lucas

and the woman had to leave the city." Peggy brought the chief up to date on all she knew, including Major Randall and Jonas Harden. Then she mentioned the senior citizens she'd observed congregating on the Mall.

"I can handle the major, but I don't want the tabloids to blow a simple demonstration out of proportion. We need to show the world that we were on the right track when we decided to bypass the military and keep our contact with the aliens peaceful." He gazed at his watch. "How long do you think you'll need to sort everything out?"

Aware she was being dismissed, Peggy stood. "I can't say, but Martin or I will call when we're ready." She headed for the door, then turned. "Sir? I—Martin and I, that is—want you to know how grateful we are that you allowed him back on the job."

"Missed him, have you?"

"Until I saw him a few days ago, I hadn't realized how much," she said with a smile. "Maybe he could stay on as a special consultant . . . or something?"

"I'll see what I can do."

Lucas sat on the gurney and tuned out the nurse reciting a list of instructions on the care of his wounds. A few moments earlier, a baby-faced physician's assistant had stitched up the front and back of his thigh, ministered to his face, and injected him with enough drugs to take the edge off the pain.

While waiting, he'd revisited everything that had occurred since last night's shower. He recalled the bathroom door slamming open as he stepped from the tub, the physical blows he'd received, the goons forcing him into fatigues and dragging him into the elevator. When it happened, he couldn't understand why they'd kidnapped him and ignored Mira. While drifting in and out of consciousness at the hangar, he'd pieced together what had happened. She'd already left the hotel suite when they'd abducted him from the Hay-Adams.

The fact that Mira had taken the first opportunity to run, that she'd lied, led him on, and lied some more, churned like acid in his gut. They'd spent several days together working out their differences. He thought she trusted him and was going to cooperate with his division. Instead, she'd decided to bolt.

It was merely a coincidence she'd seen him carried from the elevator, and sheer dumb luck that she'd bumped into Martin in the lobby. Another minute, and she would have been on a rendezvous with her ship without a word of good-bye. Damn her.

Martin had filled him in on the rest during the ride to the hospital, while Mira slept between them. As a point in her favor, he learned she'd used those stones in her precious bracelet to foil his captors, but it had taken every ounce of his self-control not to shake her awake and make her answer the other dozen questions he still had. He'd calmed some while Martin finished describing everything that had gone on inside the hangar, but he was certain Mira hadn't come on the rescue attempt willingly. She'd done so because he had saved her and seen to it she was protected. In her mind, she regarded it as a duty to do the same for him. Now that he was on the way to recovery, he didn't doubt she'd run again.

"Any questions?" asked the nurse, breaking into his musings.

"Nope. Thanks." Lucas slipped from the table and hobbled to the nearest restroom to survey the damage. It had taken a dozen stitches to close the bullet wound and two for the cut over his eye. His face was a mass of scrapes and bruises, and it hurt to breathe. Immobilizing the bastards who had done this had been too good for them, though he was positive they'd get an earful from the major, maybe even their walking papers. They'd bungled two jobs in the space of forty-eight hours, and that was more than a man like Everett Randall would tolerate.

Lucas shrugged into the rumpled fatigue jacket and headed for the waiting area. Rounding the corner, he stopped when he spotted Martin and Mira. Martin was speaking to the PA who'd seen to his wounds, while Mira slouched in a chair with a hand covering her stomach. Dark circles stained the rise of her cheeks, enhancing the paleness of her skin and the metallic silver of her eyes.

Common sense overrode the emotions crowding his heart. The woman was there because she couldn't escape Martin—not because she cared about him. If she saw a chance to get away, she'd take it and not look back. They had her over a barrel because there were two of them and only one of her. As soon as she found the resources to break free, she'd be gone.

Limping toward them, he refused to glance her way. So what if he was acting like a sullen teenager? Mira had walked out on him after they'd made a pact. She couldn't be trusted. Not now—not ever.

He nodded another thank-you to the physician's assistant. Martin gave him a once-over and grinned. "You still look like hell."

Lucas stuffed his hands in the pockets of the jacket. "I need to go home, change out of these clothes, maybe catch a short nap before we have our talk and meet with the president."

"The plan's already in motion." Martin glanced at Mira. "Peggy will stand guard while the three of us take a break at your town house, then we can all get better acquainted."

"Peggy knows to come to the town house?"

"She should by now, but I have to give her a call. I figured it would be safer there. My pal Headly has an invisible picket line on patrol around the place."

"Let them know they're not only keeping tabs on who goes inside," Lucas muttered.

"Already handled."

The two men stepped aside, and Mira stood. As if fully aware of her predicament, she straightened between them, her expression grim. "I suppose we're going somewhere to discuss strategy?"

"That's the idea," chimed Martin. "You have to go through a formal debriefing, and we all need sleep. Don't take this the wrong way, but you look almost as bad as Lucas, which reminds me." He plucked his cell phone from his pocket and dialed. "Hey, it's me."

Martin forged ahead as he spoke while Mira lagged behind. Lucas wasn't about to give her any space. He slid next to her and held her elbow in a viselike grip. "Don't think you're going to get another chance to escape."

She jerked her arm, but he didn't let go. "I thought it might be polite to allow Martin some privacy for his call."

"Nice of you to think so, but that caring attitude won't get very far with me." Lucas focused on her wrist. "I think you'd better hand over that bracelet."

"My bracelet?" She wrapped the fingers of her right hand over her left wrist. "But why?"

"Showing some cooperation will look better for you in the long run."

Mira cringed inwardly when she got a closer look at his battered face. Fisting her hands to keep from touching him, she said, "I understand you have reason not to trust me—"

"Or believe a word you say."

"But I didn't come here to cause you or any human harm. It's my duty—my mission—to return to my home. Why can't you see that?"

Lucas raised a brow. "You promised to meet with the president and answer his questions. I trusted you to keep that promise, and you ran the first chance you got. Handing over the bracelet will add back a few points."

"But I found Martin, and I stayed when I saw you were being kidnapped. Doesn't that count for something?"

"According to Martin, you had no choice. He didn't let you out of his sight from the second he realized who you were." He held out his hand and she thrust up her chin. Seconds passed before she unsnapped the jewelry and slapped it in his palm. Lucas clasped her hand and led her none too gently to the parking lot.

Mira opened and closed her mouth. There were so many things she wanted to say, so much she needed to explain, but not in front of Martin. And not in Sadie. And not when Lucas was in such a foul and unforgiving mood.

They reached the truck in silence. Martin deactivated his phone. "Peggy's cell is finally turned on. She's going to meet us at Lucas's with a change of clothes for Mira along with notes on her talk with the president. Let's get moving."

Lucas surveyed the surrounding neighborhood and spotted Martin's watchdogs before he unlocked the door to his home. A boxy gray sedan holding two men, one of whom was reading a newspaper, sat across the street. A shabbily dressed patron rested at the bus stop in front of the complex, while a beat-up dingy blue car was parked around the corner from Lucas's end unit. All the agents were inconspicuous, unless someone knew what to look for.

Once inside, Martin signaled they wait in the foyer and took off to scan the house. Lucas viewed enough of the living room to know it was safe and stepped aside to usher Mira in, hoping to disguise his sudden case of nerves with a blanket of ease. He wasn't much into entertaining, but he'd worked to make his home stand apart from the typical bachelor lair. He'd filled the rooms with comfortable-yet-modern furniture, amassed a small, eclectic array of paintings from well-known area artists, had even added a few whimsical touches in the way of table decor.

Would Mira approve? And why did it matter?

After glancing around the living room, Mira walked to the mantel, where she inspected a grouping of photographs. Lucas couldn't help thinking that the collection, a picture of his sister and her family, a photo of his parents, one of Martin standing in front of the cabin, and another of Martin and Peggy, seemed sparse when seen through another's eyes.

The slim arrangement appeared to glare at him, unhappily summing up his drab existence as well as reminding Lucas of how colorless his life had been before he'd met Mira. From the moment she'd entered his world it had become more vivid, more exciting, and certainly more meaningful. But he'd be damned before he'd tell her so, especially since she'd tried to run away and leave him looking like a fool.

Martin came down the stairs, which were located in the back hall, and peered around the corner. "Everything's clear. Peggy should arrive any minute. I'll stay down here and wait for her while the two of you get settled."

Lucas again took Mira's elbow, cursing inwardly when she pulled away. "I was going to escort you to the second floor. There's a guest bathroom you can use between the two bedrooms on the left. I'll clean up in the master suite on the right. Start your shower, and I'll bring your clothes when Peggy gets here. Then we'll come down to eat. Feel free to use whatever you find, same as you did at the cabin."

Mira climbed the steps in silence, as Martin reached his side. "Brrr," he goaded, his expression amused. "Is it me, or did someone turn on the air-conditioning?"

"Yeah, well she'll just have to live with the attitude. I'm done cutting her any slack."

At the sound of the doorbell, both men trotted to the foyer. Lucas stepped aside to allow Peggy, her arms laden with clothes and packages, entry. Martin collected a few of the parcels while Lucas secured the locks.

"Hey, Peg." The older man sat on the sofa and began opening bags. "Lunch smells great." He set the food on the coffee table and eyed the clothing. "Those for Mira?"

Peggy draped the hanger over a wing chair and turned to Lucas. "What are you doing in that outfit?" She put a hand over her mouth. "Oh my God. What happened to your face?" Brushing at the sudden tear trickling down her cheeks, she stiffened. "Those goons beat you, *and* they shot you? Wait until the president finds out about this. They'll be brought up on charges, along with Randall."

Lucas shook his head as he enfolded her in his arms. "I'm fine. It was only a flesh wound, and the bruises will fade." He glanced at Martin over Peggy's shoulder and winced. "Um, Peg? You're squeezing a little *too* tight."

She jumped back in horror. "Your ribs, too? Oh, Lucas, I'm so sorry." Dabbing at her face, she took a few deep breaths as she inspected Martin. "Are you all right?"

"Worried I'm too injured to take you out on that date?" he asked, grinning.

Peggy folded her arms, her gaze darting around the room. "So, where is our visitor?"

Martin sorted through the sandwiches and other edibles. "Upstairs showering. Lucas is going to bring her the clothes and clean up himself, then they'll come down and join us. We'll have a short discussion while we eat, and it will be my turn to get presentable. We need sleep before we meet with the president. You can play guardian angel, decide on a game plan, answer the phone if it rings. Wake us in two hours, and we'll call the boss with an ETA."

"Are you okay with that?" Peggy asked Lucas.

"I'm so tired I'd agree to anything right about now." He collected the hanger. "Give us fifteen minutes."

Lucas climbed the stairs and stopped at the bathroom door. After knocking, he inched it open and peered through the steam. "Mira. I'm hanging your clothes on the knob. Everything okay?"

When she didn't answer, he stepped into the room. The window was shut, and they were twenty feet above ground, but that didn't guarantee she wouldn't try something reckless. On the verge of panic, he thrust the plastic drape aside and met Mira's wide-eyed stare.

She snatched the curtain from his hand and shoved it in place. "Are you insane?"

"Sorry. When you didn't answer I thought—"

"I told you I wouldn't run again."

"And I told you I no longer had reason to believe anything you say."

"Fine. You've made yourself clear. Now get out."

Mira rested her forehead against the cool tiles and waited for Lucas's next verbal jab. Instead, the door closed with a thud. Sniffing back tears, she finished rinsing, turned off the taps, and stepped from the tub. After wrapping herself in a towel, she sat on the commode and stared at the window. She'd already checked the length of the drop and decided it was too risky. Not only could she break an ankle or worse in the fall, she might harm her baby.

With three people scattered about the house, there was little hope of escape. Now that Lucas had her bracelet and they knew of her mental capabilities, she was certain they would watch her carefully. Though she still had the communicator, she'd left it downstairs in her haste to get away. Maybe on her way to or from the White House . . .

Squeezing her eyes shut, she imagined that the next few hours would be her last taste of freedom. More than likely, she would be taken into custody and sent to some type of holding facility after their meeting. When that happened, she might still be able to get away, but without her bracelet there would be little point in running. And even if they didn't report her true identity, the authorities would be sure to broadcast her description and a list of charges on the television, along with a reward for her capture.

She would be a fugitive, and so would her child.

Mira towel dried her hair, then dressed in the clean undergarments, dark slacks, and pale yellow shirt from the hanger. When finished, she opened the door and tiptoed into the hall. Lucas's home was very different from hers, but still lovely, and it was obvious he'd chosen his furniture and art with care. Thinking this might be her only chance to explore his personal space and carry home more memories of him, she headed up the hall.

The first bedroom on the left was decorated in jewel-toned colors of deep blue, gold, and green. Dark furniture filled the room, while the bed had a striped coverlet and pillows that matched the draperies. The room on the far side of the bathroom held more stately pieces but had the look of an office. Overflowing bookcases lined one wall, a massive desk complete with two computers and other smaller machines graced another. A single framed photo sat amid the clutter. Clutching it in her hands, she found herself gazing at an adorable baby of no more than two months.

Kevin. The son Lucas had fathered with his wife. The boy he would never see become a man.

Mira dropped into the desk chair and held the photo to her breast. Tears welled, tightening her throat. When she was under lock and key, everyone would learn that she carried a child. Lucas didn't trust her or believe in her, but he didn't hate her. When he realized she was pregnant and had tried to leave with his son, his feelings would change.

"I see you found my office."

Startled by his voice, she sucked in a gasp. Standing, she set the photo where she'd found it and swiped at her tears. "I didn't mean to pry. It's just that beside the cabin, yours is the only home I've seen this intimately."

As if distracted, he walked to her side and stared at his son's picture in silence. Sighing, he seemed to reach deep within himself as he pulled back his shoulders and tapped a computer key. The screen grew bright with a grid of rectangular bands that varied from shades of deepest purple to lightest pink silently rising and falling in no particular rhythm.

"SETI at work. Each member has a microscopic section of space their computer monitors for sound waves, then reports the data to a base in California."

Mira tried to focus on the screen, but couldn't help noticing the perfectly tailored fit of his gray slacks and open-necked white shirt, and the light clean scent that surrounded him. "Did any of your sectors ever find anything of interest?"

"I don't know. They've been amassing data for years but were unable to calculate it until recently." He stepped closer. "Mira, about what happened earlier—in the bathroom—"

"It's all right." She inched to edge of the desk. "I realize you have no reason to trust me."

He took her elbows and turned her toward him. She gazed into his freshly shaved face, admired his tousled, still-damp hair, caught the penetrating expression in his deep brown eyes as they swept over her.

"I want to trust you. It's just that—"

The piercing ring of the doorbell interrupted him.

"Who the hell could that be?" Lucas released her arms. "Stay here until I know what's going on."

Nineteen

Lucas hobbled down the hall and took the stairs slowly. Peggy and Martin could handle anyone who arrived for a surprise visit, while he might learn more if he stood to the side instead of charging into the fray.

Two steps from the bottom, he froze when he heard his sister's chatty voice. His nosy sibling probably wanted to see if her big brother had surfaced. If he didn't rescue his coworkers, they'd be stuck sparring with Debbie until he ordered her home.

Determined not to limp, he steeled himself for a tongue-lashing as he rounded the corner. She'd be upset when she saw his face, but there would be hell to pay if she learned he'd been shot. "Hey, sis." He ambled toward her with a cocky grin, while Peggy and Martin observed the reunion as if watching a train wreck. "What's up?"

Debbie's welcoming smile quickly turned to a grimace. "Lucas! What happened?" She met him in the middle of the room. "What's going on? Where have you been?" Touching his jaw, she inspected his bruises. "Who did this to you?"

He caught her hand. "It's nothing serious. Just a run-in with a couple of idiots. It looks worse than it is."

She studied him with obvious suspicion. "Yeah, right. Just wait until Mom and Dad get a gander." Eyes narrowed, she continued to peer intently. "How the hell did it happen?"

"It doesn't matter." Lucas remained upbeat. "How about I come over for dinner one night this week and we discuss it?" By that time, the alien story would be on the front page of every newspaper in the country, and he wouldn't be breaking his oath of secrecy when he told them the truth. "You can even invite Mom and Dad."

"I wouldn't mind a family dinner, but I'm here because I had a visit from an old friend this morning. Someone you need to see."

He rolled his eyes. The last thing he wanted was another blind date, something Debbie tried to talk him into on a monthly basis. "Get it through your head. I'm not interested in meeting any more of your sorority sisters."

"Don't flatter yourself, big brother," she teased. "It's one of *your* buddies. He's waiting on the front porch with an entourage, and he says it's important."

"A friend of mine? And he stopped to see you?"

"When he couldn't locate you, yes. And don't blame Paul for arriving unannounced, because he did call. It was my idea to bring him here and see for myself if you'd returned to the land of the living."

"Paul? Paul Anderson?"

"The very hunky Dr. Paul Anderson," she said with a laugh. "I haven't seen him in a while, but he still looks like a *GQ* cover model. He arrived in DC yesterday. When you didn't return his message, he took his guests on a tour of the city. He phoned you again this morning, then called me and asked for help."

Lucas stepped back and met Martin's stare. "You remember Paul—college roommate and best man at my wedding?"

Martin shrugged. "A nice guy who should understand you have things to do. We'll wait in the kitchen." He and Peggy scooped up the sandwiches, wrappers, and other items she'd brought and disappeared from the room.

"I thought Martin retired," said Debbie. After he strode away, she spun on her heel. "Oh crap, don't tell me I've interrupted some secret space invaders' meeting." She checked out his face a third time. "Is that where you got those bruises—chasing little green men?"

His sister had made a career out of guessing what her older brother did for the government, and she wasn't shy about telling him so. "Earth to Debbie. You do not, I repeat—do not—know what I do for a living. And I'd appreciate it if you kept the small bits you've managed to invent to yourself. Now let's see what Paul wants."

He escorted her to the foyer and flung open the door. Paul came to attention, as did a giant of a man dressed in overalls, a senior citizen wearing an aluminum foil crown, and a young woman with a mop of curly red hair and a worried frown on her lovely face.

"Hey, Lucas. Sorry to show up unannounced." Paul studied his bruises with a wince, then shook his hand and stepped aside to let his companions enter. "I didn't know where else to go with my problem."

Lucas stepped aside to let them walk past, then turned to his sister. "Thanks. I'll be in touch."

"I take it I'm being dismissed?"

"Sorry, but there's no more room at the inn."

"You'll call me? And our parents?"

"I'll call, but it may take a day or two. In the meantime, don't believe everything you see on television or read in the papers."

Debbie kissed his cheek, and Lucas shut the door behind her. He limped into the living room and indicated that everyone take a seat, while he and Paul faced off in front of the fireplace. Then he gave the trio a fast once-over. The younger man smiled blankly as he gazed about the room, while the older gent seemed to be waiting for something to happen. The woman appeared uncomfortable, so he focused on putting her at ease. When she looked his way, Lucas blinked. Though her eyes weren't silver but a brilliant green, they held the same unusual intensity as Mira's.

Pushing the fantastic idea to the back of his mind, he poured on the charm. "In case you haven't figured it out, I'm Lucas Diamond, a college buddy of Paul's. I don't know what he's told you, but I doubt I can help with your problem."

"I'm Bill Halverson and this here's Harley Fogg," said the man in the tinfoil fedora. "The pretty lady sitting across from us is Lila. We need help from the government, and Dr. P says you're the fella who can point us in the right direction."

Lucas kept grinning. "I'll do my best, though I—"

"Do you still work for NASA?" Paul interrupted.

Paul was a great guy, but he had no security clearance and no business knowing what Lucas did for a living. Lucas was going to wring his sister's neck if she'd given them one crumb of information.

"I was never employed by NASA. In fact, I don't think I ever mentioned who I worked for."

Walking to the sofa, Paul plopped down next to Lila. "You didn't. But I got the impression it was an area of the government that dealt with the space program."

"Okay, let's say that's what I do."

Paul entwined his fingers with the woman's, and she smiled through trembling lips. "Lila and I need help, and we're hoping you can give us some advice on where to go and whom to see."

"And what do you need to discuss with . . . whoever it is I drum up?"

His buddy pushed to the edge of the couch, but he continued to hold his lady friend's hand. "I assume you're still a big believer in life on other planets? That you feel we'll encounter beings from another universe someday soon?"

Lucas glanced at Lila, and the hairs at the nape of his neck stood on end. "I still believe."

"Then I've brought someone you might want to meet more formally." Paul rose to his feet, and the woman stood with him. He gazed at her adoringly and her complexion turned a soft pink. "Lila is a visitor from another world."

When Peggy and Martin passed the stairway, Mira tiptoed to the bottom and took a seat on the last step. After listening to the conversation taking place in the living room, she decided she must have heard incorrectly. Lila hadn't come on this mission; it was her sister Rila who'd made the journey. Her twin sister had not been chosen as one of the final nine. It had to be Rila who was there with Lucas's friend.

But how had she been captured? And why had she given the wrong name? How much information had she let slip to Paul Anderson—and why?

She peeked around the corner and surveyed the group. Lucas's back was to her, so she couldn't read his assessment of the situation. Strange grins adorned both the younger and older man's faces, while Rila's and Paul's expressions were hopeful.

She concentrated on Rila, who appeared uninjured

and in good health. The fact that she was still wearing her bracelet and earrings was also a good sign. Then Rila smiled at Paul, and Mira gasped. The vivid emerald of her eyes sparkled, clear evidence of the success of her mission.

The sound of Mira's surprise echoed in the room. Lucas whipped around, while the men sitting on the sofa came to their feet. Paul wrapped an arm around Rila's shoulder when she sagged against him.

Now the center of attention, Mira had no choice but to make her entrance. "Rila, it's so good to see you."

"M—Mira?"

"Yes, it's me. I can't believe you—" She put a hand over her heart and stepped closer. Lucas blocked her path, but she jostled around him. Staring at the girl, she observed subtle differences—a slightly wider mouth, a deeper russet to her hair, the bracelet worn on the opposite wrist . . .

"You're not Rila."

Biting her lower lip, the woman nodded. "I'm Lila, her twin. We met during training."

"I remember. How did you get to Earth?"

Still holding her companion's hand, Lila raised her chin as if daring Mira to question her actions. "On the same ship that brought you."

The same ship? "What happened to Rila?"

Lila threw back her shoulders. "I took her place before she entered the pod . . . and I'm not going back. I plan to stay here with Paul. Forever."

* * *

Sitting back in her chair at the kitchen table, Mira tried to keep her gaze from lingering on Lila and Paul. It was obvious they were in love. No one watching them would doubt they were of a single mind.

How wonderful that one of her kind had found true love with a human. And how courageous for her to want to stay on Earth and create a family unit with him, his twin boys, and a new baby. Lila didn't even seem to care that most of the people in Preston's Ferry, never mind the world, would soon know she was an alien. As long as she had Paul's love, she would survive.

Mira endured a moment of sadness when she realized that she herself was the biggest failure of their mission. Yes, Lila had stowed away, revealed the secret of her earrings and bracelet, given the location of their planet, and wouldn't be taking home a male child to rejuvenate their species. But she was there of her own accord, and she hadn't taken the final oath of allegiance or sworn to complete her quest. She had left with every intention of staying on Earth.

The same errors had plagued Mira, but she'd been captured. The oath kept echoing in her brain, reminding her of her betrayal. Even Zara, who had been stalked, had managed to escape, while Mira had chosen to save Lucas over saving herself, and therefore, her world.

"Guess I'd better call the Oval Office and tell them we have a few more knots to unravel," said Martin to the group sitting around the table. "Lucas, it doesn't look like you and Mira are going to get the nap I promised."

"I gave up on that luxury the moment Paul introduced me to his fiancée," he answered, running a hand through his hair.

"Then you're not angry I came to you for help?" asked Paul. "Because I didn't mean to presume on our friendship."

"I'd have knocked you senseless if you'd brought Lila anywhere else," Lucas chided. "I'm just happy Debbie had the common sense to drive you to the house."

Martin cleared his throat. "I was hoping to go over our presentation to the president." A round of snores sounded from the living room. Bill had sacked out on the love seat, and Harley had stretched his legs along the sofa several hours ago. "Do you think your friends care how they'll be classified when they meet him?"

"No matter how you describe him, Bill will be thrilled," said Paul. "But you might mention he was a district leader in the Eastern Shore Alien Watch. As for Harley . . . well, he's just Harley. He'll find a corner and settle in pretty much the way he'd watch a ball game."

Martin scribbled on his legal pad. "Fine enough. Now I'd like to readdress what Edith Hammer said to you in the trailer right before you left. I also want the name and number of Preston Ferry's police chief. We have to find out if Edith's team escaped that swamp-mired trailer and where they are now."

Weary of the tactical discussion, Mira sent a subtle mental suggestion Lila's way, then rose from her chair. Soon, she and Lila would be questioned on the reason for their journey. It was important they agree in their response. In moments, she felt a presence at her side.

"You're angry with me," Lila said in a whisper, filling her glass with water. "You can't imagine why I'd want to stay here and live with humans. Or why I'd betray our people."

Mira considered her answer. This might be her only chance to speak privately with a fellow traveler before they were taken into custody and separated. Hadn't Lila thought about the consequences of her actions? Did she truly think she'd be left alone to participate in a normal Earth life?

"I'm not angry with you, but I am worried. Why do you think you'll be allowed to remain on Earth and live as they do?"

"Because Paul promised it would be so." Lila sipped her water. "I love him, and he's never lied to me. Therefore, I trust him to find a way to make his promise come true."

"But he has no credentials, no authority. He's bound by his laws, just as we are ours. If they imprison you, he'd have no way to save you. Or your baby."

"He has Lucas," Lila said, as if she trusted Lucas the same way she did Paul.

Mira glanced toward the table where Lucas, Martin, and Peggy were focused on questionig Paul. "Do you realize there are self-serving factions on this planet that would abduct you and put you on exhibit like an animal? And the military here considers us akin to criminals. They think we're a threat to their national security—their very freedom. I don't condemn you for wanting to be happy, but I am concerned for your safety and that of your child."

"I won't change my mind. I love Paul and his sons. I could never leave them." Lila lowered her voice. "I can see by the shading in your eyes that you're pregnant, too. Does Lucas know of your baby? Or how much you care for him?"

The insightful comment made Mira cringe. "No."

"How does he feel about you? It's obvious you haven't told him why we're here. He has asked, hasn't he?"

Mira eased out a breath. "Countless times. I felt it would be the ultimate betrayal if I gave him the reason for our mission."

"You've tried to escape?"

"Every chance I had." She held up her wrist, "But after I helped rescue Lucas, and he saw what I could do with my bracelet, he took it."

Lila's eyes grew wide. "He took it? Then you have no defense, no protection, no way of reaching the mother ship."

"Not exactly. Thane gave me a communicator. He knew I was coming to a populated city and thought I might need it."

"Have you used it?"

"I should have called him and left for the mother ship without a backward glance, instead of trying to save Lucas in thanks for his rescuing me. But there was never a good time." She rested her hip against the counter. "I'll ask you again. Does Paul know the truth about our mission?"

Lila set down her glass and focused on the tile floor.

"I need to know," Mira insisted, keeping her voice soft. "Once they've decided what to do about the traitors in their ranks, they're sure to start hammering at why we've come to Earth. We must be united. I'd never force you to return home, but I do expect you to keep silent on the heart of our goal."

"Paul knows, but he's sworn to secrecy on all things. The only issues he'll address are those that pertain to my welfare and our desire to marry. Now that you're with us, I plan to leave the truth about our mission to you."

"Me? But why—?"

"Because you are Thane's daughter. What better person to speak for us than the child of an elder?"

Mira placed a hand on her stomach. Thane's communicator was still in the bottom of her bag. She imagined the depth of his wrath when he learned of her capture, his disdain if he found out how she felt about Lucas. It was proper procedure that she try to reach him. Once he worked through his anger, he might be able to give her some guidance on how to proceed.

"If the humans find out why we came here, they'll

be furious," she warned. "They'll accuse us of tainting their gene pool or stealing their progeny. They may want our children for experimentation. They've just started cloning, embryonic transplants—the things we did that led to our downfall. Our psychic abilities alone will entice them into holding us and our babies hostage."

"Paul told me their current leader was understanding and perceptive. He's made it known that he believes intelligent life exists on other planets, and he's interested in making contact with any willing species. Certainly he'll protect us."

Before Mira could answer, Lucas and Paul stood beside them. Lucas shoved his hands in his pockets. "We've come to a decision. There's too much on our plate to worry about what the two of you are capable of now that you're together. Lila, Paul will hold your bracelet and return it when this matter is cleared up."

Lila's expression turned sour; her gaze darted to her fiancé. "You don't trust me?"

Paul shot Lucas a glare. "I told you she'd be annoyed." He pulled Lila into his arms. "I trust you, but Lucas doesn't know you the way I do, and he's the man in charge. I thought you'd feel better if I kept your bracelet. That way, you know it's in good hands."

The moment she heard his demand, heat raced to Mira's cheeks. Now Lila would understand what she'd been trying to explain—might even be willing to help her escape.

Lila unsnapped the clasp and passed her bracelet to

Paul. To Mira's surprise, she then allowed Paul to hold her close and press his lips to her forehead.

As if uncomfortable with the loving display, Lucas shifted his stance. "We ordered pizza. We'll eat while we finish up."

His elbows on the table, Lucas sipped a cup of caffeine-laden coffee. Escorted by one of the watchdogs from outside, Mira and Lila had gone to separate restrooms on the second floor. Martin was on his cell phone with Headly, Paul was conferring with his friends in the living room, and Peggy was pacing—not a good sign. "You've been more quiet than usual," he remarked. "Something bothering you?"

She turned and rested a fist on her hip. "Bothering me? It's a heck of a lot more than that. Let's count, shall we?" Raising her free hand, she ticked off fingers. "One, we have a pair of aliens in our midst, and we don't know why they or their seven pals came for a visit. Two, you've spent several days alone with one of them, and it's obvious you don't trust her. Three, we're about to take them to the most important man on the planet, and we have no guarantee they won't zap him like they did other humans. Four—"

"Take it easy, Peg. We confiscated the bracelets. We'll get to the 'why' as soon as our visitors come downstairs," said Martin. "And I don't think it's exactly a matter of trust between Lucas and Mira."

Lucas leaned back in his seat and folded his arms. "Oh? And what do you think it is?"

"More a butting of heads between two honorable warriors. Mira claims it's her sworn duty to return to her world, and you say it's your duty to take her to our authorities. Yet you've rescued her, protected her, and taken her to safety, and she's done almost the same for you."

"And your point would be—?"

"You respect her, and you care for her." He rested his arms on the table. "Maybe more than you want to admit."

"I'm not Paul," Lucas huffed. "I don't need a mother for my children or a—"

On his way to the kitchen from the living room, Paul reached the table in two strides. "That's not why I love Lila, and I'll challenge anyone who says differently."

"Sorry." Lucas sighed. "I didn't mean to get personal, but you know you'll be under a microscope once this story breaks. Worse things will be said than what I just suggested."

"Yeah, I know." Paul scrubbed a hand over his face. "But so what if Lila is from another planet? Why can't she be granted asylum, like we give to refugees fleeing other countries? If we plan on setting up a dialogue with these people, why can't she stay here?"

"Try worldwide panic," Peggy began, "and the fact that we have no official agreement with them, political or otherwise. If we allow Lila asylum, and they want her back, not returning her might ruin any chance we have at peaceful negotiations."

Mira and her friend took that moment to enter the

kitchen, and from the worry lines etched on Lila's face it was obvious she'd heard the last part of the discussion. Lucas thanked Headly's man and dismissed him, then pulled out two chairs. "Could the two of you take a seat?"

Mira did as he asked, but Lila walked to Paul and fell into his arms. "Please, tell them I want to stay. I won't harm anyone or get in the way or—"

"Shh, it'll be okay. You'll stay," he assured her, scowling at Lucas. "If not, well . . . maybe the boys and I could go back with you."

"Now hang on a second," said Lucas, as Lila hugged Paul tighter. "There's no reason to—"

Bill entered the kitchen, followed by Harley. The older man took one look at Lila and Paul, and gave Lucas a narrow-eyed glare. "Say, are you threatening them? Cause if you are . . ."

Lucas inhaled a breath. "Take it easy. No one's being threatened. We're simply discussing the reality of this situation. It's not up to anyone here to decide who goes or stays on this planet. Right now, it's the decision of the president. Since he's a reasonable man, and he wants to establish a dialogue between the two worlds, I think it's safe to say he'll allow Lila to live here unless her government demands we hand her over."

Mira rested a palm on Lila's shoulder. "I'll speak to my father, tell him of your wishes. By now, the council is aware you traded places with Rila. I'm sure they won't force a citizen to return against their wishes."

"Your father?" Lucas raised his voice in shock. "Are you telling me your father is in charge of your world?" And why the hell hadn't she revealed this bit of information days ago? How typical of her to lie by omission. "For God's sake, Mira."

"Take it easy," Paul warned. "It's not that big a deal."

"He isn't in charge in the same manner as your president," said Mira, her frustration clear. "We're ruled by a governing body very much like your United Nations. My father is one of the elders."

Cell phone in hand, Martin strode in from the back deck. "What's going on in here? I leave the room for a few minutes and it sounds as if World War III's started."

Bill gave a disgruntled harrumph, while Harley merely frowned. Lucas wanted to kick himself. He was being a jerk, while Paul was acting the hero. Neither woman had done a thing to threaten national security. They'd used their mental weapons only when in danger or to help a human being. And all they wanted was to return to their home or, in Lila's case, remain peacefully on Earth with the man she loved.

He thought about reaching over and patting Mira's hand or saying something to calm her, but the words wouldn't come. His ass was on the line, along with his career and everything he'd worked for. Surely she understood it was time to stop playing games and cooperate.

Martin seemed to sense Lucas wasn't ready to speak and took over. "Time to get down to the nitty-gritty, ladies. We need to know why you came to Earth."

Judi McCoy

"I've been wondering the same thing," Peggy added.

Mira heaved a breath. "I told Lucas I would explain it to your president, and he said that was acceptable."

"Did he now?" said Peggy. "Lucas, is that true?"

"It was a bargain Mira and I agreed to. She promised not to try to escape if I stopped hounding her about the reason they'd come here."

"I hope she keeps her word," said Martin. "Because I'm guessing without a plausible explanation, U.S. intelligence will advise the president to view your landing as a hostile act. That means our military has no choice but to get involved."

Twenty

$\mathcal{M}$ira and Lila walked through a metal detector, as did Lucas, Martin, Peggy, Paul, and his two friends. Then she and Lila were searched privately, and not very pleasantly, by two female guards, while another went through both their bags. She had held her breath when the guard inspected the transmitter she'd received from Thane, and quietly released it when the silver box was tossed back inside.

Now in the office of the president, she sidled next to Lucas as the rest of their group formed a semicircle in front of a massive desk. A cadre of Secret Service agents hustled in on their heels, ringing the area behind them and the world leader. Because she and Lila would soon be the center of attention, it was her duty to assess their situation and the man in charge.

The commander in chief, as Martin and Lucas referred to him, sat at attention, surveying their entrance through alert but wary eyes. Though he wore the reserved expression of a man in the throes of a possible crisis, he smiled politely when he met her subdued gaze. The gesture gave Mira hope. Against Lucas's previous order, she linked to the president's mind and detected his surprise—his shock—at seeing her and Lila. But she also felt his sharp intelligence, wry sense of humor, and a sincere desire to host a successful discussion.

Confident the man had all the positive attributes Paul suggested, Mira relaxed a bit, and it was then she noticed Lucas's clenched jaw. It was obvious he was concerned about the outcome of this meeting. But was it worry over what might happen to her or was his only concern his precious job?

The president adjusted his glasses, then moved his gaze from Mira and Lila to Lucas. "That's some shiner you're sporting. I trust you're feeling better, had yourself looked over by a doctor and all?"

"Yes, sir. I'm fine."

"Good, good."

Standing, he adjusted his tie as Lucas introduced Paul and his friends. Then Lucas placed a hand on each woman's lower back. "I'd like you to meet Lila and Mira, the visitors we spoke of."

Moving from behind his desk, the president ran his cool blue gaze over them from head to toe. "Forgive me for staring, it's just that you both look so—so—"

"Human?" Mira supplied, filling in the blank.

"Yes, and it's a—a—fact I'm still trying to get used to." He shook his head. "Sorry, I'm not sounding too coherent right now, or very much like a world leader. I'm not usually at a loss for words."

"I understand."

He smiled, then held out his hand. "It's not every day we—I—get to greet an emissary from another planet. Welcome to Earth and the United States of America."

"Thank you," said Lila, accepting his gesture.

"We are pleased to meet you, as well," agreed Mira, shaking his hand. "Though you must understand that we don't consider ourselves emissaries. It wasn't our intention to speak with you before returning to our home. Now it seems we are prisoners, forced to partake in some type of explanatory dialogue."

The president glanced from Martin to Lucas and back to her. "Why do you think that?"

She eyed the Secret Service agents standing at attention around the room. "We're being detained under armed guard."

He took in the rest of the bodies in the room and addressed the man nearest the door. "Jim, I assume our guests have been through normal inspection and clearance procedures?"

"Yes, sir."

"And you still think it's necessary all these agents be present?"

Jim leveled his gaze on the two women. "For the sake of national security and your personal safety, I feel it is, sir."

"Lucas?"

"Our guests have been relieved of whatever we per-
ceived as weapons. I don't think they could or would
do anything to harm you or endanger this meeting."

The commander in chief pursed his lips as he took
his seat. "Peggy? Martin? What's your take?"

"I agree with Lucas," answered Martin.

"I have no reason to think otherwise," said Peggy.
"But for the record, you should know that of the three of
us, I'm the most skeptical of our visitors' intentions."

"I'll take that into consideration." He leaned back in
his chair. "Jim, do me a favor. Dismiss half your men
and have them wait in the outer office." The agents
filed from the room, leaving four behind the desk and
Jim at his post by the door. "Is that better?" the president asked, directing the question to Mira.

The small victory made her sigh with relief. "Thank
you."

He gestured to Martin. "Pull up seats for everyone,
and we'll get started."

After the group was situated, Peggy reiterated their
concerns about Frank, Chuck, and the photojournalist
who'd caused trouble in Texas, and explained what
they suspected of Harden. Lucas then skated over the
manner in which he and Mira had met and revealed
step by step the reasons they'd left the District. Once
he described the incident at the cabin, and what had
occurred at the hotel and Randall's ranch, the president zeroed in on Jim.

"It's obvious the major disobeyed my direct order,

thereby putting a government operation in jeopardy. Send a team to his home and one to the compound, and bring in anyone found on either premises. I want Randall and his cronies under guard ASAP. As for the team members suspected of working with him . . ." He grinned at Martin. "It's about time we started collecting heads. Martin, give Jim a detailed list of names, and I'll take care of them personally."

"Thank you, sir," said Lucas, after Jim left with the page Martin tore from his legal pad. "Removing Randall and his pals will help make the next forty-eight hours work. First, let me tell you about what happened in Texas, then Paul can report on southern Virginia."

Mira listened with care. It was the first time she'd heard the entire story of Zara's near apprehension, and the man and boy who insisted on leaving with her. She imagined Thane and several of the council members had been furious when they'd been contacted by the mother ship, but it warmed her to know that, beside Lila, another traveler had found true love with a human.

Filled with regret over the things she and Lucas had said to each other, she wished their meeting—their entire relationship—had been different. Would they be here now if she'd given him the details of her mission when he'd first asked? What would have happened if she'd confessed her love and told him of the child growing inside her?

Mira heaved a breath, knowing she would be exactly where she was right now. No matter how Lucas felt about her, he was an honorable man with a strong sense of duty. Even if she'd told him the truth, it wouldn't have changed the tenor of this meeting.

"Sir," Paul said, after Bill entertained them with the incident in the trailer and their take on Edith Hammer. "I—that is, Lila and I—we need to—tell you—ask you something."

The president steepled his fingers and set them on his chin. "I'm listening."

"Lila and I want to get married. As we explained, she has no intention of returning to her planet. We'd like you to give her asylum so she can remain on Earth, and stay with my sons and me in Preston's Ferry."

"That's a grave responsibility," the world leader responded without a blink. "What if her planet demands her return?"

"I won't go back," Lila offered in challenge. "I've studied your world and find it as wonderful as I'd hoped. I love Paul; therefore, my place is with him. I want to become a citizen of the United States and live my life here."

"I see." The president removed his glasses and pinched the bridge of his nose. "You realize your trip here is going to cause a stir all over the world? Things may well be in chaos for quite a while. It might take months, maybe years, before it quiets down enough for you to exist in peace. The government can offer only minimal protection from the media or stalkers, and there will be hundreds of those. You'd all be living in a fishbowl, with little chance of privacy or escape."

"I know that, but I want our child to be—"

"Your child?" Lucas stiffened beside Mira. His surprised gaze jumped from the president to Lila, before it rested on Paul. "You might have mentioned she was pregnant."

Paul's determined expression never wavered. "Sorry. I guess I should have, but it doesn't change anything. I'd want to marry Lila even if she weren't pregnant. If we don't get the president's blessing, we'll seek asylum elsewhere. Hell or high water, I'm staying by her side. I love her, and we're in this together."

"You tell 'em, son," chimed Bill, resting a fist on the desk. "Preston's Ferry will protect you and the twins, and Lila and your baby. Don't you worry."

"Lila's gonna have a baby?" echoed Harley. "Hot dog."

Paul's friends continued to comment while Lucas turned red. Mira felt the bile rise from her stomach. Was he incensed with the idea of a half-alien baby? Didn't he realize that true love could surmount any problem, beat any adversity? Overcome any impossible situation?

Martin's voice overpowered the others. "Okay, let's get back on track." He waited for silence. "It's your decision, Mr. President, but if it was up to me, I'd allow Lila to stay. As Mira pointed out earlier, her world won't accept anyone who doesn't want to be there."

The president gave Mira a hard stare. "Is that so?"

"I believe it is. And I'm willing to plead their case with my father, just to be sure."

"And your father would be—?"

"Thane is one of the elders, a group very much like your United Nations. He relies on my opinion," she stated, hoping she uttered the truth.

"It sounds as if you're a person of influence in your world. Someone who can facilitate a dialogue, get the ball rolling with negotiations," said the president.

"I would be honored to try."

"Very well then. I'll call INS first thing in the morning, and see how we go about arranging citizenship. Then you can be married. I think that will go a long way in convincing your council of Lila's intentions, which should help in my granting her asylum." He leaned back in his chair. "Mira, since you seem to have some semblance of authority over your fellow travelers, I think it only fair to ask your intentions."

"My intentions?"

"I learned long ago that the best way to obtain a quick result is to be blunt. Throughout this discussion I have yet to hear a concrete reason for your visit. Why are you here?"

Mira had wracked her brain seeking an explanation for their journey that wouldn't compromise the mission. Now that the question was officially posed, she knew her options had run out. She could only hope they believed her semitruthful answer.

"We were sent to Earth on a fact-gathering expedition. Our job was to explore your country, interact with your people, and report to the council. If they approve of our findings, others will follow. They are the ones who will make arrangements for a formal meeting."

"I see." He reseated his glasses. "Any chance you can speak with your father—Thane—right now? I'd like to know where we stand before we move forward."

Mira opened her mouth to protest, then thought better of it. The president had just given her a chance to escape. When Thane received the communication, she was positive he would arrange for her to be picked up by the mother ship.

"I have a communicator." She caught Lucas's look of surprise from the corner of her eye. "May I use it?"

Three of the agents formed a protective ring around the president while the fourth approached her. "I'd like to think I'm safe with you, but my men won't allow anything of the sort unless they see what you're planning," the world leader said from behind them.

Mira reached into her bag and brought out the device. She held it up for inspection, then passed it to the nearest agent. He examined the rectangle, nodded, and returned it to her.

Mira flipped open the lid and pressed a series of tabs, then waited. Seconds later, Thane's voice, in its natural language, vibrated through the room. "Mira. I was hoping we wouldn't hear from you until you arrived home."

"Father, this is important," Mira said, speaking in English. "I'm in the office of the president of the

United States. He asked that I contact you and arrange a meeting between our worlds."

"You know what we decided if you were to reach me in this manner," Thane responded. "I expect you to obey."

"I will do as you ask." She snapped closed the device, but left it running. "I apologize for the communicator's inability to translate his words."

"What did he say to you?" asked Lucas.

"That I may speak about setting up a meeting," she answered, hoping this would be her final lie.

"Lucas, do you accept all of this?" the president asked, as the agents stepped aside.

Mira knew immediately that he didn't. She'd never mentioned that she had a way to contact her planet, and her reason for coming to Earth was no different that what she'd heard in several of the science fiction movies she'd watched on the television in her hotel room. But without Lucas's backing, it was doubtful the president would honor her answer.

She held her breath as she waited for him to counter her words. Instead, he relaxed his posture. "It's my opinion that Mira is telling the truth."

"Well, then. I think we can call it a night. Lila, I'll leave you in Paul's care with a man to oversee your safety. Mira?" He turned his satisfied expression in her direction. "I trust you're comfortable under Lucas's protection?"

Still wondering about Lucas's response, Mira nodded.

"Good. Now I have to deal with those rogue agents. Martin, how about if you, Lucas, Paul, and our new friends meet back here at 10:00 A.M.? We'll call a press conference for two o'clock on the lawn, and Peggy can meet us there with any information she gleans from the other teams in the morning."

Mira's glare shot bolts of heat straight through Lucas as they filed from the oval office. He didn't blame her for being outraged. Not only had he surprised her with his outright lie to the president—he'd shocked himself, as well. He didn't believe her explanation for a minute, but she'd taken him completely off guard with her pat answer.

He knew there was more to her story and, come hell or high water he'd figure it out, but just then he had to speak privately with Paul. Seeing as they were so close to the Treasury, it was logical they head there to talk.

Outside the building, two agents escorted them to the limousine that had driven them over. Lucas said to Peggy, "How about you take Bill and Harley to their hotel and go home? I have to pick up something from the DIA, and I thought Paul and Lila would like to see the operation. We'll meet you at the White House at ten."

"Do you think that's a wise idea?" asked Peggy, giving Mira and Lila a concerted stare.

"It'll be fine. Jim will be with us." He waited as Peggy slid into the limo and the vehicle sped into the night before he said, "Jim, why don't you and Martin escort the ladies while Paul and I do a little catching up."

Martin offered an arm to each woman, and they trotted ahead, with the Secret Service agent following. Paul slid his hands into his pockets. "You're about as subtle now as you were in college."

"Yeah, well there's no time for fencing in this business." The quartet was about a half block away before he said, "Care to answer a few personal questions?"

"You want to know about the baby?" Paul guessed. "So ask. Lila and I have nothing to hide."

Lucas didn't want to sound confrontational. He believed in true love, even if it was something he'd failed to find. If biologically possible and desired by both parties, children were a huge part of the commitment. Though he wasn't sure what would come of melding the sperm and egg of humans and alien life-forms, he now knew both species had almost identical DNA, a positive sign for offspring.

"I don't think Lila is out to deceive anyone," Lucas began, "but I am trying to ferret out the real reason the others came here. I don't buy the *fact-finding* explanation Mira gave."

"But you told the president—"

"I know what I said. Mira's been feeding me the same baloney for days, but I didn't want to call her a liar and make her look bad in front of the commander in chief. Those women are here on a mission, but it's not dangerous to our security or world peace. It's something else . . ." He slowed his steps. "Do you know why they're here?"

"I promised Lila I wouldn't tell, and I'm not about to jeopardize our marriage by breaking a confidence."

Lucas rested a hand on Paul's shoulder, and they stopped walking. "Okay, let me go at this from a different angle. Did you seduce Lila, or was it the other way around?"

"Now just a damn minute—"

"Sorry, but your answer is vital to this case."

"Okay, but what I'm about to tell you goes no further than right here, understand?"

Lucas nodded, and they continued their walk.

"I wanted Lila from the moment she stepped into my office. My ex had left me feeling like an insensitive jerk, the twins and I were having a difficult time adjusting to the town and each other, and competent help was hard to find. As soon as I hired Lila, she made it clear she was open to a physical relationship."

"How obvious was she?"

"Pretty blatant. She practically attacked me the first night we were intimate." He shrugged. "Don't get me wrong, it didn't take more than once for me to realize she was a hell of a woman." He smiled in the darkness. "There's no doubt in my mind that I love her and she loves me. Even if we hadn't started out as bedmates, I would have wanted her for my wife."

Lucas cringed inwardly at the similarity between Paul's meeting with Lila and his with Mira, but things were beginning to fall into place. "When did Lila tell you she was pregnant?"

"I'm a doctor." Paul grinned. "I know the symptoms. Besides, it seems our aliens are very much like the women on Earth when they conceive—mood swings, a roller-coaster appetite, lethargy . . . Earthwomen don't go through the eye-color thing, of course, but that's probably one of the differences between the two species."

As if sucker punched, Lucas swallowed his surprise. "Say that again."

"There are minor differences between—"

"Before that."

"The eye-color thing?"

"Yes, that. Explain what you mean."

"Lila's eyes were an attractive but sedate green when we first met. One morning, after a particularly energetic bout of lovemaking, I noticed a subtle difference in their color. The green was brilliant, almost luminescent. I didn't get it until I put the pieces together and guessed she was expecting. The color of her eyes has toned down, but the intensity is still there. I imagine it will fade as the pregnancy advances, but it's a real tell."

Mira eyes had been a lovely, silvery gray when they'd first met, but had turned a deep, polished pewter after their last encounter at the cabin. It was something she'd refused to explain, and now Lucas knew why.

"Mira's eyes have that same quality," continued Paul. The men locked gazes. "Oh, hell. I should have figured it out sooner. She's pregnant, isn't she? And the baby is yours."

Lucas fought the tidal wave of emotions rising from inside of him. Mira was carrying his child, yet she'd done everything in her power to escape. "All she ever talked about was going home. We can't have a rational conversation without fighting, so detailing her physical condition was out of the question."

Paul shook his head. "You are a fool."

"What the hell does that mean?"

"Sorry. Some things work out better when you come to your own conclusion."

"Can you at least tell me if the pregnancy was on purpose or accidental?"

"Not without betraying the confidence," muttered Paul, as they strode through the doors to the Treasury. Thanks to Jim's status, the security detail had cleared Mira and Lila. He did the same for Paul, and they ambled to the elevators while Lucas ordered his brain to put an impersonal, analytical spin on the latest bit of information.

He had to forget he was going to be a father again, forget about having another life to care for, and concentrate on his job. That Mira didn't want him in her world or their child's was clear as crystal.

Damn, but he hadn't seen it coming. Based on Paul's experience and his own, plus what he'd heard of the situation in Texas, the aliens had come to Earth on a baby-making expedition. He, Paul, and the other men had been used for their semen supply and nothing more.

But why?

Twenty-one

As they left the elevator, Mira thought about Thane. She had no doubt he'd arranged an emergency rescue, and the vessel had already homed in on the transmitter. With luck, it was hovering somewhere nearby, shielded by its cloaking device. She'd studied the architecture of this building and knew its large flat roof would be best suited for a pickup. Once she was on board, she and Zara would figure a way to collect the remaining women.

When the doors to the elevator slid open, Lucas grasped her arm. "Mira and I have things to go over. Martin, why don't you take Lila, Paul, and Jim into the tracking room and show them what we do here."

Surprised by his actions, Mira stumbled alongside him to a room that contained a large table and many chairs. All she had to do was get Lucas to stay put while she reached the roof. If she were clever, it would take a few minutes for him to figure out where she'd gone. She simply had to distract him, keep his mind on other things while she focused.

Before she could begin her assault, he crossed his arms and glared. "I guess you think you're pretty clever, pulling the wool over the president's eyes."

She tugged on her ear to be certain she understood the accusation. "Me? You're the one who said I was—if you hadn't told him you believed me, he never would have—" Realizing what she'd just admitted, Mira scowled. "That was deceitful and unnecessary."

"Guess I was right about your lying," he said, dripping sarcasm. "It's time we got to the truth. The real truth."

"I don't know what you're talking about."

Lucas stepped close, backing her into a corner. "You're pregnant, Mira. With my baby."

She closed her eyes. Soon she would be gone. It had been too much to hope he would never know. "How did you find out?"

"I compared notes with Paul. When he mentioned Lila's eyes changing color, I was certain." Resting his palms against the wall, he caged her between his arms. "When were you going to tell me?"

"You were never supposed to know."

"And the other women? They're all here to be impregnated?"

"Yes." She raised her chin. "Is that such a bad thing?"

"It might be to the men they've used."

"Your men don't care. Each of them sold their sperm years ago. If it wasn't important then, I doubt it will be now."

"People change, things happen that shape our future. Did you ever stop to think how they would feel— how I would feel if I learned I'd created a life and someone had taken it a million miles away?" He didn't move. "I lost one child, Mira, I won't lose another."

"I didn't know about Kevin until the cabin. By that time it was too late. I never meant to hurt you."

"Which made it acceptable?"

"You don't understand—"

"Then make me understand." He speared his fingers through his hair. "Trust me enough to tell me everything."

As Lucas took a step of retreat, Mira eased out a breath. His eyes held anger, but more than that, a profound sadness that cut to her heart. How she loved him. If only there were some way to come to terms. "We stopped producing children ninia ago—your equivalent to centuries. We're a planet of frustrated women and despondent men with little hope of producing a healthy generation."

"How did it happen?"

"Progress," she said harshly. "An experiment to create a super race that went out of control. It began with our decision to manipulate genes and choose the qualities of our offspring. Our scientists moved to cloning, not realizing that the males were growing more damaged with each successive round. By the time they learned what they'd done, it was too late."

"Surely there were a few people who conceived in the natural way?"

"Some, but the gene pool is small, and there are inbreeding problems. We've stopped all reproductive methods and now work on finding a way to bring our men back to potency. We also concentrated our efforts on finding a race with whom we could breed safely."

Lucas dropped into a chair. "How did you locate us—me?"

"You and Paul—all the men—sold sperm in college. When scientists determined our two species were compatible, citizens were put in place to locate those who produced an inordinately high number of Y chromosomes. After finding the nine brightest and most promising, we matched them with nine women from the thousands on our world who had volunteered. You and I are 99.9 percent compatible, guaranteed to create a male child."

"A son? And you were going to take him from me?"

"I had no choice," she whispered, swiping at a tear. "It's my duty."

Mira sensed Lucas's distraction, his utter bewilderment, and decided this was the moment she'd been waiting for. Though her heart was breaking, she gazed into his eyes and willed herself to be strong.

Stay here and meditate on Kevin. Remember the joy

you felt when you first held him. Know that I love you and our child. If there's a way, we'll meet again, and I'll show you your son. Trust that I will take good care of him and tell him of the man who fathered him.

Without a backward glance, she trotted from the room and shot to the elevators. After the car opened, she reached inside and pressed the DOWN button as a ruse. Logic would tell them she was on the street looking to escape. Heading to the stairs, she raced skyward.

Precious minutes passed while she sped up each flight. At the top, she heaved in gulps of air. Checking the door, she found it propped open by a small wooden wedge. Improper security maintenance, she decided, would work in her favor.

She walked onto the roof and focused on the stars, hoping to discern the familiar hum of the mother ship.

"I had a hunch you'd find your way up here."

She jumped when she heard the voice and spun on her heels. "Martin?"

"Maddox? I'm insulted you'd think so."

Guns raised, two men in fatigues appeared from around an air vent. Mira scanned the area and saw the outline of a huge helicopter waiting on the far side of the roof.

"Come along quietly and you won't be harmed," said the disembodied drawl. "And don't try any more of your mind games."

"Only a coward hides in the darkness," she spat.

The owner of the voice stepped from the shadows. Dressed in full military regalia, he gave a smart salute. "Major Everett Randall, United States Army, at your service."

"How did you get up here? I thought this city—all government buildings—was secure."

"I'm an officer of some importance. It's amazing how far a uniform and a bit of military bluster will go when one puts his mind to it."

Mira turned to the door, but two men blocked her way. Inching backward, she continued to the middle of the roof. She only needed to be clear of her surroundings to be beamed up.

Randall signaled, and all four of his henchmen skulked in her direction. "Walk to the helicopter. We're taking a ride."

Lucas pulled himself awake and shook his head to clear his fuddled senses. Damn, but she'd done it to him again! Anger screamed in his brain. Pushing from his chair, he lunged for the door and met Martin and Jim coming inside.

Eyes narrowed, Martin glanced around the conference room. "She's escaped?"

Lucas didn't speak. Shoving past them, he reached the elevator and saw that it was on the first floor. "You and Jim go topside. She's out there somewhere, and Randall is still at large. I'll join you in a minute."

The two men disappeared behind the sliding doors just as Paul and Lila entered the hallway. Lucas concentrated on Lila. "Does Mira have anything I don't know about? A weapon or some kind of device that will aid in her flight?"

Lila opened and closed her mouth, then shook her head.

"Honey, Mira could be in danger." Paul hugged her to his side. "Lucas has to know."

Standing tall, Lila said, "Just the transmitter. I imagine if it's turned on the mother ship will track her."

"You two stay put." Lucas took off at a sprint. "I'm going to the roof."

Ignoring the ache in his leg, he ran up the stairs at full speed. Mira was going to have a hard time getting anywhere with the exit to the outside locked. At the top of the final landing, he saw the door open a crack and caught his breath. Something was definitely wrong.

Lucas peered through the slit. Streetlights and a three-quarter moon cast eerie shadows across the area. He spotted a frightening shape on the far side of the roof, then a murmur of sound caught his attention. To his left, Mira and Randall were arguing, while armed commandos stood guard.

Fisting his hands, he considered his predicament. With his lame leg and no weapon, he had nothing to overpower the men or show himself as a threat. He dropped his hands to his sides and felt a rustle in his pocket. Mira's bracelet. If she had it, she could do her immobilization trick, or whatever else the gems were capable of.

He slipped onto the roof and sidled to a large air

vent, then squatted and duck-walked toward the group. Now behind a second vent, he could read their expressions and hear clearly their conversation.

"What are you going to do with me?" demanded Mira.

"There's big money to be made with you, my dear, and I intend to retire on it," crowed Randall. "I already have bids in hand from several private organizations who are salivating at the thought of owning their own personal alien."

"I'm not a commodity to be sold or bartered," said Mira, her voice stony.

Randall snorted. "I don't think you have much to say about it. The Russians are interested, as is a cartel of scientists in Buenos Aires. There's a group in the States bidding, but I'm afraid they're going to find their morals before the deal is concluded. I suggest you cooperate with the winner. Tell them everything about your mode of travel, the type of fuel that powers your vehicles, where you come from, and that fancy jewelry you—" He latched on to her wrist and held it to the light. "Where's the bracelet?"

"It's right here," called Lucas. Stepping from the shadows, he dangled the prize and walked to the edge of the roof. Swallowing his fear of heights, he refused to look down, but held the bracelet over the side. "All you have to do is come get it."

Randall swung Mira around. Two of the gunmen crouched and raised their weapons. "Don't shoot him, you idiots. We'll lose the gems."

"That's right," Lucas said in a jaunty tone. "So how about you and I make a deal?"

The major pulled Mira in front of him and held a pistol to her head. "Hand over the bracelet, and I'll see to it she goes to a good home."

"A good home? She's not a pet up for adoption."

"Isn't she?" Randall ran the pistol lovingly down Mira's cheek. "Though she may look it, she certainly isn't human. What else would you call her?"

My soul mate. The woman I love. Lucas bit back the words, though he knew them to be true. If Randall thought he cared . . .

"How about I trade you the bracelet for her? She'll explain how it works, and you can sell it to the highest bidder."

"The money I'd get for it wouldn't compare to what I'd receive for an alien. Besides, how would I know she was telling the truth?"

"You won't get away with taking her, but a man with your connections would be able to make a killing with the bracelet. Let her go, and I'll give it to you. You can sell it for millions."

"I have a better idea," Randall hissed. He jammed the gun in Mira's temple. "Drop the bauble, and I'll think about sending you the name of the winning bidder."

Lucas slid the bracelet back into his pocket.

"Very well," said Randall, dragging Mira toward the helicopter. "Kill him."

Lucas ducked and dived for the nearest air vent. The entry door opened and Paul and Lila rushed in.

Greeted by a hailstorm of bullets, they dropped and rolled for cover. He scrambled around the vent as Lila raised her arm. Without hesitation, she pressed a stone in place and closed her eyes. Lucas peered around a corner and saw the two commandos stalled in a weird half squat.

Mira wrestled with Randall while the two remaining gunmen separated. Lucas read the frustration on Lila's face and realized she couldn't work her magic on both of them.

"Let her go, Major. The game's up," he bluffed. An icy tendril of fear tripped through his mind, then he heard Mira's trembling voice. *Lucas, save yourself. I'll find a way to escape.*

The words came to him automatically. *Not a chance, sweetheart. I love you. I'm not letting you go.*

Oblivious to the mental interchange, Randall shouted, "A second alien. How fortuitous for me." He cocked his head and the man nearest Lila took off in a crouch. Just as he got to her, he, too, froze.

Moments passed. Lucas knew the fourth man was being cautious. Did Lila have any more usable stones? He slipped from behind the vent. He couldn't worry about Lila or Paul when Mira was still in danger.

Slowly, he walked toward the major. "Let her go."

Lucas, don't be foolish. I'll find a way—

Trust me, Mira. Just trust me.

Randall raised his gun, aimed it at Lucas, and shook his head. "I was hoping it wouldn't come to this. It seems I'm going to have to kill you myself."

"Nooo!" Mira screamed. Jerking from his grasp, she slammed the gun from his hand and ran toward Lucas.

Lucas pulled Mira against his chest and slipped the bracelet onto her wrist. "Here, do something with this thing."

Crouched by his side, she hurriedly fiddled with the gems as Randall and his last henchman climbed into the chopper. Lucas felt her stiffen and looked up to see the major and his pal suspended in place, frozen as they tried to climb into the helicopter.

Gazing at her, he grinned. "That's an amazing trick. Remind me to have you show the president tomorrow."

Mira smiled through quivering lips. The tendril of ice in his mind turned warm, caring. "You love me."

"I do. But you have to stop poking around in my head. It takes all the fun out of things." Lucas narrowed his eyes and drew her close. "Are you all right? The baby—?"

"We're fine, but I have to go." Mira struggled to her feet. "Please understand."

Lucas thought his heart would shatter. Mira tugged from his grip and he grabbed for her hand, but she edged away. The *thunka-thunka-thunka* of a helicopter filled his ears. Bright lights strobed the sky. Sirens screamed, and he heard voices. The rescue chopper churned the air around him, throwing the rooftop into chaos.

I love you, Lucas. You are the man of my heart. Whatever happens, remember that one thing is true.

Mira's words rang in his head, cut into his soul, and pierced his very existence. Her eyes never leaving his, she continued to walk backward.

Paul and Lila reached his side. "Let her do what she has to do, Lucas. She'll be back," said Paul.

Martin stepped from the group of officers who'd surrounded the major and walked to his side.

Lucas swiped at his face and felt the tears. "Talk to her dammit!"

"It's not for me to decide, son. Or you," said Martin, clasping his shoulder.

Suddenly, a huge craft encompassed the heavens above the building. Blinding lights pulsed, strobing in rhythm from the underbelly of the massive vessel.

All around them, men dropped to their knees and aimed their weapons. "Hold your fire," Martin ordered, his voice a sharp crack of command.

The ship hovered directly over Mira. A hatch opened and a beam of light radiated downward. Lucas shrugged from Martin's grasp and ran toward her, but it was too late. Mira broke into a million tiny pieces and disappeared upward into the streaming beam.

He stared as the behemoth disappeared into the night, taking with it his very life.

Epilogue

Six months later

*D*ull humming filled the air, throbbing in an almost silent rhythm with the inner workings of the spacecraft. A small, inlaid string of lights shone over one of several tables in the center of the massive room. Each table held a stellar chart, a star map of sorts, that could be studied as the ship traveled through space. Ingeniously designed, the map showcased a dime-sized dot that represented the conveyance as it slid along a faint, pulsing line that marked the route the vessel was taking on its journey through the heavens.

Mira pressed a series of keys and the time line for touchdown at the projected sight was displayed in a corner of the map. She smiled at Zara across the table's broad expanse. "Can you believe we're almost there?"

"No. I can hardly wait to see Lila and meet her husband. The way she sounds in her transmissions, you'd think Paul was the only man on the planet." Zara tucked a curl of burnished gold behind her ear, then checked the trajectory of their flight for herself. "As if our men don't count."

"With the new twins, Lila will soon have five men in her life. Can you imagine it?" Mira patted her rounded belly as she leaned into the map. "If you ask me, it's going to be hard enough handling two."

"And don't forget about my three," Zara reminded her, settling in a large, cushioned chair with a high back. "Of course, Will is easy. He's already playing the doting big brother. I hated that we had to leave him behind. He really wanted to meet the president."

"Too much to do this trip. Setting up an interstellar council will require countless hours and effort. Are you sure you want your baby born on Earth?" asked Mira, walking around the table and taking the seat next to Zara. "Your mother is upset she won't be with you."

"Though our sister travelers are willing to wait out their time at home, I want my son to have dual citizenship. I'm told the best way to do that is have him born in the United States. I plan to stay on Earth and await the event even if we're finished with meetings." Zara smiled. "What about you? Are you happy that you'll be living on Earth so much of the time?"

Mira spun in her chair, her heart light, her mind racing. Since her appointment as one of the delegates to Earth, headquarters were being readied in a new complex near the White House. Martin had been in charge of the DIA's move to the same structure, so she and Lucas would be sharing space in the building.

"I'm looking forward to it, though my father didn't agree at first. But Lucas appealed to Thane's common sense. Since he'll be a delegate as well, it's the best way for our two worlds to work out the details of our alliance. Thane is planning to visit soon."

She stood at the sound of a door sliding open. Daniel Murphy and Lucas walked in side by side, both men wearing smug grins. Lucas came to her and pulled her against his chest, hugging her to his pelvis. Mira giggled when their son kicked, and he jumped back.

He gazed at her belly. "Place kicker for the Giants, is my guess. Either that or another Dave Beckham."

"No contact sports," chided Mira, poking him in the ribs. "He could get hurt."

"Told you so," said Daniel, his expression all knowing. Holding Zara tight, he kissed her cheek. "Hi, Mrs. Murphy. How's your day going?" Before she could answer, he gazed out the window that took in the passing skyway at an amazing rate of speed. "Almost forgot, it's impossible to tell whether it's day or night on this traveling bucket. Don't know if I'll ever get used to that."

Zara rested her head on his shoulder. "I miss Will."

"Well I don't. The kid's been driving me crazy with questions I can't answer ever since we arrived on your planet. Let him antagonize your scientists for a while . . . or Mira's father."

"It's good he'll be staying with Thane," said Mira. "He needs to get used to being around children. Will is a perfect challenge for him."

They exchanged a few more pleasantries, then Daniel and Zara left the map room hand in hand. When the door closed, Lucas sat down in her chair and pulled Mira onto his lap. Giggling, she hoisted her baby-filled self onto his thighs and asked, "How are you feeling? Has the medication helped you to deal with your fear of heights?"

"It's better when I don't think about it. Like I told you on the trip to your home, all I have to do is steer clear of the viewing screens during hover phase and I can handle things."

She nestled into his chest, determined to ask what had been on her mind for five months, ever since Thane and the Council of Women had allowed her to return after the altercation on the roof of the Treasury. So much had happened since then. Major Randall and his men were in prison, as were Edith Hammer and her crew, Jonas Harden, and the team from Texas. Jack Farley's newspaper had hired a prime litigator who'd gotten him off on a technicality, and Farley had vowed to write a book on his experience.

Better still, Paul, Lila, and the twins were living in

relative peace on the eastern shore, with Bill and the entire membership of ESAW standing guard.

Lucas had been named one of three ambassadors to her world along with Daniel and Martin, while Peggy was made director of the DIA. Of course, with the older couple planning a wedding of their own, there would be no problem with the two organizations working hand in hand.

In the midst of laying out the logistics for a compatible galactic union, Mira and Lucas had gotten married. On this trip, they were having a ceremony for his family, along with all the pomp and publicity that accompanied a media event.

"Someday you'll want to watch touchdown," she reminded him. "If only to share it with our son."

"Don't count on it," he said, with a laugh.

"There's something I've been meaning to ask you . . ."

He placed his lips on her forehead. "More questions?"

"Just one or two. Do you ever think about Kevin? Or worry about our son?"

Lucas knew the concern she spoke of, because it had invaded his thoughts on several occasions. As for Kevin . . . he would never forget his firstborn, but Kevin was his past. Mira and this child were his future.

"If you're talking about SIDS, the affliction did cross my mind. But your doctors assured me this baby was going to have a long and healthy life, and I believe them. It seems that while our genes will strengthen the

DNA of your people, yours have done the same to ours."

She sighed. "That's not exactly what I meant."

"Okay, I confess I am a little concerned about how this baby and all the children we have will handle living in a fishbowl, just like the president said. And our private life won't be simple, either. I had to jump through hoops when I met Thane, and I'm sure the press will try to horn in on the wedding. At least you'll have an easy time of it with Debbie and my parents."

Snuggling closer, she rested her head in the crook of his neck. "I know you've told me a dozen times, but I have to ask once more. Are you pleased with the way things turned out?"

Lucas drew back and took in the softly lighted room and the huge window that opened to the full expanse of the universe. Martin had been right about grabbing true love when it found you and holding on for dear life.

Mira raised her head, and he gazed into her eyes, pools of liquid silver that reflected the overhead lights. He'd been a fool when he'd first discovered who and what she was, and he'd vowed to spend the rest of his life making it up to her.

She'd returned to Earth after a confrontation with the Elders, taken him to her planet, and paved the way for him to meet an entire alien race, as well as experiencing space travel and life on an unknown planet. But realizing his career dream was just icing on the cake.

His arms tightened around her, and Mira gave a moan of contentment. "What about—?"

He grinned. "Being happy?"

"Yes. Are you?"

"Truth?"

"We promised always to tell the truth and believe what the other said, no more lies ever again, remember?"

His chest rumbled with laughter. He seemed to laugh quite a bit lately, and that always made Mira smile.

"I remember. Then again, telling the truth was never *my* problem."

"Very funny," she said, swatting at his chest.

Lucas lifted her hand and kissed her palm. "I am the happiest man on two planets, my love. I doubt there will ever be a guy more ecstatic. Now, what about you?"

"My life is perfect. Thank you for our son. Thank you for believing in me. And thank you for loving me. After all, what more is there in life?"

"Not a thing, Mira." He spun the chair toward the viewing screen and gazed at the star map, noting the vast expanse of heavenly bodies that seemed to part magically as they plowed through space. "Not one damn thing."

Don't miss October's offerings from Avon Romance. . .

A Matter of Temptation by Lorraine Heath

An Avon Romantic Treasure

Victoria is nervous, yet thrilled, to be plucked from the many debutantes who vied for the hand of Robert, the Duke of Killingsworth. What Victoria doesn't know is that the man who she became engaged to is not the man she has married. But what will happen when she finds out the truth?

Flashback by Cait London

An Avon Contemporary Romance

Haunted by the suicide of her sister, Rachel Everly goes back to the place where everything went wrong, only to find Kyle Scanlon, a man who seems to hold all the answers. But the closer Rachel comes to getting the truth, the closer she draws to the path of a horrifying serial killer.

Scandalous by Jenna Petersen

An Avon Romance

Katherine Fleming is devastated to discover the nobleman she's engaged to has a secret he's kept from her: a wife! Suddenly Katherine is tainted by scandal, and is forced to accept a most unconventional proposal from the notorious seducer Dominic Mallory, her faithless fiance's brother. He is precisely the sort of rake she has always tried to avoid, but can't resist!

Rules of Passion by Sara Bennett

An Avon Romance

Marietta Greentree could care less about society's restrictive rules—not when she can become a courtesan like her mother. But when Marietta sets out on her first task—to seduce the darkly handsome and aloof Max, Lord Roseby, she finds that falling in love can often be an unavoidable consequence of seduction. . .

Avon Romances
the best in
exceptional authors and unforgettable novels!

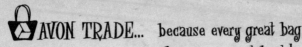